Echoes of the Rising

The Watchers Series: Book 3

Eilidh Miller

Cover Photography by Paul Macdonald

Cover Design by Matthew Weatherston

Griffith Cameron Publishing

ISBN - 978-1-7364148-0-4

GRIFFITH CAMERON
PUBLISHING

I dedicate this book to Euan and the memories of my Scottish ancestors — the Camerons, the Stewarts, and the rest in just about every Jacobite clan — those brave men who took up arms for a cause bigger than themselves. Those who died at Culloden, and those who fled to America to fight the English in a new rebellion, were all with me as I wrote and researched this book. May it keep the flame of your memories burning for another generation.

FOREWORD

Scottish Borders
March 2021

History can catch us in a myriad of ways. It can be through hearing lore of the land around us. It can be inspiration from the country of our forefathers. It can be in seeing or feeling some kind of personal connection to a relic behind glass in a museum, or it can be by means of transportation.

The latter may be delivered by the mediums of screen, publication, or storyteller, and any of these might be based entirely in fact or in fantasy and inspire equally well. It takes, however, a magical combination in any storyteller for them to alchemically weave together historical fact with fiction and bring history to meaningful and colourful Life in our mind's eye. For here, might we find ourselves more directly there.

One value in this portal to the past is by learned scholars recognising the factual places, names, dates, and historical characters and enjoying them all the more with personalities, experiences, and detail unfolding through them. Another, possibly greater, value is by readers fresh to these histories learning of them for the first time so vividly, only to find themselves more curious in learning and research, and perhaps sometime later, finding themselves standing at these very same locations, with the clearest of historical contexts, events, and characters already secured.

Eilidh presents us here with that rare gift of breathing Life into history's own pages and carries us through many prominent events during one of Scotland's most turbulent times. The Rising of the '45 was the last big push to restore the Stuart throne. We are no strangers in Scotland to rising once again following defeat, which was what the previous three risings had proved for us.

In such do-or-die eras, emotions run high throughout the land. Loyalties and friendships are ultimately tested to be broken or withstand the tests of time. Honesty and trust are valued above all when breaking bonds of secrecy carries a high price. The entire clan system of the Highlands was presented in this time with its greatest cause and greatest threat together.

'Echoes of the Rising' expresses through its characters those very real concerns, fears, doubts, grief, and pain that lay behind every honourable step and action taken throughout the campaign. At the Heart of this work, however, lie the facts behind those prominent names, places, and events that took place in real time, and many of them in exceptionally well-researched detail. And Truths of any matter will always hold value in our own Hearts.

It is my hope that this story might in itself catch you, and yet transport you on a greater journey. One where you might just shake hands with history and perhaps even hear the Echoes of the Rising.

Maestro Paul Macdonald,
Macdonald Armouries
Macdonald Academy of Arms
The 1745 Association

CHAPTER 1

LE HAVRE, FRANCE 1736

EUAN HURRIED UP THE ladder steps and onto the deck of the ship, dodging crew as he made his way to one of the railings. They were to dock today, at least that was what they'd been told, and after so long at sea, the idea of being on land once more held great appeal. It wasn't that he hated being at sea — he quite liked it — but he was ready to be on solid ground and eat a meal that consisted of more than tack rations. John and James had, of course, been fed better meals, but that was to be expected as the sons of Lochiel.

More than anything, there was the excitement of a new beginning and a new place, with his having been sent to France with Lochiel's sons. John, who was five, and James, who was three, were returning to their mother and to the life that awaited them there with their exiled grandfather. Euan, who had been educated at Achnacarry far more extensively than was normal for someone of his standing, was sent along to continue his education, and the thought thrilled him to his core. He loved learning, loved reading anything the tutor had let him. The others in Lochiel's service had been less thrilled about the basic learning required of them, but he hadn't let their schoolboy complaints deter him. What might he learn here? What was there to see and to do? He knew he was to go to King Louis' court to serve and learn from the men there who guarded the king, but the schooling would make up for those long hours; he was sure of it. There was excitement in that, too, the thought of serving a king and moving amongst the court. Him, Euan, serving a king!

Taking in a deep breath of fresh sea air, he closed his eyes and listened to the waves crash against the hull of the ship. He found it stifling below decks and was out as often as he could be, while the two older men sent as guardians often stayed below with the younger boys. He very much wished his mother could've come along, and the thought made his heart ache. She'd wept when he'd left, not knowing when or if she'd see her only child again. She hadn't, however, had a choice in whether he stayed or went. He was in Lochiel's service and had been since he was four years old, with Lochiel in complete control of the young man's path in life. Then there were his closest friends: Duncan, Iain, and Malcolm. He'd miss them a great deal, too. Opening his eyes, Euan caught sight of land on the horizon and grinned, turning and hurrying back below.

"John! James! I see it!" Euan blurted out as he entered the cabin.

"See what?" John asked.

"Land, of course," Euan said.

"Thank Christ," said George, one of the men with them. "I am tired of being on this ship."

"Yer problem is that ye dinnae see it as an adventure, George," Euan said, dropping into a chair. The easy familiarity from years spent with these men was obvious in the lack of formality he used toward those older than he was.

"Only ye are daft enough to see it as one," George groused.

"Only ye are short-sighted enough nae to," Euan retorted.

"Aye, well, ye would nae say so if ye were nae —"

"George!" said Alexander, the other man with them, in a stern tone, silencing George before he could say something he shouldn't.

George's lips settled into a thin line before he looked away.

"Dinnae mind him, Euan; he is only bitter because he has been unwell most of the journey."

Euan glared at George, knowing what he'd been about to say. His position was often used against him, a common barb used when nothing better could be thought of as an insult. He was poor, his father had been a farmer, and he was only where he was due to Lochiel's generosity.

"If that is his reason now, what excuse does he have any other time?" Euan asked pointedly.

Alexander had no answer, and Euan knew it was because there really wasn't one. George could be petulant and cruel if he wanted to be, and it was something which had always irritated Euan. In a way, Euan envied his position. As one of Lochiel's officers, George was now set, his life devoid of the struggles someone like Euan might face, or anyone in his clan for that matter, because his position within the clan was a high one. It never ceased to amaze Euan that anyone in such circumstances could have any reason to be so grim, but it was the way George was. Even so, he could be charming and funny most other times.

"Sorry, Euan," George said, his apology genuine. "Ye know I dinnae mean it."

"Then why do ye say it?"

"Because it shuts ye up."

Euan frowned. "Why do I need to?"

"Ye can be entirely too happy."

"Too happy?" Euan repeated, astounded.

"Excited, maybe."

"Why are ye nae? I dinnae understand it. Ye get to see France!"

"Because nae all of us are as excited about other places as ye are," Alexander said with a wry smile.

Euan scoffed and rolled his eyes. "I came down to tell ye that ye should be ready to leave, and now that I have, I am going back up."

Standing, Euan left the room, shutting the door behind him, and Alexander looked over at George.

"What is wrong with ye?" Alexander asked. "Why do ye have to do that to him?"

"Come on, Alex, ye cannae tell me ye dinnae get fed up with him at times."

"Actually, I can because I dinnae. Or, if I do, it is nae enough to provoke cruelty."

"Need I remind ye that he is nae these lads' brother? That he is only here because their father wants him to be?"

"He may nae be *their* brother, George, but he is a brother to *me*, even if it is by association and nae blood. We have taken care of him since he was but a bairn, looked after him, groomed him to be an officer. Now he is a young man, and Lochiel wants him here because he feels as though Euan deserves a chance to be more than what he was born into, and Euan is taking advantage of that as he should. Ye should be happy for him, but instead, ye seek to pull him down."

"Seek to remind him of his place, more like."

"His place? What place is that? Below ye?"

"The same as us, Alex. Maybe less because he is nae yet a man, but he is no better than we are, and it would serve him well to be reminded of it lest he start to think too highly of himself."

"In case ye have nae noticed, Euan has never been one to think highly of himself. In fact, he is far more likely to think less. Ye need to mind yer tongue, for if ye dinnae, some of the other lads or even Lochiel might see fit to watch it for ye."

"Is that a threat?"

"It is a warning ye would do well to heed, George. Euan is here for a purpose, sent by Lochiel specifically to learn how to guard a king and bring that knowledge home to guard his chief. Clearly Lochiel knows something ye dinnae, has a plan, and if ye interfere with it, he will nae be merciful."

George sighed in annoyance but said nothing, and Alexander nodded.

"John, James, get yer things together lads. As Euan said, ye will be docking soon, and it is certain yer grandfather awaits ye."

As the ship made its way into the port at Le Havre, the deck was a flurry of activity. Euan found a safe place to stand out of the way where he could watch the goings on. Men were in the rigging, tying sails, gathering lines, and he watched them in fascination. They were exceedingly high up, and he wasn't sure if it was something he could or would want to do. He was quite happy on the solid wood of the deck, and happier on solid ground. As they neared the docks, he turned his attention to the bustle of the wharf. It was filled with shops and warehouses, mongers, carts, carriages, ships, and any other number of things. Euan's eyes scanned for any sign of the Camerons who were meant to meet them there but saw nothing familiar amidst the teeming mass of humanity around the docks.

Turning away, he hurried down to grab his belongings, meager though they were, and went back above with Alexander, George, and the two boys. There was a strange sort of silence now, the sailors on deck looking apprehensive. Alexander and George slowed, looking at them and then at each other. Before anyone could ask what was wrong, the reason for the silence appeared at the top of the gangplank: French soldiers. From their uniforms it was easy to see that they were not just any soldiers, but the king's men.

"Which one of you is Euan?" the ranking officer called out in English.

"I am," Euan said, though he was tempted to remain silent. It was a thought he'd immediately dismissed, as he didn't want to endanger anyone else.

The officer gestured to the men behind him, who stepped

around him and seized Euan by the arms. Euan pulled back, resisting in his confusion as to what was happening.

"Wait, what are ye doing?" Alexander asked.

"He is coming with us," the officer replied.

"And who are ye?"

"We have been sent by the king, and that is all you need to know."

"I dinnae think so," Alexander said. "He is still our charge, and he is meant to go with these young lads to their family. Ye need to release him."

The man laughed at him, shaking his head. "I do not care what you think or say. This boy is coming with us. Your master sent him to learn with a particular group, and that tutelage begins now. Take him."

"No, wait!" Euan cried out as they yanked him roughly forward even as he continued to resist them. "Alex!"

"Stop fighting us!" shouted one of the men holding him.

The lead officer turned around and sent his fist into Euan's gut, taking the wind out of him and leaving him unable to breathe. Euan doubled over, which stopped any sort of effective resistance he might mount. Little John screamed in fright and started to cry, while James dashed behind George.

"What in Christ's name are ye —" Alexander began, but his words were stopped when the point of a rapier appeared at his throat.

"I suggest you cease with your questions," the lead officer snarled as he held the point on Alexander. "He is no longer your concern."

Alexander raised his hands in surrender, and George looked on in anger and shock.

"Euan!" John sobbed out.

"Be strong, Euan!" George called out in Gaelic. "Show them that ye are a Cameron and that a Cameron never can yield!"

Euan could say nothing, still coughing and gasping for air

as they dragged him down the gangplank. He could hear John and James screaming in protest and fear, and it infuriated him. They could've just explained, and he would have willingly gone, but this was entirely unnecessary. Euan felt like he might be sick once he could breathe again, but he didn't have long to think about it. As he started to stand up, a blow to his face buckled his knees and caused his vision to swim before the officer grabbed his hair and yanked his head up, forcing Euan to look at him.

"Welcome to training, boy," the man said with a cold smile. "Lesson number one: life is pain, and you must learn to keep going no matter what."

Euan retched involuntarily.

"I swear to the Holy Mother that if you vomit on me, I will slit your throat and dump your worthless carcass in the Seine."

Managing to keep himself from doing exactly that, Euan closed his eyes.

"Very good. Put him inside and let us be on our way. We have a long journey to Paris."

A carriage door was opened, and Euan was thrown inside, the door slamming shut behind him. The sound of a heavy lock being turned made him panic. The windows were all covered with heavy drapery, and there were no seats, leaving him lying in the dark on a hard floor. He began to cry, though he kept it silent, refusing to give these men the satisfaction of his fear and his pain.

Euan had no idea what time it was when he awoke again, the covered windows preventing his ability to even guess. It was hard to say how long he'd been asleep, or even if he'd fallen asleep rather than lost consciousness. Pain radiated through his face, making him groan, and he had no desire to open his eyes. He felt the carriage slow and then stop, heard movement outside, and almost forgot to breathe. He strained to hear every sound, to deduce where he was. The bits of French he caught didn't tell him much, and he cursed not knowing it better. His lessons in French had been interrupted by his departure.

The sound of the lock turning made Euan sit up in a single, quick movement, though it made him dizzy, and he forced down the nausea just before the door opened. Hands reached in and yanked him out, throwing him to the ground, and Euan glared up at them.

"Ye could have asked me to come out, ye know," Euan said.

"Did I tell you to speak?" the man from earlier said, slapping Euan across the mouth.

Euan winced but bit back the sound of pain he wanted to make.

"Look, he is learning," said one of the others before they all laughed.

"See how pretty a youth he is?" commented another. "We could sell him to a brothel and he would make a killing."

"How about it, boy? Care to earn a living in buggery?" said yet another.

Euan said nothing, but the fury in his eyes was plain.

"We need to set up camp, but first, some more learning for our young charge," the lead officer said.

There wasn't even a moment for Euan to process the words before blows were suddenly being rained down upon him from all sides. He covered his head and screamed as hands, feet, and heavy objects crashed into him. The pain was immediate and intense, his screams unable to be held back and out of his control. After what seemed like an eternity it stopped, leaving Euan panting and sobbing on the ground for a moment before trying to push himself up. His arms gave out beneath him as he tried to crawl away, only to be grabbed by the ankle and dragged back.

"NO!" Euan screamed, now unable to check his fear.

"Lock him up again."

Euan was grabbed from the ground and once more shoved into the carriage, the door slammed shut and locked.

Everything hurt and he couldn't stop his tears even if he wanted to. He could taste blood in his mouth, breathing was painful, and his own tears stung the wounds on his face. This exciting experience had, in an instant, become a horrifying nightmare from which there was no escape, and he wondered if he would even make it to Paris at all. The world and its sounds began to fade in and out, until there was nothing but darkness and silence.

CHAPTER 2

THE NEXT FOUR DAYS were a hellscape of travel in that darkened carriage, followed by a beating at night when they stopped. By the morning of the third day, his eyes were swollen shut and he could barely move. He choked on the wine they poured into his mouth in an attempt to at least make sure he was drinking something, but it didn't stop the onslaught. Euan no longer tried to fight being pulled out of the carriage and didn't have the strength to try to defend himself. He had no idea what was happening or why they were doing this, but he knew they'd never tell him if he asked, and were instead more likely to beat him for daring to question them. He almost wanted to beg them to kill him, to put him out of his misery instead of killing him this way, slowly, but managed to keep that to himself. George's words floated to the surface of his pain each time he felt that desperation: show them that a Cameron can never yield.

When next he woke, he realized he was no longer moving and no longer in the carriage. Beneath him was a bed, though he could feel that his eyes were covered. Moving his hands to touch his face, he found them strapped down, and it brought immediate panic. What torture was he in for now?

"Easy boy, easy," someone near him said in English, his voice different from any of the others he'd heard over the last four days. "You are fine."

"Where am I?" Euan asked, almost afraid to hear the answer.

"At the palace. Well, more specifically at the barracks, but close enough."

"When did I get here?"

"About a day ago."

"Untie me!" Euan demanded, his panic beginning to give way to anger.

"Cannot do that, I am afraid, for it is for your own safety. You need to stay where you are, as you are in rather rough shape."

"Aye, because those men tried to kill me!"

"They did go a bit overboard, I think."

"That is an understatement!" Euan snarled.

A soft laugh emanated from the unseen person beside the bed. "It is the only statement I can give. You will recover, but you did well. They tried to break you, but you would not give in."

"I did nae realize giving in was an option. What was it they wanted me to do?"

"Beg them to stop, plead with them, bargain, things of that nature. You did not, however."

"I will nae give anyone such satisfaction," Euan replied with far more determination than he felt.

"Ah, and that is why you are here. You are strong and strong-willed, a soldier. Now you will learn how to harness that to your advantage."

"Who are ye?"

"My name is Jacques, and I am the captain of the king's guard. You need not tell me who you are; I already know."

"I dinnae want to be here!"

"You have no choice, I am afraid."

"This was nae —"

"Was not what you thought?" Jacques interrupted. "I am sure it was not. However, you cannot leave. You are here now, and you will learn what you were sent to learn, though we will all speak to you in English for the time being. You have a few days to rest, to let some of that swelling go down, and then

11

we begin again. Take advantage of the time while you can; you will most certainly need it."

"Please, uncover my eyes," Euan asked, his voice now absent of the determined edge it had held only moments ago and betraying a child's fear.

"It is for your own good. You could not see out of them anyway, as swollen as they are. You must begin to heighten your other senses, Euan. Without your sight you must instead learn to hear, to smell, to feel."

Euan heard Jacques' footsteps walking away from him, and the panic rose once more. "No! Wait! Please!"

Silence was the only response to his plea, and Euan struggled against the ties that bound him before he fell back to the bed, letting loose a scream of anger that made his breathing ragged. The moment he was free, he was leaving this place. This was not what he'd been sent here to do, and he was sure Lochiel wouldn't have allowed such treatment of him.

"Let me out of here!" Euan screamed in fury.

"And if we do not?"

Euan went still, barely breathing, the fear of that voice creeping into his heart and clenching it with an icy grip.

"That is what I thought. Nothing," he said with a chuckle. "Jacques, we should send this petulant baby back home. He will not make it."

"Now, now, Alain. He is just a boy, and though you will never admit it now, you were this way, too. We all were. Answer the question, Euan. What will you do?"

The calm of Jacques voice was maddening, making it impossible to tell what was going through the man's mind or giving any hint as to what answer he was expecting. Euan was silent for a long moment before he spoke. "Ye will let me go sometime; ye have to, for ye have a job to do. But I promise ye this: when all of this is over, I am going to make ye pay for what ye have done to me."

"Are you? Fascinating," Jacques said.

"I would like to see you try, boy," Alain sneered.

"Especially ye," Euan hissed.

"If I do not kill you first."

"Do it," Euan said, his tone cold. "Go on. Either way I win. If ye kill me, I am free, and ye hang for murder. Dinnae think for a moment I would nae be missed."

There was a silence that left Euan to wonder if they'd left before Jacques spoke. "Have a pleasant day, Euan."

The two men turned and departed, at least as far as Euan could tell. He growled in anger, but even with his temper as high as it was, decided to do as Jacques had suggested: begin to heighten his other senses. Taking deep breaths, he calmed himself and went as still as he could, his breathing becoming slow and quiet. The sounds he hadn't noticed before came to him then, dripping water, echoes of distant voices, footsteps. The water was near him, but the rest were not. Those were muffled as though they were outside of a wall. The scent of wet stone filled his nostrils, followed by the mossy smell that usually accompanied a place where water was constant.

The following day, neither Jacques nor any other man came near him, only women. Their footsteps were lighter, their touches gentler, but none of them spoke. They helped him sit up in order to feed him broth, the restraints allowing only enough movement for that purpose, and Euan was grateful for it. He was ravenously hungry, not sure when he'd last eaten; he wasn't even sure how many days had passed or if he was where Jacques said he was. When the women left him after helping him to relieve himself, he lay there doing recitations in his head of any poetry or songs or other pieces he could remember so the silence wouldn't drive him mad. He refrained from doing so out loud, for if they could keep silent, so could he, and if they were trying to break him and make him talk, he wouldn't.

It became easy to tell by the routines what time of the day it was. He began counting how many times he was fed, paying attention to the change in temperature that suggested nightfall. It occurred to him that they were teaching him how to survive if he were ever taken prisoner, and he wanted to prove to them that he wasn't weak, that he would survive it. Though his body ached with being stuck in one position for the majority of the time, he gritted his teeth and refused to cry out. He counted three days before he realized he could see the inside of his blindfold, meaning the swelling had gone down.

On the fourth day, he heard heavy footsteps and went perfectly still as if he were sleeping. He subdued the urge to smile when he felt them loosening the ties, and when they were sufficiently undone, Euan made his move. Able to tell where they were by the sounds they made, Euan landed a punch to someone's jaw before he ripped the blindfold off. Someone tried to grab him, and he dodged it, sending an elbow into the man's back before he sprinted out of the door. Running down a stone hallway, he slid to a stop as someone stepped out to close off the end of it. Euan pulled one of the sgian dubhs they hadn't found, clutching it tight in his hand.

"And just what, pray tell, do you think you will do with that?" Jacques asked, an amused smile on his face. He was tall with blonde hair, in his thirties at Euan's best guess, with a soldier's fit build.

"I am getting out of here," Euan replied.

"You have gotten as far as you are going to go, I am afraid."

"Nae yet."

"If you really believe you are going to stab me and get past, you might want to reconsider. Even if you did, you have no idea how many men are here or where to go. If you did manage to get out of the building, you do not know where you are. How would you find your way? Where would you go? You do not even know the terrain. Think strategically instead of emotionally."

Euan heard footsteps swiftly approaching behind him and

darted out of the way, putting Jacques on one side of him and an angry group of men on the other. Looking between the two, he knew he wouldn't get any further, but he didn't want to surrender either.

Jacques seemed to understand what Euan wouldn't say and held up a hand. "Leave him be," he said to the others.

"What!" Alain shouted. "He deserves another beating for that stunt!"

"Why? Because he did precisely what he should have done? Euan took our advice even if we did not know it. He should not and will not be punished for that. I will handle him."

Grousing, the others backed off and walked away, and Euan looked over at Jacques. "What are ye going to do to me?"

"Nothing, my young friend. Stand down, I mean you no harm."

"How do I know this is nae a trick?"

One corner of Jacques lips twitched in something like a smile. "An excellent thing to consider, to be sure, but you have my word as an officer. This time there is no trick; I really do mean you no harm."

Euan's heart was racing at almost the same speed as his mind, but he lowered his blade, forcing himself to trust Jacques.

"Good. I understand you have little reason to trust anyone here, and for that I do not blame you. I, however, have yet to give you any reason not to trust me. Come, I am sure you are hungry?"

Euan nodded.

"I thought as much. This way," Jacques said, gesturing toward the way he'd come.

Euan made his way down the hall, following Jacques at a slight distance until they came to a door. Jacques opened it and went inside, with Euan behind him. Inside was a quite simple room with varied things sitting about, showing it to be a guard room where they might sit for a meal or a break. On the table sat a platter with what looked like chicken, along with wine, bread, and cheese. The rumble from Euan's stomach was audible, but he refrained from making an immediate attack on the food despite his clear desire to do so.

Jacques laughed at the young man who was almost salivating in front of him. "Go on, boy. Eat."

The words were half a second from having left Jacques' mouth, and Euan was already at the table putting food on a plate. Euan was careful to not take much, as he was used to making sure there was enough for everyone.

"Thank ye," he said as he sat down to eat with well-mannered restraint.

"Why did you take so little?"

"I did nae wish to be greedy. Everyone else must eat, too."

Jacques looked at him in curiosity. "With the way you have been treated, why do you care?"

"Habit. Also, I am fairly certain my mam would appear out of nowhere to slap me for such a lack of manners."

"Ah, yes," Jacques said, laughing. "I forgot you are still young enough to fear your mother's wrath."

"Dinnae know I will ever be too old to fear that. Dinnae ye?"

"No, but I did not really know my mother. I do, however, fear the nuns."

Euan smiled; he couldn't help it. "Aye, I have heard stories about them and dinnae blame ye."

"There is something very important you must understand, Euan, and it is important you realize it from the start," Jacques said, his expression becoming serious once more. "From this moment on, you must distance yourself from those you love, and you must do this in order to protect them. If anyone sets out to harm you, they will search for those you love and make those people the first victims. Do not give them that ammunition. Do not act overly fond of anyone publicly. To show affection is to mark them for death. I would even suggest marrying a woman you care little for, so if she falls in such a way, it will not damage you."

Euan stared at him. "Are ye saying nae to embrace my own mam?"

"Not in public, at least."

Euan frowned, this command not sitting at all well with him, though he understood it at the same time. His love meant death to those he held dear now, and the thought bothered him a great deal.

"Feel free to eat as much as you need; this is for you alone, though I do admire your restraint," Jacques said, changing the subject as he sat down in one of the other chairs. "You did a very good job in getting away."

"Ye told me to heighten my other senses, so I did."

"Yes, you did, and you did it far more effectively than we had expected you to. That bodes well for you."

"Were ye trying to teach me how to handle it if I get taken prisoner?"

"Not exactly, though that is certainly a bonus. You had to trust yourself, to let go of your fear, and you did that. When fear is gone, *that* is when you become truly dangerous. There must come a moment where we realize there is more to the world than what we can see."

"What am I really to do here?"

"That, my young friend, is far more complicated. You are here to learn how to be a soldier of a different sort. Any brute with a weapon can fight. Only a certain kind of man can be the weapon himself. You will learn the way we guard the king, but it is not in the way you think. We are the elite, and though we stand watch at his side, we stand watch in the shadows as well. When you leave us, you will have a set of skills that will make you more valuable than any money could buy."

"How does what ye did help any of that?"

"This is a brutal business, Euan. There is pain, exhaustion, danger. You must learn how to get past and work through all of it. I will not lie and tell you that this is the end of the pain you will suffer, for it is not. It will be your constant companion for some time to come. Every mistake you make will earn you more until you stop making mistakes."

"What if I dinnae want to do this?"

Jacques looked at him in an almost sad and sympathetic way. "You have no choice. This is what you were sent here to do, and you can either do it or die because you failed. Those are your options. By all means, resist and drag your feet, then watch what happens to you. You will find no mercy here, and I promise you those men will beat the life out of you if you try it."

"I thought I was going to have lessons," Euan said, the words followed by a heavy sigh.

"You will," Jacques said, smiling. "You must be educated in a great many things to do this work well. One of those things is fluent French."

Euan smiled in return. "At least I have that to look forward to."

"Ah, so you are one of those, are you? Find the bright spot to get through the dark."

"It is the only way I know."

"It is as valid a way as any. Now, eat up. Afterward you will have a bath, be given your training uniform, and shown to your room. Tomorrow it all begins again, and you must be ready for it."

CHAPTER 3

THE SPECIALIST SAT IN silence for so long that Euan opened his eyes to look at him in curiosity. "Are ye all right?"

"I should be asking you that question, I would think," Specialist George replied.

"Ye were silent, so I wanted to make sure."

"Yes, I was, for a couple of reasons. One was to be sure you had nothing else to say, the other was to absorb what you've told me. Companion Cameron —"

"Euan, if ye dinnae mind," Euan interjected. "Companion Cameron sounds so formal."

"Very well. Euan, I must first say that I'm deeply sorry to hear such a tale. It's terrible that anything such as that was inflicted upon one so young."

"It was a different time."

"That doesn't make it right, does it? Do you feel as though any of what you've related to me was a good thing?"

"No," Euan replied. "Which is why I never want to speak about it. It was a horrible time in my life that I wish I could forget."

"But you cannot."

"No, I cannae. Every time I use what they taught me, those moments return."

"I'm sure being back there on your last mission didn't help matters."

Euan sighed. "No. Everywhere I looked there was a memory of those years."

19

"Were they there? Did you see them?"

Euan gave a gentle shake of his head. "I did nae see any of them. They might have retired, or perhaps they died. That was always a very real possibility. It is also possible that I was seen, and word got back to them that I was there. Such a thing would cause them to avoid me at all costs, for they would have known I was there on a task and not put me in danger of exposure."

"Did anyone else there recognize you?"

"No, thankfully. Well, one person I sought out did, but I have no ill memories of him."

"It was very clever of you to occupy your mind by reciting poetry and songs in order to keep from having a mental breakdown," George said.

"I dinnae know what made me think to do it, but it worked."

"Sometimes our minds know what to do to help themselves even if we don't. Tell me, do you think Lochiel should've sent you there?"

"If he knew what was to happen to me, no. If he did nae, I cannae fault him for it."

"But you were just a boy. Do you think he could have or should have waited longer?"

"I dinnae think he could have. As terrible as it sounds, I needed to go into that situation as malleable as could be, or I would nae have survived it."

"Does it make you angry now to think of these things? To think of the boy who watched the shore come closer while dreaming of a new life?"

"Aye," Euan admitted. "It angers me that the dream was snatched from him, that his life was nae ever going to be what he had dreamed it would."

"You spoke of yourself in the third person there; why?"

"Because that boy does nae exist any longer. He died on that ship."

George raised an eyebrow. "Why do you say that?"

"Nothing was ever the same from the moment Alain stepped onto the deck. When they threw me into the carriage, they had already struck the fatal blow to the child I had been. That life, that dream? Dead and gone."

"What was the dream?"

"What does it matter?"

"It's somewhere in your mind. What did he want? What did he dream of?"

Euan sat in silence for a few minutes before he was able to speak. "An education more extensive than he could find in the Highlands. Perhaps something rivaling a university. He dreamt of serving a king while wearing a fancy uniform and moving amongst a glittering court. There was the chance of staying on in France and serving Lochiel's wife and father, of sending for his mam and giving her a better life."

"Did he dream of his own life as a man?"

"Aye, but in that way his dreams were far exceeded by what the man he became found."

"In what way?"

"My Grace," Euan said, the smile that spread across his lips instant and natural. "Never in a million years would that lad have dreamt of someone like her. Such a creature could nae even exist, much less be within his reach, yet she is here. She is mine, my heart and my soul, everything good in me. As much as I hate what I went through, I would go through it again and again if it meant I had her."

George smiled. "That's the only time I've seen you smile today."

"Cannae help but smile when she is in my thoughts."

"What other parts of your life now exceed what you wanted then?"

"All of it, really," Euan replied with utter honesty. "I have a home of my own, a fine, grand home. It is a home on the estate where I spent most of my life, something I never could have owned in my previous station. My mam is safe, healthy, and happy in a way I have never seen her. I have a study full of more books than I could have dreamed of, and more money than most of the nobles I encountered."

"So, perhaps he didn't lose his dream after all and instead came by it in a different way than expected."

"Perhaps," Euan admitted in a quiet voice.

"But you're still angry."

"I think I have every right to be."

"No one is saying you don't. Who are you angry with?"

"Everyone."

"Everyone?"

"Well, nae everyone. Lochiel, Jacques, Alain … all of the ones who conspired to do this to me."

"Jacques? By your telling, he seemed to at least have some care for you."

"Aye, he did, somewhat. He still had a job to do, and he did nae hold back in his punishment. He was nae, perhaps, as cruel as the others could be, but dinnae mistake that for care."

"I see. You said something at the end that I found curious. Jacques told you that this wouldn't be the end of the pain you suffered. What did he mean by that?"

Euan's expression darkened at the memory. "What he meant was that I would still take constant beatings. The following day, though I was still quite injured, they started physical training. I was to learn how to keep going no matter what, no matter the pain. It would inflict more injuries or let others linger, and if it did nae, they would cause some new ones. If I cried out in pain at any point, it would all start again. They starved me for several days once so I could learn to think and work through hunger. They deprived me of sleep so I could learn to go without it and go longer without feeling the effects the lack of it might cause."

"How old were you then?"

"Still sixteen. This all happened within the first few months of my being there. It was the period where I made the most mistakes, and any mistakes I made would bring physical punishment."

"Can you explain? What sort of mistakes? What punishment?"

The small laugh that came from Euan was full of bitterness. "Ah, well, the true question is what was nae a mistake? Everything was. Anything they decided. I never knew when it would come. Nae until I started anticipating their thoughts, where they might go next, did it begin to taper off."

"When you began to make a study of them and learn their traits, their cues," George said.

"Aye, precisely. This was, of course, the start of the other part of my training, though I was doing it long before they were ready to teach me."

"Did they realize it?"

"Eventually, but it put me far ahead of where they thought I should be. It was when Jacques really seemed to notice I would be suited for more ... specialized ... things."

"I see."

Euan couldn't help his smile. Though the man didn't intend for it to be there, there was a tone in the Specialist's voice that conveyed not only how concerned he was, but also how disturbed and slightly fearful. Euan couldn't blame him, really. He had no idea what Euan was able to do, how well he was able to read people no matter how well-trained they might be at trying to conceal it.

"I think that's enough for today. There's a lot to process, a lot stirred up. What I want you to think about before our next session is how these things play into your daily life. Sit down and evaluate your behaviors, your interactions. Do you hold back? Do you approach things differently? Is there a difference between your first impulse and what you actually do because of what was done to you? Think about the way you are with Watcher Cameron and evaluate how your behavior changes with her, if it does."

"Aye, I will."

"Excellent. I look forward to seeing you again next week."

"Thank ye," Euan said, standing as George did the same and shaking his hand. "Nae to worry, I will come back to see ye and nae another."

Specialist George smiled at him. "Good. See you then."

Euan left the room and made his way out, where he found Caia waiting for him. "Ye have nae been waiting here the whole time, have ye?"

"No," she said, smiling at him. "They called me when you got ready to leave."

"Ye are quick."

"Transport takes only a split second."

Euan chuckled a bit. "Aye, I suppose it does."

"You seem well."

"Mostly, aye. Nae sure I will always be, but this is a start."

"I'm glad to hear it. I know Grace is waiting for you; shall we take you home?"

"Of course. Cannae keep my Watcher waiting, can I?"

The way he said it, followed by his teasing smile, made Caia laugh. "You say that as if you don't wish to see her."

"Well, we both know that is a lie, dinnae we?"

"Indeed, we do."

"In all honesty, I dinnae want to keep her waiting if she is missing me. We are apart enough as it is."

Caia's smile softened. "I love to see how much you love her."

"She deserves no less. From anyone."

"True, but it's special with you, something no one else can give. Come on, let us go."

Euan took her hand and, in the next moment, found himself in their bedroom. Caia was gone again before he could thank her, leaving him a moment alone. Closing his eyes, he took a deep breath and released it, sitting down in a chair and rubbing his forehead as if it would clear the aching brought on by the stress he was so adept at hiding. For now, he could let his guard down and not need to pretend to feel the way he didn't. He'd told Caia he was fine, but he wasn't, and he was certain she knew it but was too kind to press him. The memories shared today were unpleasant, and having them dredged up brought with them a darkness he'd neither expected nor wanted. He could see all of them so clearly, those men of his past, hear them as though they were standing right at his side even now. He wondered what he would've done if he'd seen them on this last mission, what *they* would've done. Would they have found a way to speak to him privately, or would they have ignored him? One thing he was certain of, there wasn't one of them who stood a chance against his wife. They wouldn't have known what to make of her, but that was at her best, something she hadn't been while they were in France together only recently. A large part of him was tempted to take her back there and pit her against them just for the sheer pleasure it would give him to watch her wreak utter havoc and leave them in ruins.

"Euan, are you okay?"

The sound of her voice, soft as it was, made him jump, and his eyes snapped open as he looked up. She could sneak up on him in ways he still found unnerving because his training had taught him to be better than that.

"Aye," he replied, attempting a small smile.

"Hmm, nice try, but I don't believe you," she said as she walked across the room to him.

She placed a hand on his cheek, drawing a soft sigh from Euan as he felt the peace her touch and her presence instantly afforded him, and closed his eyes again. "Sometimes I do wish ye did nae know me as well as ye do."

"Even if I didn't, I can still feel how bothered you are. Did you want to talk about it?"

"I have done enough talking for today, I think, at least about the past."

"I understand that feeling far more than I'd care to admit. Did you want me to leave you alone?"

"No," he said almost before she'd finished speaking, opening his eyes and looking up at her. "I want ye to stay, as ye are perhaps the only person in the world I would want near me just now."

A small frown settled over Grace's delicate features. "That bad, huh?"

"Aye," he replied, reaching out for her and pulling her down into his lap once she took his hand. Resting his head against her shoulder, he felt the gentle pressure of her resting her cheek against the crown of his head an instant later.

"I'm sorry," she said, untying his long, dark hair and then running her fingers through it in slow, gentle, repetitive strokes. "Is there anything I can do?"

"Just be here, be ye," he said, drawing a fingertip down the inside of her forearm and over the Watcher's mark on her wrist. "That I dinnae want to speak of it is nae personal; I hope ye know that."

"I never thought for a minute that it was. I'm not sure I've ever felt you so bothered as this."

"I think the last time I was is when we were cut off from each other."

"Our last mission."

"Indeed. How are ye feeling?" he asked, wanting to shift the subject away from his own feelings for now.

"I don't know, really. It's the strangest feeling, because something massive has happened to me, and yet, at the same time, none of it feels real. How do you process what feels unreal?"

"I understand that better than ye know, and the truth is that ye cannae. Instead, ye simply wall it away because there is naught else ye *can* do. It is too big, too painful, and ye just want things to be as they were before."

"Even when they aren't."

"Even then. All ye can do is try to make it as close to what it was as ye can."

"I suppose. I wanted to tell you about … um … about …"

Euan looked up and watched the sudden fear leap into her eyes even as he felt her panic within himself when she couldn't remember what she'd wanted to say. "*Leannan*, dinnae panic. It is all right. It is nae what ye think, just give yerself a moment and breathe."

"I can't remember! Euan, I can't remember!"

"No ... Grace ... shh ..."

"What if ... no! I have to remember what it was!"

Whatever he might have been feeling was shoved aside in an instant in the face of her anxiety. He stood up and switched their positions, sitting her down in the chair and then kneeling before her. Taking her hands in his, he could feel her shaking.

"Grace. Grace, listen to me. Look at me. Ye are fine."

"I can't remember!" she said in distress, looking at him but not really seeing him as her mind raced with the frantic need to recover the intended words.

"I know, but that happens all the time to everyone. Ye forget what ye meant to tell someone about, we all do it, and it will come to ye if ye relax and give it time. This is nae the same; it is nae happening again. Those were nae the things they were taking from ye. Here: where did ye go to university?"

"Oxford."

"Aye. And where did we have dinner my second day in California?"

"Blue Plate Taco."

"What did my mam chastise me for saying in front of yer mam?"

"That you weren't Jesus Christ as far as you knew, but you did come back from the dead, so maybe?"

Euan laughed. "Aye. Ye see? Ye do remember things."

Grace smiled as her panic began to ease a bit. "You're right."

"My poor love," he said, reaching up to stroke her cheek. "Ye are still so frightened, but I cannae blame ye in the slightest. I do miss that restaurant, though."

"We could always take a quick trip with Caia."

"Tempting."

"You could have more tequila."

"Even more tempting."

"Margaritas?"

"Only problem with this plan is ye would have to hope ye did nae see anyone ye knew."

"Ugh, right. Wait! We could order to go and see if Caia would pick it up."

"I like the way ye think."

Grace laughed softly. "It will have to be for supper, though. They aren't open yet."

"Fair enough."

"I hope this doesn't keep happening."

"Christ, Grace, give yerself a bit of time, would ye? We just got back yesterday. The previous day ye were dying in a bed, unable to remember anything. Things will nae be normal for a while, no matter how much ye want them to be."

"You're right, I know you are, I just … I hate this."

"Ye are as bad as I am. Ye hate to be down for long."

Grace made a face at him, and it brought laughter from Euan because he knew she was irritated that he was right. "Aye, exactly. Love, maybe ye really should see a —"

"No," she said, cutting off his thought.

"Grace."

"No!"

"Why nae?"

"Because I don't want to! Euan, please."

"I will nae push ye, at least nae yet."

"Thank you. You don't know what it's like to have people playing in your head."

Euan gave her a look.

"Okay, but not the same way."

"No, that is entirely unique to ye; ye are right."

"The point is that I don't want to talk about it, I don't want anyone else in my mind, I don't want anyone else to have any of my memories, and I definitely don't want to share it with The Council."

"Oh?"

"I just … they have so much already, Euan. As it is, they took all those memories from the mission to study. They have access to other things. I want to deal with this on my own, in my own way, with you."

"All right, all right, calm yerself, Wife. I understand ye."

"Don't sound so exasperated."

"Ye try to deal with someone just like ye, and ye tell me how ye dinnae get exasperated, hm?"

"Seriously? You're going to go there?" Grace retorted, raising an eyebrow.

"Well, nae … I mean … ach, ye see? We are just like each other, and it is like arguing with yerself. I get to see how I must be to argue with, and it drives me mad."

"No way, you're far meaner."

"What!" Euan exclaimed, not needing to fake his astonishment at the accusation.

"You are! You have a sharp tongue when you want to."

"I have nae heard ye complain," he shot back before his lips spread into a wicked grin.

"Euan!" Grace gasped. "That is totally not what I meant!"

"No, but it is what *I* meant," he said, and to his great amusement, she rolled her eyes at him. "And I dinnae have a sharp tongue that way."

"Oh, yes you do."

"No."

"Fine, I'm going to record you next time we have an argument."

"Good, because then ye get to hear how sharp ye can be as well."

"You are impossible!"

"So are ye, but this is why we are made for each other, is it nae?"

Grace scoffed in playful annoyance and gave his shoulder a small shove.

"Oi! Watch yerself!"

"Aww, did I hurt you?" she asked with an exaggerated pout.

"Oh, ye are going to be that way about it, are ye?"

Grace grinned and then laughed. "You know I love you. Stop it."

"Aye," he said, chuckling. "I do know, and it is the only thing in the world that matters to me."

Grace leaned forward and kissed his forehead. "Want some ice cream? Maybe with a whisky drizzle?"

"Ach, now, that is a language I understand."

"Then we can binge-watch something on television?"

"Oh aye, keep talking."

"And maybe I can give you a back rub."

"Uh-huh."

"Then maybe *not* watch television?"

Euan grinned. "Ye had me at ice cream, but I am happy to do all the rest."

"Argh!" Grace said, reaching out and placing her hands around his neck in joking exasperation.

"Careful, I might like it."

"EUAN."

The way she said it brought a loud laugh from him before he leaned forward and kissed her. "Come on, let us go get that ice cream, shall we? Then ye can pretend to choke me some more."

"No way!"

"Ye are no fun."

Grace rolled her eyes again and stood up, walking past him to the door, where she paused and looked back at him over her shoulder. The smile she flashed at him was one of pure teasing, the type of smile that immediately sparked a desire in him to drag her into their bed before she shook her head and left. Euan wasted no time in scrambling up to go after her. If anyone could make him forget today, it would be her, and he found that right now it was all he wanted.

CHAPTER 4

PARIS, FRANCE 1742

THE SOFT PATTER FROM the drops of wax hitting the paper was oddly satisfying, reminding him of the sound the rain made when it hit the leaves in the woods at Achnacarry. Lifting the stick and holding it back over the flame, Euan let his eyes become unfocused as the oranges and reds in the fire danced and turned the hardened wax back into liquid. It was soothing; the sweet scent of the wax swirling around him, mixed with the slight acrid hint of the wick itself. Pulling the sealing wax from the flame, he added more of the liquified substance to the already generous portion on the paper before setting it aside and picking up a scalpel. The blade was small and fine, not particularly useful on humans, but perfect for the task Euan was about to undertake.

With a steady hand and intense focus, he began to carve a design into the wax. When it hardened too much, he held the scalpel to the flame to heat it so that it cut easily through the wax. The details were small, but these tiny details would make or break this work. It didn't matter how long it took to get it right, so Euan paid no mind to it, singularly attentive to his task. When he sat back and looked at his handiwork, he smiled at the perfection of it before glancing at the window to see the sun starting to turn the very horizon pink. Rising from his chair, Euan swept the tools into a bag, along with the sealed letter, and blew out the candle.

Pulling a greatcoat over his shoulders, he left the room, and though the hallway he stepped into was dark, he needed no candle to find his way because he already knew it like the back of his own hand. He'd studied it since the moment he'd arrived, after all. In complete silence, he made his way down the hall, careful to avoid the areas where he knew the floor might squeak and give his presence away. He crept down the stairs and then out to the stables, where he saddled his own horse, walking it out a good distance before mounting up so that no one in the house would hear the hoofbeats. Taking in a deep breath, he relaxed as he put distance between himself and the chateau, finally able to be Euan again and not Bastien de Clément, though he had to admit he quite liked the name. He had more than a few aliases he would use again if he needed them, and this one would be added to the list.

The dark stillness of the pre-dawn road was comforting, and it left him time to relax himself. There would be no peace when he returned — there never was — so he must take it where it came, and his thoughts drifted toward home, as they often did when he was alone. He prayed everyone there was all right, especially his mother. There had been no word sent that anything had befallen her, and he certainly hoped someone would've let him know if she'd died. Did she miss him? He wondered if she'd given up hope of his ever coming home, even though at times he felt as though *he'd* given up hope of ever doing so. What had they told her about him? He hadn't been allowed to write to her, or to anyone, and he knew it must have broken her heart to go so long with no word from him.

The thoughts brought a heavy, sad sigh from Euan. He'd been here for five years now, and Achnacarry was becoming more and more a distant memory, a thing to hang onto when he had nothing else. Those initial days of desperation, too, were long past. He was no longer the scared sixteen-year-old beaten to within an inch of his life on what had seemed like a near-daily basis. He was now twenty-one, a man, tall and broad-shouldered, someone to be feared instead of frightened of others. It was strange, but there was a comfort in the ability to inspire that fear, a testament to how far he'd come here. With Euan now a captain in the king's army, even Alain grudgingly respected him, or at least kept a respectful distance.

As Euan rode into the city an hour later, he didn't go directly to the palace or to the barracks, instead making his way down a narrow street and tying his horse outside of a bookseller's. The windows were dark and shuttered, but Euan knew that made no difference. Where others might be afraid to leave their horse tied here, much less be here at this time of day, there was no concern about either thing in the young man's face. Everyone in this small area knew to whom this horse belonged, not one of them would dare touch it, and any who didn't know and tried to steal it would be swiftly warned by others. Lifting a fist, Euan pounded firmly on the door, but not so hard as to seem as though it were the gendarmes come to call. Within moments he heard shuffling within, and the bolt slid back, the door opening a small amount to allow a bespectacled older man to peer out.

"Oh, it is you. Come in," the man said when he caught sight of the visitor, stepping back to let Euan inside before shutting and bolting the door behind him. "Let me fetch Pierre."

"Thank ye, Cyrille."

A moment later, another man came down the stairs, rubbing his eyes. "Euan? What are you doing here at this time of day?"

Pierre Faussaire was one of the best in France at his craft, and his craft was just what his surname suggested: forgery. A man of thirty-five, his head bald and his face clean-shaven, Pierre didn't appear unusual in any way — which was precisely as he intended it to be. Not drawing attention to oneself was key in this business. As part of his training, Euan had apprenticed with Pierre to learn the fine art of forgery, a critical element in the types of jobs Euan often did. The two men had taken a great liking to each other, and it was the only reason Euan would even think of calling on him at this hour.

"Sorry to wake ye, Pierre," Euan said as he pulled the letter from his satchel and held it out.

Pierre took it and looked it over, then looked up at Euan. "A letter from the Marquis d'Anglure?"

"Nae exactly," Euan replied, a sly smile appearing on his lips.

"Ah. So, le Métamorphose Écossais has struck again, has he?"

Euan laughed and gave his head a gentle nod. The Scottish Shapeshifter had long been what Pierre called him due to Euan's almost preternatural ability to become anyone he chose and have no one be the wiser. "Oh, aye."

"Who sent you for this?"

"Who do ye think?"

"Mmm," Pierre groused. "Why did you bring it to me then?"

"I wanted ye to check it to make sure it was right."

"For Christ's sake, boy, are you really that unsure of your own talent?"

"What harm does it do to have the best eyes on it?"

"Because the best eyes after mine are yours, and if you are satisfied with it, then it is perfectly acceptable to anyone else who knows no better. As I have told you many times, you are one of the best forgers I have trained, *the* best if I am honest, and you will not always have me to check your work. You should trust yourself!"

"Maybe someday I will nae have ye, but while I do, I will make use of ye."

"You are an idiot," Pierre said before he smiled and then laughed. "Who were you this time?"

"Bastien de Clèment, at yer service."

"Oh, very nice. Quite genteel sounding."

"I liked it."

"I will not ask you what this is about."

"Ye should nae."

"You would not tell me anyway even if I did."

"No, I would nae."

"What else have you gotten up to since last we spoke?"

"Most recently? Explosives."

"I hope you are as good at that as you are at forgery."

Euan held up his hands, grinning. "Everything is still attached."

"That is good, at least. It would be hard to relieve yourself with no hands."

"I could always have someone else hold it," Euan replied with a shrug.

"And knowing you as I do, you would not lack for volunteers to do so."

"Indeed nae," Euan said, chuckling. "At least nae now."

"In that same vein, you would not have to worry about other relief either."

"I should think nae. The same one holding it can handle the other parts as well."

"We are a vulgar pair."

"It is why we get along, aye?"

Pierre laughed. "I agree. Did you want a cup of wine?"

"I would love one if ye can spare it."

"For you, anything. Come."

Euan followed Pierre into the workshop behind the counter, pulling off his gloves, coat, and hat before taking a seat. Pierre poured two cups and handed Euan one of them before sitting down.

"You look tired, but I am sure it has nothing to do with your most recent assignment. Have they still got you working with the Prussians on Austria?"

"Ye mean the never-ending war? Aye. I was pulled away from strategy planning to do this, much to my irritation."

"Clearly you were needed for something a bit more specialized, and I am certain you are the best they have when it comes to this sort of espionage."

"I am also quite good at the other. I prefer it."

"Sometimes we all do things other than what we prefer. I know perfectly well that you prefer the more direct methods, but I assure you that the Austrians have no idea who you are and do not care, so it is just as faceless as the rest."

Euan rolled his eyes before he drank deeply from his cup.

"You do so hate it when I am right."

Euan gave Pierre a wry smile over the rim of the cup and shook his head.

"However, at least you have a real war to cut your teeth on, hm? If your country is ever at war, they will have your experience to help them."

"Maybe."

"What does that mean?"

"Ye are assuming I will ever be sent home."

"You will be. I am sure your Lochiel will be asking after you if he has not already."

"And he would be easily overruled by a king who decides I am now far too valuable to him to return."

"That is a possibility, yes."

"So, you see?"

"I would think that, if such a decision is made, your value to the king and to Jacques would give you a bit of leverage to use in negotiation to bring your mother to you here. Would you?"

"Aye," Euan replied, his voice softening along with his expression.

"You seem to like it here."

"At times, yes, but at others, no. I miss the open spaces of my home. The people, the places, the language with which I am familiar."

"I can certainly understand that," Pierre said as he studied the young man before him.

Euan stared out in front of him, eyes unfocused and unseeing, and he knew it was clear to Pierre that Euan's time here was wearing on him. He knew it had always bothered Pierre that Euan was kept here almost like some sort of prisoner, that he'd been allowed no contact with anyone from his homeland, never knowing if he would ever go back there. It was cruel, Pierre had said, and something Pierre had raised with Jacques, only to be told that these were the orders. Euan was perfectly aware that Pierre knew him well enough by now to see the strain in Euan's eyes no matter how he tried to hide it, so he'd long ago stopped trying.

"None of it matters," Euan said, giving his head a tiny shake to clear it. "I have a job to do and I will do it."

"Of course you will, just as you always do. Would you like a couple of hours to sleep here? Far more peaceful than going back to the palace, I am sure."

"Normally I would say aye, but this needs to get into the king's hands. He is waiting for it."

As Euan pulled his hand back from the cup, Pierre grabbed his wrist to stop him. "Hold on a moment, are you telling me the king asked you to forge this letter?"

"In a sense. He asked me to provide proof of something, I have done so, and the only thing forged is my signature and the marquis' seal."

Pierre frowned. "Euan, what have you gotten into?"

"It is better ye dinnae ask, Pierre, for the less ye know the less danger ye are in," Euan replied, pulling his hand free of Pierre's grip and standing. "Thank ye for checking it," he finished as he pulled on his outerwear.

"As I said, for you, anything."

Euan gave a small nod and a smile before heading out. Untying his horse, he mounted back up and turned toward the palace, making his way there with no further delay. Once he was off the horse, he handed the reins to a stable hand and entered the palace. The halls were deserted at this hour, and it allowed him to reach his destination with no interference. Reaching the door that led beyond the watching chamber and to the passageways to the meeting rooms for the king's council, the king's rooms, the queen's — and whoever the mistress of the moment happened to be — Euan was greeted at the door by two guards who immediately stepped aside to allow him entry. After he nodded in acknowledgment as he passed them, Euan continued down the hallway, coming to a stop outside of a door and knocking.

When the door was opened, a man looked out and smiled when he saw Euan. "Well, well. Back already? Do you have it?"

Euan held up the letter, and the man's smile grew wider.

"You, monsieur, are an incredible asset, and the king will thank you."

"Only doing my duty, monsieur," Euan replied, bowing before handing over the letter.

"Indeed, you are Captain, and you never fail us. Go, get some rest and return by ten. We will need you in chambers."

Euan bowed once more, then turned to make his way out and back to the barracks. None of the others bothered him when he came inside, or even spoke to him. They noticed his arrival, but it was crystal clear to anyone who saw him that he was in no mood to speak. Once he reached his room, he tossed his bag aside and lit a fire in the small grate before he lay down and fell quickly asleep. By ten in the morning, he was back at the palace as commanded, still out of uniform, and standing out of sight as a man was brought into the room looking confused and worried.

"Monsieur Denis," he said, bowing to the nobleman who stood waiting for him, the same man Euan had delivered the letter to only hours before. "What is the meaning of this? Why have I been called here?"

"Good morning to you, Marquis d'Anglure. Judging by the look on your face, I think you already know."

"If I did, I would not have asked you."

"As you seem to want to play coy, I shall enlighten you: have you been conspiring with the Austrians?"

The face of the marquis went white. "No, of course not!" he sputtered. "Why would I do such a thing?"

"Lands, money, and titles from the Hapsburg king for a start."

"I have all of that here!"

"Not enough, it seems."

"This is ridiculous slander!" the marquis shouted.

Denis held up the letter, and the marquis fell silent. "Is it slander if it is your own words?"

"I ... I wrote no letter."

"Monsieur de Clèment, if you would?"

Euan stepped out into the open, his face serious. "You did," Euan said in French, any trace of his Scottish accent vanished, just as it had been for the whole of the time he was with the marquis.

"Monsieur de Clèment?" the marquis stammered. "But ... I never ... no. I did not have anything to do with that!"

"Your signature is on it," Denis said, "along with Monsieur de Clèment's. All you needed was to believe that someone felt as you did, that someone was willing to conspire with you against your own king."

"I never sent it! I threw it away!"

"And Monsieur de Clèment brought it to us, concerned as he was by your actions. You sealed it, so you were serious enough."

"I did not!"

"Is this not your seal?" Denis asked, holding up the letter once more.

"It is, but ... he must have stolen it!"

"How would I have done that?" Euan asked. "You never take your ring off; it would be impossible for me to steal it."

"Guards! Take him!" Denis shouted to the men at the door.

"No!" the marquis shouted as the men surrounded him and ushered him from the room.

Euan knew that perhaps he should feel bad, but he didn't. The truth was that the marquis was a traitor, dancing with treason, courting it, but never having the gall to set it to paper until Euan had shown up and pretended to be sympathetic to his cause. It was best he was taken care of now before he could do any actual damage.

"Captain Cameron, you are dismissed."

"Thank ye, Monsieur Denis," Euan replied, letting his own speech return before bowing and walking out.

As he left the palace, Euan didn't hurry, allowing the slower pace to give him time to put away the identity of Monsieur de Clèment and become Euan once more. When he arrived back at the barracks, however, Jacques was waiting for him.

"Euan, come speak with me," Jacques said before walking toward the guard room.

Without a word, Euan followed him, silent until the door shut behind them. "What have I done wrong, and what is the punishment to be, Captain?"

A small smirk crossed Jacques' lips. "Nothing, my boy. I hear you did a very fine job with the marquis."

"I did what needed to be done, as ye taught me."

"Yes, you did. It will, however, be your last assignment here."

Euan froze. Whatever in the hell did that mean? "My ... what?"

"If you think I mean you are about to be executed or something, you really need to relax. You are going home, Euan. While we are loath to lose you, your time here is finished. There is nothing more we can teach you and, quite simply, you have outstripped us. As it stands, in your five years here, you have already reached the same rank I hold, though I do appreciate your continuing to treat me as your superior instead of your equal."

"Then why are ye sending me home?"

"Because you were never meant to be ours to keep."

"But the king —"

"Does not even know you exist and will not miss you. We, on the other hand ..."

"Who will protect him? Who will do my tasks?"

"We will, just as we did before you arrived. Are you trying to stay?"

"I —" Euan began before he stopped, not knowing what to say. He *did* want to go home, but he wasn't expecting to feel so conflicted about doing so. He'd convinced himself for so long that it would never happen and now had no answer when it had.

"Pack your things. You leave now."

"I dinnae even have a chance to say farewell?"

"To whom?"

"I did make friends here."

"Write letters and I will see to it that they are delivered. Go on."

Euan bowed and left the room in a state of disbelief. He was going home.

CHAPTER 5

SCOTTISH HIGHLANDS, 1742

THERE WAS NO ONE waiting to meet Euan when he arrived in Inverness, but he wasn't at all surprised by that. He knew it was unlikely any notice had been sent ahead that he would be returning. What he'd not expected was the rush of emotion he felt upon setting foot on Scottish soil once more. It was overwhelming, that feeling of reality, of knowing he was in his own country and such a painful chapter of his life was finally at an end. Euan wanted to weep with relief, but everything instilled in him these last years prevented him from doing so.

After a short wait, his horse, Absalon, was brought up from the hold of the ship, and his reins passed to Euan. Absalon was the one thing he'd been truly thankful for during his time in the king's service. Absalon had been Euan's for the last few years, a fine Arabian stallion from the king's own stables and quite an expensive gift to thank Euan for his service. The murmurs at the docks as Euan led Absalon through the crowd were amusing but not unexpected. Absalon, with his shining, onyx-colored coat, was a rarity anywhere, much less here. The pure black was what made the animal as striking as he was, but his beauty wasn't Euan's favorite thing about him. Absalon was loyal to Euan alone, a horse bred and trained for war. Arabians were, as a general rule, fussy about anyone who wasn't their master, and Absalon was no exception to that. He did, however, tend to be more extreme about it. Absalon was obedient and well-trained, but it wasn't until he came into Euan's care that he'd found his true master and bonded with him nearly instantly. Now, if someone who wasn't Euan tried riding him, it wasn't going to happen, and Absalon would ensure that outcome in any way he could; something a good many people had discovered the hard way.

Once he was out of the docks, Euan mounted the horse and took to the southern road. The journey wouldn't take him long, less than two days, and Euan had left France with plenty of coin to not only provision himself for the journey back to Achnacarry, but also take care of himself and his mother for quite some time if they were careful. He'd taken side jobs with Pierre, his earnings stashed away in the hope of this very thing, and if Jacques knew, he never spoke of it.

As he turned onto the road that led to the castle, he took a deep breath and closed his eyes. The scent of it was so familiar to him, something that lived in his soul, it seemed, no matter how long he might be away from it. The smell of the trees, the damp of the leaves on the ground, the moss, the wood smoke from fires. He smiled and opened his eyes, urging Absalon into a fast trot. Riding through the gates sent a wave of excitement and relief flooding through him: he was finally home.

Coming to a stop, Euan dismounted and patted Absalon's neck. "Here we are, my friend. Home. This is where ye will stay, what do ye think of it?" Euan smiled as Absalon made a sound. "Aye, the stables are quite fine, and ye will be well treated. Maybe nae as fine as the palace, but they will do."

A young boy from the stables came out, eyeing Euan warily.

"Ah, thank ye lad," Euan said, handing the reins over to him.

"Will ye be needing him back, sir?"

"No, he will remain here, as I will," Euan said to the boy before turning to the horse. "Absalon, ye be a good lad and let him see to ye. Dinnae ye give him a hard time."

"Aye, sir," the boy replied, leading Absalon away and casting glances back at Euan as he did so.

Euan smiled and shook his head, pushing open one of the great doors and stepping inside. All activity ceased, people staring at the man who'd so brazenly made his way inside without waiting for Lochiel to arrive and invite him in. It looked much the same to Euan, everything where he remembered it: the iron stands of candles, the roaring fire in the massive fireplace of the great hall, the people scattered about preparing for the next meal, and it was comforting to know that his memories hadn't failed. It didn't, however, take Lochiel long to appear, flanked by men Euan knew well.

"May I help ye?" Lochiel asked as he approached Euan.

Euan was confused for a moment as his chief and his own friends seemed to fail to recognize him, and not only that, spoke to him in English. It was only as he watched them all taking him in that he realized why they wouldn't. Euan stood before them in the officer's dress of the French military. The deep blue of the coat made Euan's blue eyes stand out, and the vibrant red of the waistcoat popped with the shine of the silver facing and polished silver buttons on both. He wore riding boots, something only those of higher status wore here, though they were covered by knee-high white gaiters with obsidian buttons. The broadsword at his hip denoted a seeming wealth, the basket polished and shining. Euan was now far taller than he'd been when he'd left Achnacarry and seemed to tower over the others, though it was only a few inches difference. His chest and shoulders were broad, thanks to all the training and work he'd done, and there was an intimidating strength in his bearing.

Euan gave a deep bow, removing his hat. "Lochiel. It is good to return to yer service once more."

The other officers looked at him in confusion, and Euan realized, to his great irritation, that he'd spoken in French. Lochiel, however, understood him and answered in the same. "In my service, lad? May I ask who ye are?"

Euan stood upright and smiled. "Ye know me well even if ye dinnae think so. It is me, Euan," he said, this time making sure he spoke Gaelic. "Hello, Malcolm, Iain, Findlay," he continued, with a nod to the officers.

The surprise on the faces of all of them made Euan want to laugh as they looked him over once more and tried to reconcile what they were now seeing with what they remembered.

"Christ in heaven! Euan, my boy!" Lochiel bellowed before laughing and stepping forward to embrace him. "Look at ye!" he said, stepping back to look him over. "For a moment I swore I was seeing the ghost of yer father."

Euan was more than happy to return the embrace. "Aye, a bit different from the sixteen-year-old lad who left ye."

"That is an understatement, lad. It looks as though the time in France did ye quite a bit of good!"

Euan kept the anger out of his expression at the mention of France, knowing Lochiel had no idea what Euan had gone through there. "Aye, I learned much."

"They made ye an officer, did they?"

"Aye. I have been helping with the Austrian war for the last few years and earned my promotion to captain in such a manner."

"Ye have been at war?" Lochiel asked in surprise.

"No, I was setting the strategy for those who were. The king found it a much better use of my talents, though I would have gone to the front if he had sent me."

"That is ... well, that is far beyond what I sent ye to learn, and I look forward to hearing all about yer time there."

"I look forward to telling ye."

"Fetch Aileen here but dinnae tell her why," Lochiel said to one of the girls in the hall.

Malcolm grinned. "Euan Cameron, no longer a boy but a man."

"A giant of a man at that," Findlay said.

"I am surprised they found a uniform to fit ye," Iain said.

Euan laughed and stepped forward to hug his friends, the men he'd always considered his brothers. He'd missed them, and being in their company again had been something he'd very much looked forward to once he'd learned he was returning. Their faces had never faded from his memory, though at the worst of times he'd wished they would. It was its own kind of torment then, reminding him of what he'd lost and torturing him with the sure knowledge that none of them had any idea what was happening to him so far away. He'd often wondered in those moments if they missed him as he missed them, if they could hear him crying out for them in his heart.

"Welcome home, lad," Malcolm whispered to him as they embraced. "Ye were much missed."

"As were ye," Euan whispered in return. "More than I could possibly say."

"Ye sent for me, Lochiel?"

The familiar voice of his mother took Euan's breath away, and he felt unable to move, keeping his back to her.

"Aye, we have someone come to see ye, Aileen," Lochiel replied.

"Me? Who would want to see —" her words were cut off in a loud gasp as Euan turned to look at her, her hands covering her mouth.

"Hello, Mam."

Aileen said nothing, dissolving immediately into hysterical sobs. Euan hurried forward, catching her in his arms as her knees gave out and hugging her tight against him.

"It is all right, Mam, shh. I am home now, back home with ye," he whispered to her.

Aileen pulled back to look at him, cupping his face in her hands and crying before she hugged him again. Her tears brought them to Euan's eyes as well, his own swirling emotions mirrored in the outward face of hers.

"Let us go into the study, and ye can have a moment alone there," Lochiel said in a gentle voice.

Euan helped his mother to stand and followed Lochiel, who opened the door to let them in and then shut it behind them, truly giving the two of them time alone.

"My Euan! My own sweet bairn!" Aileen sobbed.

"Aye, it is me," he said as a soft smile appeared on his face. "Home where I belong."

"I dinnae understand what ye are saying," Aileen said, shaking her head.

Euan swore softly to himself. "I am sorry," he said, forcing himself to speak Gaelic. "I have been speaking French for so long it is now the first thing I do. It will take me time to adjust. What I said was that aye, it is me, and I am home where I belong."

"Aye, ye are," she said through tears. "But look at ye! I hardly know ye!"

"I have grown up a bit."

"More than a bit, but ye are the spitting image of yer father."

Euan smiled. "Does that give ye joy or pain?"

"Both, for I am overjoyed ye are here, but pained I did nae see ye become the man ye are now."

Euan winced. "Ye would nae have wanted to witness it."

"Euan, what happened?"

He shook his head. "Dinnae ask and let us just be happy I have returned."

"Are ye to go back to France?"

"No, I have been dismissed to return home and to Lochiel's service."

"Thank God for that," she said, stepping back to look him over. "Look at that beautiful uniform! Ye look so handsome in it."

"Thank ye," he said. "It will be odd nae to wear it now after so long."

"Why would ye nae?"

"No reason to do so here. Here it means naught."

"I suppose ye are right, but ye will have to wear it until I can make ye some new clothing. Oh, love, it is so good to see ye," Aileen said, though she hadn't stopped crying.

Euan embraced her once more, which only increased her tears, but this time, Euan didn't stop his own. It was all too much, this relief, this emotion. No one recognized him, and while he thought coming back would be easy, it was going to be far from it. He had no place here, not yet, and it made him feel like an outsider. The looks, which had been amusing initially, now hurt when he recalled them, the lack of recognition from his own friends painful.

"Oh Euan," Aileen said. "I know. Ye dinnae have to say it. This must be so hard for ye after so long away, but ye are home and I will take care of ye. It will all be right again in no time, ye will see."

"Aye, it will be."

"I dinnae know what Lochiel will have planned for ye tonight, but I am sure it will nae be going home and resting so ye can get yer mind straight."

"Probably nae," Euan conceded. "I am sure he will want me at supper at the very least."

Aileen sighed. "Ye have just returned, and yet ye are already at work."

"It could nae be any other way, and we both know that. I dinnae know what sort of plan Lochiel has for me now that I am back, but I am sure I will find out soon enough."

"There is something different about ye, Euan. Ye are so distant and ye dinnae seem as free as ye were when ye left."

"To show affection is to mark them for death."

Jacques' words echoed in his mind, but he forced them away. "I am nae, but I cannae be, Mam. I am different, very different. I am nae the boy ye knew, nae anymore. The things I have done, the things I have learned, all of it has changed me in ways ye cannae possibly understand. No matter what it may seem like outwardly, please always know that I love ye, truly and without measure. I thought of ye every day, prayed for ye each night. Ye are all I have."

Aileen stroked his cheek. "No, ye are nae my sweet young one now, and I know I should nae expect ye to be so."

Euan covered her hand with his own. "I want to keep ye safe from harm, and to do that I may have to sometimes seem distant to ye, but I promise it is nae so. Please, tell me ye understand."

"I dinnae, but I trust ye."

Euan squeezed her hand and sighed. "I suppose I should go now, but I swear the moment I am finished I will come home. I am going to ask for a bit of leave so I can help ye around the cottage and do what ye need me to do."

"All right, son," she said, letting go of his hand. "Ye watch yerself."

Euan smiled then, and her shock at how it changed him showed on Aileen's face. He was, in an instant, dark and full of danger. "No, *they* will need to watch *themselves*. I fear no one here because there is no one here who can harm me."

"But —"

"Trust me," Euan said firmly. "There is nae a man here who stands a chance," he continued before he kissed both of her hands and bowed to her. "I will see ye soon, Mam."

"Aye," Aileen whispered as he walked away, leaving her to wonder what man had replaced the son she'd known.

As soon as he exited the study, Euan was directed to another room where he joined Lochiel and the others. The rest of the officers were also gathered there now, and Euan bowed to all of them, a gesture which was returned.

"Well, Euan," Lochiel said. "I am surprised no one sent word ahead that ye would be returning. I had rather lost hope of ye coming back at all."

"So had I, if I am honest. There was no warning, I was simply told I was leaving."

"And here ye are."

"Aye," Euan said. "Here I am, back to serve ye."

"Tell me, what did they teach ye while ye were away?"

"Many things. How to guard a king, but how to do so from the shadows as well as from the front line. How to stop threats from becoming a reality. Explosives, forgery, spycraft, strategies, tactics."

"Spycraft?"

"Aye, how to become another person entirely in order to do whatever must be done. I am quite good at it and was often sent to do such tasks."

Lochiel smiled. "All things that are very useful to any leader."

"Indeed. Just before I returned, I made sure that a threat to the king was stopped before it could become a liability. A nobleman had conspired with Austria, and I made sure we had the proof."

Euan watched as the effect of the words and the way he spoke them gave both Malcolm and Iain pause, the looks on their faces unambiguous. To them, there was something almost frightening about Euan's nonchalance, the way it seemed as if doing what he'd done was as simple and insignificant as tracking down a lost cow.

"Excellent. I am sure we will have great use for such skills. In the meantime, I want ye as part of my constant escort. Wherever I am, there ye are as well. Where I go, ye go. Understood?"

"Aye, Lochiel," Euan said with a nod. "Though I ask for a few days to adjust to life here once more and to assist my mam in anything she may need. I have been long away, and it will take a bit of time to remember that I am home again. I know she is already set to work on a new suit of clothing for me."

"Aye, I assume it would be quite a change from what ye were used to these last years. No longer at court with a king in a shining palace, but back here in the remoteness of the Highlands."

Euan saw the eyebrows of the officers shoot up at the mention of the king and the court, and it told him they'd had no idea where he'd been or why.

"And, of course, remembering to speak Gaelic first instead

of French," Lochiel said, chuckling. "Yer request is granted, and I am nae surprised she has set to seeing to yer clothing, for Aileen has always been on top of such things. However, for that, she will need these," Lochiel said, producing a small bag and tossing it onto the table between them, where it made a clinking sound as it landed.

Euan picked it up and opened it, then looked up. "Silver buttons?"

"Aye, silver buttons to go on yer new uniform, along with this," Lochiel said, opening his hand to expose in his palm the shining silver badge with the Cameron crest that denoted an officer.

All the men gathered in the room let out a collective gasp. Euan was young, only twenty-one, and the youngest officers in the room were almost five years older than he was and newly promoted themselves. This promotion would make Euan the youngest man in the clan to be so elevated, and it was something Euan himself had always dreamed of and wanted. Now, his dream was about to become his reality.

Euan gingerly took the badge from Lochiel's hand, smoothing his thumb over the raised surface. "Thank ye, Lochiel. This is a great honor," he said with a deep bow.

"An honor ye have well earned, Euan, and will continue to earn. We should celebrate with a dram, and ye shall be the guest of honor at supper tonight."

The others cheered and congratulated Euan as Lochiel poured a serving of whisky for each man so they might toast Euan's return and his promotion. While Euan was happy and excited for both things, he was also uneasy. There was part of him that longed to be the person he'd once been, but the child who'd left Scotland was no more, and he could never come home again. All that was left was the man who'd risen from the ashes of the hopes, dreams, and broken spirit of that child; and as they all spoke, it became clearer and clearer to Euan that he was a stranger. They knew nothing about his life, nor he theirs, and they'd been some of his closest friends once. More than that, there was a massive divide in education that prevented Euan from expressing many things in the way he ordinarily might because he knew they wouldn't understand it or recognize the things he referenced. Philosophy, literature, the finer arts of warfare; all of those things that would be hard for anyone but Lochiel to understand, and it only served to deepen his feelings of isolation.

Supper was a blur of toasts, laughter, introductions, and reintroductions, and the merriment helped to banish some of those feelings, at least for a while. It was good to be home in that sense, and he found he still knew the routines and how things at Achnacarry were run because those were things that would never change. When Euan was finally released to make his way home, he took his time to breathe in the night air as he walked, reacquainting himself with the landscape he'd always known. The sound of the river, the leaves of the trees rustling in the night wind, the way the light from the lantern he carried made scant difference against the darkness of a Highland night when the clouds covered the moon. The realization that Jacques, Alain, and the others were now an ocean away from him and unable to cast their pall over his life was so overwhelming in its emotion that by the time he got to the cottage he'd been born and raised in, all he wanted to do was sleep. He could tell his mother about his promotion in the morning. Aileen didn't stop him when he expressed his desire to go right to bed, though she wondered aloud how long it had been since he'd last had a good night's sleep, a question he acted as though he hadn't heard rather than answer.

Euan felt as though he'd just fallen asleep when the sound of footsteps on a stone floor reached him through the darkness. Stone floor? That wasn't right. Their home's floor was packed earth and nowhere near large enough for that many steps to be taken. His eyes fluttered open, and he was surprised to find himself not in his home but in the castle. How had he gotten here? He could've sworn he'd gone home. Sitting up from a bench with a concerned frown, he looked around at the empty great hall. Where was everyone else?

"Gone," a soft voice said, answering his silent question.

He almost forgot to breathe when the sound reached his ears. It was a voice with which he was intimately familiar, but one he hadn't heard since his early years in France, and it set his heart to racing even as he smiled. "Hello, Grace," he said in quiet reply.

"Hello, Euan," she said, and he could hear her smile in her tone. There was, and always had been, something soothing in the sound of her voice. Though she sounded English, there was something slightly different about it that he'd never been able to place.

Euan turned around and took in the sight of the figure standing there. Her white dress seemed to glow, her golden hair loose over her shoulders, and those hauntingly beautiful blue eyes that were hers alone. She'd always been a beauty, always the same age he was whenever they met, and she stood before him now as a stunningly beautiful grown woman. An angel, *his* angel, his protector. Whether she truly was an angel or a figment of his imagination, he couldn't say, but it had never mattered anyway.

"It has been a long while since ye have come."

"It has been a long while since you have truly needed me."

"Aye, I suppose it has been, has it nae? Yet, ye always know when to appear."

She made her way forward and sat down beside him, sitting the opposite way to him on the bench so that they still faced each other. "Of course I do, and I always will."

Euan reached out and took one of her delicate hands in his, letting the warmth of her skin wash through him and warm him, too. "I am thankful for it."

"I know, as I always am when you need me. I miss your company when I am away."

"Do ye?" he asked, looking up at her with curiosity. She'd never said anything like that before, and it intrigued him. In an instant, all he wanted to do was reach out and let one of those golden tendrils slip through his fingers to see if it was as soft as it looked.

"I do, but at the same time, I know being here means you are troubled, and that is not something I am happy about."

"Ye always take it away, and ye have always done so. Ye are the only one who can."

"What is it that sits heavy on your mind and heart?"

"My return. All I wanted for so long was to come home, but now ..." he began before letting the thought trail off.

"But now you are not sure if you belong."

"Aye, that is just it."

"You do belong; this is your home. Your mother is here, your friends."

"Do I? Do I really? Grace, they dinnae know me now. I am nae the same as I was; I cannae be, and I feel the gulf between us all so keenly that I wonder if they are still my friends. I cannae tell them why I am this way, cannae tell them what I have done or what I know. I cannae speak with them in the same way I might speak with ye, or the way I spoke with Jacques or Pierre."

"The depth of your education places a river between you, I know. But, Euan, you will learn how to bridge it and mend your relationships. You will adapt, as you always do and have always done, and you will find your way here once more. It is only temporary though, for someday you will be free."

"Free? From what? When?"

"I cannot say."

Euan let loose a heavy sigh. "For now, I am a stranger in my own home."

"It will be brief; you must have faith in yourself."

Euan stroked her hand in soft, slow movements. "Ye are so ..." he began before shaking his head. "I dinnae even have the words for it," he murmured in an almost absent-minded way.

"Close your eyes," she whispered.

Euan felt his eyes close, out of his control, and found he couldn't open them again when he tried. "Why?"

"Because," she replied, taking his hands and lifting them up.

Euan gasped at the first touch of his fingertips against the silken skin of her face. This had never happened before, not like this, and the undercurrent of intimacy that had been present since the moment she'd arrived tonight seemed to intensify in an instant. When last he'd had need of her, he was seventeen. Things were far different now, with the man before her able to notice the thoughts and feelings she stirred in him that the boy had been too broken and scared to see. He let his fingers slide over the contours of her face, heard her breathing quicken to match his own. They slipped along her cheekbones and the line of her jaw, then down her delicate neck. It was there that he felt the brush of that golden hair against the top of his hand and gave in to the need to touch it, finding it soft like velvet. He moved his free hand and traced a fingertip over her lips.

"What have ye done?" he asked in a near whisper. "God help me, ye are the softest thing I have ever touched. I will always crave this now."

"So will I."

"Grace, I —" he began, but any further words were silenced when he felt the gentle brush of her lips against his. As the shock tingled through him, Euan felt as though he might die of need right then and there. He'd never wanted anyone this much in his life. "Oh, sweet Christ …"

There came a quiet chuckle from her. "I am sorry."

"Dinnae be. Do it again, for I realize I have longed for it. All of those visits in that year and I just … please."

"Will you be brave enough to claim what you long for? There will come a time when you must trust, fully trust, in order to have all you want."

"Ye speak in such riddles."

"You seek someone you will not find here. She will come from far away, and when she does, you will have a choice to make. You will have to summon all of your courage to follow your heart to your destiny."

"I know I will forget this, as I always do, left with just the peace ye bring me when I wake. I hope that I will have that courage when it is called for, but no one will compare to ye. How could they? Nae to mention I have been taught never to love."

"She will compare, fear not, and she will get past those lessons. You will be defenseless against her."

"I am defenseless against ye," Euan whispered as he used his hands on her face to pull her toward him. When her lips fully touched his, the feeling that tore through him was intense and immediate, drawing a small moan from his chest against those lips.

She responded to him without hesitation, and he slid his hands away so he could wrap his arms around her and hold her to him. The feel of her body was sheer perfection, the soft floral scent of her skin intoxicating. All of it felt right in a way he couldn't begin to explain, but he didn't care. All that mattered right now was this. Her lips were soft and sweet, and it felt as though he could linger on them alone for days. He didn't want this to stop even though he pulled back from her just a bit in order to catch his breath.

"I have never felt … I know I should nae have …"

"You should have. You claimed what you longed for, and you will do so again when you must."

"Kiss me again," he murmured against her lips. "I need it."

When she obliged him, it made him feel weak, and he prayed for God to forgive him for sullying one of his celestial beings, but she was too much for him to resist. Her lips left his, and she placed a small kiss on his jaw, but he gripped the bench with both hands and groaned when she kissed his ear and followed it with a gentle bite.

"Jesus," he breathed. "Dinnae stop. Please, dinnae stop."

He felt her lips curve into a smile against his cheek as she nuzzled it before she ran a line of kisses down his throat, her fingers deftly untying his neck stock and parting the shirt he wore to allow her to trail those kisses down to the center of his chest, and Euan felt as though he might pass out.

"Until then," she whispered, flattening her hand over his heart, "this is mine, as are you."

"Aye. God forgive me, aye."

"We cannot go further than this," she said, and he heard her soft laugh at what surely must have been the disappointment on his face. "It will be worth it."

"I am nae so sure about that."

"Do you not trust me?"

"Oh, I do, but right now I know what I want, and nae being able to have it does nae seem worth it to wait for a mystery."

"You must trust me."

"How will I know?"

"You will feel it when she is near you," she said before she kissed him again.

"Ye doing that does nae help."

"I cannot help it, for I have wanted this as much as you have."

"Have ye now? Then it sounds as though ye are as much mine as I am yers."

"I will not deny it, for I have always been."

Euan smiled. "I wish my waking mind could remember ye."

"No, you do not, for if it did you would be miserable. It is better this way. Our time tonight is ending."

"No! Please, nae yet!"

"I have no control. I want to stay, but I cannot."

Euan sighed in resignation. "Then kiss me once more, my beautiful *leannan*, and let my dream body die upon yer lips only to wake in a darker world without ye."

"What poetry you can speak."

"I mean every word when it comes to ye."

"I know."

"Please," he whispered.

Euan took a deep breath in when he felt her lips on his again, this new kiss between them now full of longing and desire. It was passionate and set him on fire, spurring him to bury his hands in that gossamer hair and hold her to him.

"Euan," she breathed as she pulled back from him.

Euan opened his eyes with a small gasp, blinking as he stared up at the ceiling of the cottage. He smiled as the warmth of the dream wrapped around him, knowing this feeling, and knowing it well. Whenever he'd felt at his worst in France, there had always been a dream to pull him back and give him the strength to keep going. After he'd had it, there was always this same feeling: love, warmth, and comfort. He never remembered it, which saddened him, but the feeling always seemed to linger long enough to soothe him. He wished he knew what it was about, this dream that served him so well, but as long as it still came to him when he needed it, he wouldn't question it.

CHAPTER 6

"YOU HAD THESE DREAMS often?" Specialist George asked.

"Only in my first year in France. There were so many times I wanted to give up, so many times I wanted to just let them end my life so the torture would be over. Any time I got to that point, I would have that sort of dream and would wake up feeling better."

"But you don't remember anything about them."

"I did nae," Euan said, his voice becoming so quiet as to be near a whisper. "But now …"

"Now?"

"It was her."

"Who?"

"Grace. I know that now."

"How, if you don't remember it?"

"There were flashes of things that would come back to me, things which made no sense at the time, but as a whole, they do. I remembered golden hair, the way her hand felt in mine, the way it felt when she held me to comfort me, or how it felt when she stroked my hair to ease me. It all meant naught until she came, and then all of it came together. I feel the same way now as I did in those dreams when she holds me, when she strokes my hair, when her hand is in mine. Whenever she is near, I feel that same warmth."

"How do you think such a thing is possible?"

"I am nae sure, but all I can think is that God sent her to me to show me what waited for me if I just held on. My patience and my will would bring a wonderful reward. As I tell her, ye dinnae always have to understand everything for it to be real."

"Have you told her about this?"

"No, and I dinnae know yet how I would. The time will come for me to say it, and I will when it does."

"You had these dreams when you were at your lowest points: were you truly that troubled upon your return?"

"Aye, far more than anyone there could understand, and I hid it from them because I knew they would nae. There was only one other time that I —" Euan said before he stopped, his eyes widening.

"Euan?"

"Falkirk," he whispered.

"What?"

"She was at Falkirk. She came for me there, she …" Euan said to himself in a rush as he sat up. "I wanted to … but she … no, no, it is nae time for that yet."

"What do you mean?" George asked, trying to draw Euan's attention back to him.

"We are nae there yet, but we will be and … I cannae," Euan trailed off as he gave a gentle shake of his head. "Nae yet."

"Very well, let's change topics. Let's instead discuss the things you learned."

"The things I learned. I learned how to destroy people, to end lives."

"You also learned how to save them through the use of strategy."

"Did I? Or did I just learn how to save the lives I wanted to save, those *we* deemed worthy, by ending the lives of others?"

"Quite a narrow distinction."

"But an important one. In war there is no safety without the death of others. Ye must kill to be safe, kill to keep others safe. There was no right side in that war or even in our own rising later, no matter what anyone involved wanted to think."

"You were, you said, trained in espionage."

"Aye. I was very good at it and still am. It is what allows Grace and me to work so effectively together. We are the same in that sense; we understand each other without having to say so. I can become anyone I choose, and I can do it easily. I can make ye believe me, but so can she; she is a master at it. Jacques and the others would have worshipped her for such skills."

"Does such an ability make you feel powerful?"

"Of course it does. How could it nae? It is nae something I am comfortable with, and it is why I am happy to have the chance to turn it to good instead of other ends."

"Do you ever use it to hide things from Watcher Cameron?"

Euan looked up at him, and his expression made it clear that the very suggestion offended him. "Never. I have *never* done so and never will. Nae that I could, for such things dinnae work on people like us. She would see through me in a second."

"Do you mean Watchers and Companions?"

"No," Euan replied, a hint of a smile on his lips. "I mean people who do what we do, who become others and play the necessary parts to get what we need. Ye call them spies, dinnae ye?"

"Interesting. Do you worry she can or would use it to hide things from you?"

"What are ye trying to say?" Euan asked, his expression matching the sudden darkness in his tone drawn out by the mere suggestion that Grace was anything but straightforward with him. No one would imply or speak ill of her in his presence without him challenging it.

"I'm just asking if the thought has crossed your mind," George said, reading Euan's tone and taking the chance to clarify his question.

"No, because I know she would nae. Even if she wanted to, she cannae hide from me that well, nae anymore, nae with the bond we share. I would know, the same as she would with me."

"Very well. Let's talk about your last assignment in France

before you were dismissed from the king's service. What was it you did?"

"Information reached us that the marquis was attempting to contact the Austrians to provide them with information about nae only the king's movements, but also what strategies and formations were being set in the war councils. He was willing to provide information on any holes he could find in the king's security to assist with an assassination. I was tasked to make contact with him and pretend to be willing to assist him, to be on his side, and provide the proof needed. I did so."

"Did you forge the whole of the letter?"

"No," Euan said, chuckling. "Ye would be amazed at how brazen people will be when they believe they are nae alone out on the limb. He wrote the letter himself that night while we were sitting together. When he retired, he left it upon the desk, and that was his mistake. I retrieved it, and the only thing I forged was his seal."

"How did you forge it?"

"I carved it by hand in the wax. I made a study of the seal on his ring and was able to replicate it."

"You carved the seal by hand?" George repeated, eyebrow raised.

"Aye. Best way to do it if ye are able and have a steady hand. It was how I got the missing seals on our last mission. I made them."

"Clever. Did you feel at all badly for what you had done?"

"Nae at all. His actions would have meant chaos for France. If the king were assassinated, what then? It would pull us from the war, the kingdom would collapse on itself over the succession, and it would make us vulnerable to enemies. He needed to be stopped, and he was."

"Let's circle back to the day you came home. You mentioned that you felt like a stranger when you returned to Scotland."

"Aye, and I was. No one knew me, and I had this whole

other life they knew naught of, nor could I tell them."

"Coming back far more educated than they were must have also been difficult."

"It was. I could nae discuss things with them that were nae clan related, farming, soldiering, or the like. I did nae know their lives or the families they now had, but as time went on, I fell back into life again. I knew the people and their struggles, the families, all of it. Through that I connected with my friends again and set all else by the wayside."

"Were you able to have those discussions with Lochiel?"

Euan's smile at the question was half-hearted and sad. "Aye, and we did on our many travels. It was why what happened a few times during the rising and what happened during our last mission was so jarring and painful. That was nae the man I knew, and I could nae reconcile it."

"Were you pleased with your promotion?"

"Aye and no. I was happy to have it, for I had wanted it my whole life, but then I had spent that time away. I was already an officer when I returned, an officer under a king, guiding his army, nae for a clan chief. My perspective on where people sat in the world had vastly changed. While my position was important within my clan, within the wider world it meant naught."

"And now you're something even greater still."

"I am, and it is more important than either of the other two, but it still is nae my most important position."

"What is, in your opinion?"

"Being a husband to my wife. Being a son to my mam. Making sure they have the things they need, that they are safe, loved, and happy. Being a Companion to Grace in every sense of the word and being everything she needs me to be to work at her side. Being the man she believes me to be."

"You don't think you're that man?"

"Nae yet, but each day I strive to come closer to it. I am nae sure I will ever feel as though I am worthy of her, but there will never be a day where I dinnae thank God and the universe for bringing me to her. It was only then that I could begin to become the man I am truly meant to be."

Specialist George smiled. "You have quite the way with words."

"I have been told that before," Euan said, amused.

"Is there anything else you'd like to discuss from this period before we're done for the day?"

Euan sighed and dropped back against the arm of the couch. "Aye, one more thing."

Euan sat in silence at a table in the great hall of Invergarry Castle, surveying those gathered within. Lochiel was here to meet with the chief of MacDonell of Glengarry, John Mac-Donell. He didn't know what they were to speak of, but it wasn't his business, so he hadn't asked. His job was to protect his chief, though he'd been dismissed from standing watch at the door and sent to the hall to take his ease with the other men. Seated at the table with him were Malcolm, Iain, and Findlay, and all four were enjoying mugs of ale.

"Why so serious, Euan?" Findlay asked.

"It is my job to be serious, Finn," Euan said, bringing his eyes back to his friend and smiling. "And even if I look serious, it does nae mean I am. Anyone else here does nae need to know that."

"It is his job to look menacing, more like," Iain quipped.

"That too," Euan replied.

"Tell us a tale of France, Euan," Malcolm said.

Euan raised an eyebrow. "What do ye want to know?"

"What was it like guarding a king?"

"A lot like this but with fancier surroundings and stuffier clothes."

The three men laughed, which made Euan do the same.

"Surely it was more interesting than this," Finn said, gesturing about him.

"Sometimes it was, I suppose. There were a lot more of us, and for all the men ye could see, there was an equal number of men ye could nae."

"What do ye mean?" Iain asked.

"There were men always lurking in the shadows of Louis' court. Watching him, watching the men tasked with watching him. Layers of security to ensure the failure of one layer did nae mean total disaster. If ye were on that duty, ye blended in."

"Surely ye were never on it then," Iain muttered into his mug.

Euan laughed. "Iain, would it surprise ye to know I was almost always on that duty?"

"How! Ye dinnae blend in at all!"

"Ye would be amazed at what I can do," Euan said, becoming quiet. "Who I can become if I must, how I can disappear in plain sight if I wish to. It is possible if ye know how. Unfortunately, that duty often means more time watching the king bed varying women than ye would like to be privy to."

The three laughed again. "I dinnae think I would want that duty," Finn said, rolling his eyes. "Unless, of course, I get access to them, too."

"Depending on who it is, ye probably could," Euan said, shrugging. "I never did."

"Why nae?"

"I prefer an honest whore."

"Ach, Euan, that is sharp," Malcolm said.

"It is also true. Some of these women were offering themselves up for position, money, titles, and the like. Bedding a man for that reason does nae make ye any less a bawd just because he is a king. Give me a woman who is at least honest about the reason she is riding ye."

Iain choked on his ale and started coughing, which made Euan laugh a bit harder.

"A bit crass," Finn said.

"Dinnae act so scandalized, Finn. Nae as though ye have nae said worse," Malcolm chided.

"And nae as though Euan has had any shortage of that type of sport since he returned," Iain coughed out.

"No, I have nae," Euan said, grinning, before he took another drink. "It is amazing what women are willing to do when ye let them know that fancy ladies in France are doing it."

"Oh? Like what?" Finn asked.

"Like share a bed with ye two at time."

"No!"

"Oh aye. If ye have nae tried it, I suggest ye pay for it the next time ye are near a brothel."

There was a commotion at the other end of the hall, and it got the attention of everyone else. A young woman, held by the wrist, was backed into a corner with a man yelling into her face.

"Stop it!" she shouted.

"Ye will give me an answer, Janet!"

"No! I dinnae want to wed ye! There is yer answer! Now leave me be!"

"Ye lie! No one else will have ye, slut that ye are!"

"How dare ye!" she shouted, lashing out with her free hand and slapping him across the face, the sound reverberating through the now silent hall.

Without a moment's pause, the man struck her back, not with a slap, but with a fist, bringing a scream of pain from her as she crumpled to the floor in front of him. "Ye bitch! If ye will nae wed me then —"

"Then what?" Euan asked from behind him, having gotten up as soon as the shouting had started. He knew full well where such a thing would be going; he'd seen it far too many times.

The man turned around and looked at Euan. "Mind yer business," he sneered.

"This *is* my business since ye made it the business of all of us when ye did it here in the open. Now, let the lass be.

She has said she has no wish to wed ye, and that is all."

"And what will ye do? Who are ye anyway? Some other man she has bedded?"

"I dinnae even know the lass, and I am a guest here."

"He is right, lad," one of the other Glengarry men called out. "Dinnae be foolish! Ye will be in enough trouble with the chief as it is!"

"Shut yer mouth!" the young man shouted before turning back to Euan and stepping close to him. "I will do what I please, and I suggest ye sit down."

"Do ye? And if I dinnae take yer suggestion?"

"Then I will challenge ye."

"Feel free," Euan said, a dark smile appearing on his lips.

"Euan," Iain called out, but Euan held up a hand to silence him.

Janet pushed herself up from the ground, leaning against the wall while holding her face and sobbing. Euan stepped around the young man so he could help her, pulling a piece of cloth from his sporran and offering it to her for her bleeding nose and mouth.

"Dinnae ye touch her!" the young man screamed in fury.

Euan turned just as the other man charged him, now holding a knife he'd pulled when Euan's back was turned. Without thinking, Euan caught his wrist, shoving it upward and ducking under his arm to come out behind him. Extending the arm fully and turning it, Euan viciously pulled it backward while bringing the flat of his free hand forward toward the elbow. The sickening snap of the arm breaking was, in the next second, followed by a shriek of pain. Euan snatched the knife from the assailant's now useless hand and brought the blade across the backs of his opponent's hamstrings, severing them and causing the man to scream again. Euan released his arm, and he dropped to the floor, his legs now completely unable to hold him up. Euan fixed a cold glare on him as he bled and writhed in pain on the stone floor.

"Well, that was stupid of ye," Euan said, the timbre of his voice as calm as the tone was sinister.

The hall was silent, all of them staring at Euan in shock as well as fear. They'd never seen anything like what he'd just done and had no idea what to make of it. It had all happened in such quick succession, so smooth that it seemed unreal and impossible. On the faces of his friends, the astonishment was greater: this was not the boy they'd known, and they'd just seen it proven in the most brutal way.

"What in the hell has happened here!"

Euan turned around to see the chief of the Glengarry standing there with Lochiel and swore to himself.

"The lad tried to attack one of Lochiel's men when he came to the defense of the lass," one of the Glengarry men said before anyone could try to suggest Euan was to blame.

"What!" Lochiel exclaimed in anger.

"It is true, sir," Janet sobbed to her chief. "He was just trying to help me!"

"I am sorry to have caused a disruption in yer hall, Chief MacDonell," Euan said, bowing. "I just could nae stand to watch the lass be struck."

"Of course nae," MacDonell replied. "Get this lad out of here and to a surgeon!"

The order was obeyed with immediate effect, the screaming young man lifted and dragged from the hall, leaving only blood on the ground where he'd been.

"I thank ye for the assistance to one of mine, Euan Cameron."

Euan bowed again. "If I may, I would like to take a moment out of doors."

Lochiel nodded, and Euan swept past him, hurriedly making his way out. Leaning against the wall in the darkness, he let the bite of the night air soothe him, giving him something to focus on in order to bring himself back from the dark place such things always sent him to. Closing his eyes, he took in a deep breath and released it. There'd been no choice, he knew that, but he hated that he'd had to do it. The man would never walk again, or at least he wouldn't if he lived through the fever that was sure to come. The sound of footsteps got his attention, and he looked up to see Malcolm coming out to find him.

"Are ye all right?" Malcolm asked as he leaned against the wall beside Euan.

"Aye, fine," Euan replied. "Just need a moment, as I always do."

"What in the hell was that?"

"Training. A lot of training."

"Ye learned that in France?"

"Amongst many other things, aye."

"That man in there, that was nae the Euan I know."

"It is, for it is the Euan ye know now. The Euan who left here as a boy is long gone, Malcolm."

"That is unfortunate."

"I agree. Parts of me are still the same, but nae this, never this. I am nae just any soldier and never will be."

"How many lives have ye taken, Euan?"

"So very many," he said, his voice softening. "More than I can count, and I am sure there will be more still before my own life is over."

"Why?"

"Varying reasons, and all of them necessary. I never committed murder, but I had to protect a king, Malcolm. I could have killed that lad tonight so easily and nae been sorry for it, but I chose nae to."

"Meanwhile, yer own life was taken from ye."

Euan said nothing, the words ringing true and bringing a deep hurt with them.

"Anything ye could have been was wiped away to make ye into what they wanted, into *this*."

"Ye speak of me as though I am a monster."

"No, ye are nae, I know that, and forgive me for making ye think that was what I was suggesting of ye. Ye are still the Euan I cared for all of those years, deep down. I just feel so much anger for what was done to ye."

"What was done to me," Euan repeated flatly, his voice remaining quiet in the darkness. "Ah, ye have no idea, my friend."

"What does that mean?"

"Ye dinnae just become this. They must destroy ye first, everything ye were, and I was no exception to that. My first four days with them were a haze of beatings that left me so injured I could nae stand or see. For the next year, I did nae know a time when I was nae injured in some way, nae stuck in some hell of endless torture and praying nae to wake up. I was forbidden from contacting any of ye, and though I survived, it changed me forever. Now I am someone who trusts no one, loves no one, and will nae flinch when it comes to doing what needs to be done. *That* is what was done to me."

"Ach, Euan, I ... I dinnae know what to say other than that I am sorry."

"Ye are nae the one who should be sorry."

"The ones who should be never will be."

"Why would they be when I am what they wanted," Euan said, the bitterness he felt quite clear.

There was a heavy sigh from Malcolm. "No matter who ye are now, ye are still my little brother, and ye always will be. Naught will change that."

Euan closed his eyes, unbidden tears sliding down his cheeks.

"Euan," Malcolm said as he stood up and stepped forward, cupping the younger man's face in his hands and pressing their foreheads together. "I mean what I say. Every word. Ye will be fine. Ye are back at home with yer kin, and ye will find yer way back to at least some of what ye once were with our help. It will take time, but I am with ye; we all are."

"Thank ye," Euan whispered.

"That being said, those were some brutal moves ye showed us."

"And here I thought I was being kind."

"Ye are kidding ... right?"

"No. I could have done far worse."

"Jesus. Remind me never to sneak up on ye."

Euan laughed. "I wish ye all the best of luck in doing so."

"That sounds like a challenge."

"Perhaps. Ye want to try it?"

"No. After that? Are ye out of yer mind, lad? Come on, get back inside and have some more ale with us. I know the Glengarry lads have some whisky for ye to thank ye for what ye did, and God knows ye have earned it."

CHAPTER 7

"GRACE?" EUAN CALLED OUT as he came downstairs after returning home. "Mam?"

Silence was the only response, and he sighed, walking into the kitchen to find his phone sitting on the counter where he'd left it. Picking it up, he saw a message from Grace saying she'd gone into Fort William but would be back soon, and his mother had gone somewhere with friends. He put the phone back down and frowned; being here alone was the last thing he wanted right now. More than anything he wanted Grace ... no, more than wanted, he *needed* her. Bringing up those moments had been difficult — more difficult than he'd expected — as had been confessing to another about the dreams he'd once had but couldn't explain until very recently. In truth, he still couldn't explain them. He had no idea how he'd managed to dream about his wife so many times before he'd even met her, but at the same time, he was grateful because it was what had gotten him through so many of those dark days. The realization about Falkirk, however, had been stunning, though he wasn't ready to even think about that one yet. Falkirk still hurt in so many ways ... far too many.

He sank into a seat, resting his head in his hands. He thought of Malcolm, of Iain, of Finn, and of Duncan, his friends and brothers gone forever in a way they never should've been. They had been cheated out of their lives just as he had, but in a different way. He'd long ago resolved within himself to live for all of them, and though the weight of that resolution sometimes felt too intense and heavy, he refused to put it down.

The sound of the back door opening and closing caused him to look up, and in the next moment, the very person he'd been craving with every part of his being came around the corner. "Ah, there ye are."

Grace's smile was bright when she saw him, and it still astonished him how far such a small thing could go in beginning to ease his tension.

"And here *you* are," she said as she crossed to the table and gave him a soft, loving kiss in welcome. "How'd it go?"

"Fine," he replied. "Well, mostly."

"It's never easy, is it?"

"No."

Grace shot him a curious look, setting the bag she carried down on the table. "What are you hiding?"

"What? Naught."

"No, you are. You're trying to act so calm, but you aren't."

Euan cursed how well she knew him in this moment. "It is nae something I wish to discuss is all. As I said before, it is nae personal, and someday I will tell ye all, but I need to make sense of it myself first."

"I understand that perfectly."

"Of anyone, ye would understand me."

"I would."

Euan stood up, not breaking eye contact, the movement swift and putting him very close to her. He heard her breath catch just a little, saw her eyes widen for the briefest of moments, and smiled. There was something in the way he'd moved that she understood and read instantly. She knew what was on his mind, and it had nothing to do with talking.

"Euan ... I ..." she stammered.

"Hm?" he said as he reached out to take a lock of her long hair and let it slide through his fingers. Something about the movement made his heart clench, pulling at the edges of a memory he couldn't quite reach.

Grace closed her eyes as he moved his fingertips to her cheek as the last of her hair slipped away from them. "What are you doing?"

"Touching my beautiful wife."

"Yes, but —"

He pressed a gentle fingertip to her lips and closed the distance between them. "I need ye," he whispered against her ear.

"Clearly," she whispered in return, smiling and looking up at him.

"No, it is more than that. I need ye to save me."

Grace's brow furrowed in concern. "From what?"

"Myself. My past. The world. Everything," he said, the sentences murmured against her skin and coming between the kisses he was placing on her neck. "Ye are the only one who can."

Grace's eyes closed as he kissed her neck. "Tell me how. You know that whatever it is, I'll do it."

"Command me, control me," he said, his tone seductive and his lips still against her skin.

Euan felt Grace tense against him, knew she was fighting to hide how much his words and his actions were twisting her insides.

"Please," he whispered in a gentle but almost desperate plea.

Grace stepped back from him and out of his arms so quickly that it both surprised and confused him. He looked at her with curiosity, wondering if he'd said something wrong and if, perhaps, he shouldn't have asked for what he just had. The slow smile that spread across her lips as she backed away from him said otherwise, however. It was teasing, tempting him, and as he stepped toward her, she stepped back once more before turning and dashing from the room. Euan grinned when he heard her footsteps on the stairs and chased after her.

He got no words out as he stepped into the bedroom, the door slamming shut behind him. Whirling around, he was immediately met with the point of his dirk placed dead center against his chest. Euan looked down at it and then back up at her, his eyes glazing over with desire. In the next instant, he grabbed her wrist, pulling it to the side and the dirk away from his chest as he yanked her against him in the same motion. The moment he completed the movement, he felt the point of the sgian dubh he'd given her in France come to rest against the opposite side of his throat, and he couldn't help the small groan it brought from him. Closing his eyes, he tilted his head back, offering himself to her, reveling in the sensation of the cold metal against his skin and the very slight sting from the gentle pressure of the sharpened edge, savoring the surrender.

"Sit," Grace commanded as she walked him backwards to the bed.

Euan wasted no time in obeying her. "As ye command."

She smiled, turning the knife and drawing the flat of the blade down his throat in an almost torturously slow gesture, watching him shudder. "Mmm, very good Captain. Is this what you want?"

"Ye know it is."

"Do I? Say it."

"Aye, it is."

"Such a good officer, following my orders. How *obedient* you are."

"Sweet Jesus, Gr —" he breathed, but his words ended in a moan as she leaned forward and gave his earlobe a gentle nip.

"I didn't give you leave to speak," she whispered in his ear. "Mind yourself, soldier."

Euan gripped the duvet tight in an involuntary and desperate manner as a bolt of need shot through him at those words, fighting not to make a sound. Her lips moved from his ear to his jaw, then down his throat, and something about it once more brought that tingle of memory with it. Euan's eyes then flew open and he gasped as he heard the unmistakable pop of threads being cut followed by the soft click of a button hitting the floor, realizing she was now cutting him out of his clothing. Grace placed a kiss on his chest in the space opened up by the missing button, then proceeded to cut the next one, and the next, following each with a kiss. Euan squirmed beneath each one, fighting himself as she subjected him to this perfect torment.

Grace stood and stepped back from him, and he knew she noted the look of supreme disappointment on his face by the smile that spread on hers. "Take them off," she said, gesturing to his jeans.

The order was obeyed without a moment's hesitation, and once it had been, Grace returned to him. She gave him a deep kiss but, as soon as he touched her, she stepped back.

"Don't touch me."

"But —"

"Don't touch me until I give you permission to do so. That's an order, Captain."

Euan's jaw tightened, and he almost wanted to scream. He was already struggling with himself as it was, and she was making it worse every moment while giving him exactly what he craved. He was desperate to touch her, but his hands wound themselves in the duvet once more in an attempt to hold off. She came back to him, kissing him once more, drawing an almost pleading sort of moan from him as she kept any other part of herself from touching him. Unable to stand it any longer, he grabbed her and pulled her onto the bed. With a movement he couldn't even begin to comprehend at that moment, she turned it around and put him flat on his back before straddling his hips. Before he could even process that part, he felt one of her hands on his throat and the point of the knife she held in the other pressed under his chin.

The loud groan the combination pulled from deep within him was surprising, but he didn't care about that now. There was no pressure from her hand whatsoever, she was fully in control of herself, but it was the mere threat of what she could do that was turning him inside out. The power she had over him in this moment, the control and his lack of it, all coalesced into a fervent hunger for her. Alongside it was an almost frantic need to be controlled by someone, as he had been his whole life. Even though he was very much his own man, he wanted to be possessed by someone, under their command, and to be in control over whom he gave such power to.

"Impatient, are we?" Grace said, the teasing tone in her voice driving him mad. "Tell me you want me."

"I want ye; dear God ye have *no* idea how badly."

"Tell me you belong to me."

The words made him want to scream, but instead, his response came in a voice almost hoarse with desire. "I belong to ye. Always."

"What belongs to me?"

"Everything. Everything I am."

The knife left his skin for a moment and he felt the heat of her hand as it flattened on his chest over his heart. The sensation made him want to weep in remembrance of something his mind no longer had images of. It was all feeling, intense and consuming, reckless.

"And this? Is this mine too? A lover's heart? A warrior's?"

"Aye, my heart, my soul, all of me."

Euan hadn't realized until that moment that she'd managed to undress herself while kissing him earlier, so when she took him at that moment, he thought he might die from the relief, the pleasure, and the still unmet need. He swore loudly and arched into her without even thinking about it, but as his hands moved to grasp her hips, she tightened her hand on his throat the slightest bit and stopped moving.

"No."

He almost whimpered in frustration, but he dropped them

back to the bed as ordered and she ceased the pressure, moving without his guidance, making him completely helpless in his own ravishing — which was just as he'd wanted it. The cries it drew from him were almost feral in their foreignness, and he allowed himself to give in to the powerful release of his submission and surrender.

Euan couldn't think clearly as he lay there trying to catch his breath. It had been perfect, what he'd wanted and needed. He'd never asked for this before, had never trusted anyone enough to do so, or felt comfortable enough to relinquish total control. The memories brought forth today had stirred in him a need to hand that power to the one he loved above all else, the only one who would never hurt or betray him. Giving it to her meant that no one else could ever have it, and no one else would ever own or command him again.

"Are you okay?" Grace asked, her voice as soft as her hand on his cheek, the knife now put aside.

"Aye, more than," he said with a smile. "That was amazing, and ye can be sure I will be asking for it again."

Grace chuckled and lay down, her head on his chest even though she still straddled him. "I'm glad."

"Ye did nae think me strange?"

"No, why?"

"It seems an odd thing to ask."

"Not as odd as you think."

"Hm," he said, reaching out to touch her but then stopping. "May I?"

"You most certainly may."

He drew a hand down her back and felt her sigh. "I am nae through with ye yet," he whispered.

"No?"

"Absolutely nae," he said, pressing her to him and rolling them over to put her beneath him. "I know my darling was nae as satisfied as I was, and that is unacceptable."

"No, really, it was —"

Euan placed soft kisses along her collarbone, and it stopped her words. "My angel, my *leannan*, deserves her worship," he murmured against her skin, "and I am her devoted and willing disciple."

"Then kiss me once more, my beautiful leannan, and let my dream body die upon yer lips only to wake in a darker world."

A tiny gasp left Euan's lips, making him pause for a moment as the memory found its way back to him. It *was* her. He was more than certain now, and the surety overwhelmed him. She had no idea what she'd done for him. She'd saved his life so many times before the one she knew about. She had no idea how long she'd been with him, in his heart and in the reaches of his mind that daylight couldn't touch. Of course she'd seemed so familiar to him when they'd met on this earthly plane: they already knew each other. All of those moments made sense now, the sense that she was returning to him, the power of their draw. It *was* more; there *was* a reason she'd come to him, and it had nothing to do with God, of that he was certain. Whether he'd ever find out what it was seemed irrelevant now.

"Euan?"

Her gentle voice called him back to her, and he looked up at her before he smiled and then kissed her in a way he knew would turn her to liquid heat beneath him. It was time to repay the favor.

CHAPTER 8

ACHNACARRY, JULY 1745

"Euan!"

Euan stood up from where he was working outdoors and turned around at the sound of his name being called. "Lochiel," Euan replied with a bow.

"I need ye to fetch yer things here. We leave at first light."

Euan gave a small nod. "Aye, Lochiel. Where are we going?"

"Borrodale."

Euan's eyes widened for a moment. "But, is that nae where —"

"Where the prince has set up camp, aye. Archibald did nae succeed in convincing him to return to France, and the prince has stated that honor requires me to provide my counsel to his face. So, we go."

Euan wanted to sigh but refrained, knowing full well what this meant. War was coming to the Highlands once again, and whether he believed in the cause or not was irrelevant. He would be fighting alongside everyone else because his allegiance and position required it, and his training assured it. Now a young man of twenty-four, he'd been back at Achnacarry for a few years, with plenty of opportunity to demonstrate how skilled he'd become in France. Not only that, but he'd been able to teach some of the combat skills to the other officers, only making them more formidable and feared as a unit. More than once Lochiel had borne witness to someone underestimating Euan only to learn they'd made a terrible mistake. It was easy for some to dismiss Euan because of his youth, his handsome face, or his seemingly gentle nature, but to do so was absolute foolishness.

Also helpful was the simple fact that Euan drew eyes and attention any time he entered a room, and did so without even trying, his presence not easily missed because it commanded any room he was in or place he was found. Lochiel had found this to be quite useful, because with Euan beside him, most people found it prudent to think twice about even considering a move against Lochiel, and that second thought more often than not led to them deciding against it.

"I should have sent ye, lad," Lochiel continued. "Ye might have had a better time of it. The prince may be silver-tongued, but I feel ye would have been a fine match for him, for I have seen ye use such yerself more than a time or two."

A half-smile crossed Euan's lips, and he shrugged. "Perhaps, but usually to woo a lass to bed and nae a chief to war. Nae that I am in any sort of position to be yer representative to the prince, Lochiel. There is a rather large difference between royalty and lasses."

"Ye are what I say ye are, Euan," Lochiel said.

The smile left Euan's face as the chastisement checked him. "Aye, of course, Lochiel. That is nae what I meant."

"I know ye dinnae think as highly of yerself as most others do, but perhaps ye should. As I have always told ye, ye are more valuable to me than most of the rest of them put together. Ye are a brilliant asset to this clan, and to me, with experience in dealing with nobility. If I wanted to nominate ye to be my emissary, then that is my own business."

Euan nodded, though he knew it would never come to that. There were plenty of others that could and would go before Lochiel would ever even think to send him. "I would do my best."

"Aye, ye would, and it would probably still be better than what I got. Now, get ye gone and bid yer mother farewell. I expect ye back by tonight for supper, and I would rather ye stayed here so all is ready."

"Aye, Lochiel," Euan replied with another bow before he turned and headed for the gates.

Euan made his way quickly home, his mind spinning with the thoughts of what might come. He could only do so much, of course, as he was Lochiel's to command as he would. There was no chance of his not going wherever Lochiel went even if that was into battle, because that was his job. It wouldn't please his mother, he knew that, but her upset over it mattered just as little to Lochiel as Euan's thoughts on the matter did. He threaded his way through the woods and up over the crest of the small hill, smiling when the cottage where he lived with his mother came into view. It was humble, to be sure, but it was the place where he'd grown up, and the same place his father and his grandfather had. It was nowhere near as fine as Achnacarry or the quarters he slept in when he was required to be there overnight, as he would be tonight, but that didn't matter to him. This place held the love and memories the other could never rival, and that is what made it home. It was the place he had so often allowed himself to return to in his mind in order to survive that first year.

"Mam?" Euan called out.

"Aye, son!"

Euan followed the sound of her voice around the back of the cottage to the small garden of herbs and other vegetables she tended faithfully. Aileen was a small woman compared to her son, who favored his father in looks and size, but his mother in personality and wit.

"Ye are back early," she said as she stood and smiled at him, wiping her hands on her apron before she placed a hand on his cheek and pulled him down to kiss the other.

"Aye, I am here to collect some things, and then I am back to Achnacarry."

"Off again, are ye?"

"I am to ride out with Lochiel at first light."

"To where?"

Euan hesitated. "Borrodale, to meet with the prince."

Aileen's eyes went wide before she frowned. "I thought ye said he sent his brother, Dr. Cameron, to meet him?"

"He did, and Dr. Cameron was nae successful in convincing the prince to return to France. Instead, the prince sent the message back that honor requires Lochiel to give his counsel and his refusal in person."

Aileen rolled her eyes and shook her head. "Men are the most ridiculous creatures God ever made."

Euan chuckled. "I have no say in the matter, Mam."

"Of course ye dinnae, and yer honor and position require ye to go. I understand that, but it does nae mean I have to like it, does it?"

"No," Euan replied, his lips twisting in an amused half-smile. "We will nae be gone long, I am sure."

"This is a dangerous business, Euan. Ye know what is happening here as well as I do, perhaps better. What they are about is treason, the same as what they have all been about for almost sixty years. If Lochiel is caught up by the English, ye will hang for that crime right alongside him, because they dinnae care that ye were only there on his orders. Lochiel is a wanted man, and ye know they will be looking for him. If the government finds him while ye are with him …"

"Then they will have to get through us to reach him, but we will do our best to make sure they dinnae find him. If they really wanted him that badly, they would have sent men from Fort William by now. It is nae as though they dinnae know he is here or that we have nae left here often. They have had their chances all this time and have nae bothered."

"There is war brewing."

"More than," Euan replied, his voice quieting. "If the prince has landed in Scotland, then war is already here."

Aileen looked at him, her expression a mixture of sadness and worry. "I fear what this means for ye."

"It means what it has always meant, Mam. We always knew this was possible; it is why I am where I am and why I learned what I did."

"Ye swear to me ye will be safe and nae take foolish chances to save someone who would nae do the same for ye."

"I promise," Euan said, knowing she meant Lochiel. Euan, however, was sure Lochiel would save him if he had to.

"Get yer things then. Ye dinnae want to be late getting back."

Euan pulled his mother into a tight embrace. "I will be all right Mam; I swear it to ye, and I will be back before ye know. Ye be safe, keep an eye out, and if ye sense trouble, ye know where to go."

"Aye, I do. Now, go on."

Euan kissed her cheeks and then released her, walking back around the cottage and inside to pack what little he needed. When he emerged with his saddlebags slung over one shoulder, he turned to give her a small wave, walking backwards. Aileen waved to him, and he bowed deeply to her in return, placing his hand over his heart in a gesture of respect and love in case he never returned to her.

Once he arrived back at Achnacarry, Euan proceeded to the barracks where the other men would be. Entering the low building, he made his way to his cot, slinging the saddlebags onto it before pulling his coat off and going to the wash basin to clean his face and wipe himself down. If he was eating supper with the chief tonight, he wasn't about to go in looking like a boy who'd been out playing in the dirt. Surveying himself in the small looking glass, he went to his bag and pulled a comb out, running it through his hair before re-tying it. As he was finishing, the others came inside after being dismissed to get ready for supper.

"Ach, Euan! How did ye get here before the rest of us, eh?" Malcolm asked.

Euan laughed. "Dismissed earlier than ye, that is how. I had to go home and collect my things."

"He needed time to look pretty for the lasses in the hall," Iain teased.

"One of us needs to, Iain," Euan answered, "and it certainly is nae ye."

"Why bother? Ye have bedded at least half of them already," Iain quipped.

Euan rolled his eyes. "No, I have nae."

"If ye have nae, ye are wasting those good looks, lad," Malcolm said. "I would be doing just that if I were ye."

"I just said it was nae half; I did nae say it was none or even that it is nae more than half," Euan said with a wicked smile that made the others laugh.

"Ye smug bastard," Iain said, even though he was laughing just as much as the rest were.

Euan grinned and grabbed his coat before walking out of the barracks. It wasn't entirely untrue, as the number of Achnacarry lasses he'd entertained was nowhere near half, but that didn't matter. They always liked to tease him about such things, and he didn't mind, because there were far worse things to be accused of than sleeping with half the women working at Achnacarry. As he entered the hall, he greeted those he knew who were already present, stopping for conversation with them. One of the women walked by him and dragged her hand along his as she did so. When he looked over at her, she smiled at him and gave a gentle nod to a hallway to indicate she wanted to speak with him. Euan waited, remaining in conversation for a few more moments before excusing himself to follow her. When he stepped into the hallway, she grabbed him by the front of his coat, pulling him into a doorway and placing her lips on his.

"I heard ye are staying here tonight, Euan," she said when she released him.

"Aye," he replied, his smile teasing. "Why?"

"Care to spend it somewhere other than the barracks?"

"Perhaps. Are ye offering, Brenda?"

"Would I have mentioned it if I was nae?"

Euan chuckled as she drew a fingertip along his jawline. "I will see what I can do."

"Same place."

He nodded before she pulled him into another kiss. He didn't remain in it long before he stepped away from her, walking back to the hall. It was strange to him, the way he felt about any of the women he'd spent time with. It wasn't that he didn't care; he did. He'd never intentionally be cruel to or harm any of them, but they didn't move him in the ways he sought. He enjoyed the women and their company, was aware that some of them likely wished more of him, but he wouldn't promise more than he could give. He was always honest and upfront about it to avoid hurt feelings. Jacques' words still lingered — he'd never want to put any of them in danger — but it was also more than that, far more. He'd long felt there was something — no, *someone* — waiting for him, someone who promised a far deeper connection than anyone here could offer him. If asked, he couldn't explain why he felt such a thing, but it colored his actions all the same whether he intended it to or not.

Euan made his way toward the officer's table, sliding into a spot on the bench. Across the hall he saw one of his oldest friends, Duncan, and acknowledged him with a nod. Duncan returned the gesture and then went back to his conversation with the others near him as Euan joined in conversation with the other officers until Lochiel arrived. When Lochiel made his way into the hall, they all stood, waiting for him to be seated before returning to their places so supper service could begin.

Now that he'd been back a while, Euan found it was easy to get lost in laughter and conversation, and he always did. To be around the other men and talk about the day, or to joke about things they'd heard or seen, was something he appreciated. It put him at ease, much as those same moments had once done when he was away, something normal in the midst of all of the abnormal his life had become there. It wasn't the same talk as when he was at home with his mother, but he liked those intimate conversations with her, too, where he introduced some philosophical topic and listened with amusement to Aileen's no-nonsense answers.

When supper was finished, they rose to return to the barracks, shaking hands with friends and saying their goodnights while engaging in brief pleasantries. Malcolm took the time to say goodnight to his wife and his children because he, too, was staying in the barracks tonight. As they headed back as a group, Euan split off from them.

"Euan, where are ye going, lad?" Malcolm called out.

Euan turned, raised an eyebrow, and grinned, causing the other men to laugh and jeer him before he turned back around and proceeded on his way. Brenda was one he'd never had to worry about as far as her feeling more for him than he did for her. She was after the same thing he was, and that made moments like these easy for them both. It also made her the one he spent the most time with in this fashion, because it meant he needed to have no concern about wounded hearts. Brenda, for her part, was already waiting for him and wasted no time in pulling him into an embrace, kissing him before he turned them and pressed her against a wall. He should probably be getting rest, he knew that, but right now he didn't care. He could sleep when he was dead.

In the predawn darkness, Euan and the other men saddled their horses and prepared for their imminent departure. The officers would all accompany Lochiel to the meeting, with the junior officers remaining behind to make sure the estate was protected. There was no need for a large traveling party, as that would only serve to attract unwanted attention, and given that their path took them very near the Fort William garrison, less attention was a good thing. It was two day's ride to Borrodale House, and they'd stay the first night at the home of Lochiel's brother, John Cameron of Fassifern, then camp overnight at Lochailort before Lochiel met with the prince the following morning.

Lochiel emerged from inside, looking none too pleased, and gestured to the waiting men. "Right, lads, mount up and let us be on our way. The sooner we get this over with, the sooner we are home."

Euan mounted his horse in one fluid motion, patting Absalon's neck as the stallion danced nervously, ready to go. Moving forward, he took his place with Malcolm at the head of the formation.

"Ride out!"

The group moved forward together, officially underway as they made their way out of the yard. At least there would be fine weather for the journey, and that was always something Euan appreciated. Riding anywhere in rain or snow or sleet was miserable, and they rode in that weather most of the time. Summer journeys anywhere were always far more pleasant, and most times he welcomed the opportunity to be out. This time, however, that was far less true, and he knew he wasn't the only one who felt it.

Once they were underway for a time, everyone fell into conversation behind Malcolm and Euan, who fell into conversation with each other. Riding vanguard meant that your focus was forward, and your only talk was with the other person on the same duty. They could hear some of the talk behind them and would laugh and glance at each other, but they didn't participate in those conversations. Eventually, Lochiel joined the two men up front, though even that conversation remained light. It was clear that Lochiel had no desire to discuss the upcoming meeting or what might follow it, a desire

Euan understood. There was still hope this could all be avoided, and to say otherwise felt as though he might be cursing the endeavor before it began.

When they arrived at Fassifern House, Euan and the others greeted the men there that they knew, but Euan's summons to Lochiel's side was immediate as he went into conference with his brother. Although Euan felt badly for it, the grooming and stabling of Absalon would have to be handled by the others because duty called him elsewhere. Entering the study, Euan bowed to John before the two brothers greeted each other.

"Good to see ye, as always, Euan," John said.

"And ye," Euan replied.

"Donald," John said as the door shut. "Tell me true: has the prince landed with men, money, and arms?"

Lochiel was silent for a long moment and then shook his head. "No, he has nae, at least that is the report from Archie and the MacDonalds. They all tried to tell the prince to go back, but he has been steadfast and insists the Highlanders must and will stand by him."

John scoffed. "Donald, I beg ye, ye cannae do this. Ye cannae have any part in this ridiculous venture! He has naught and is showing up here expecting us to do all the work for him in supplying men, money, weapons, and support! If ye have no desire to be pulled into this, then dinnae go to Borrodale and send him a letter from here."

"John, ye and I both know I am duty-bound to go to his royal highness now that he has called me, but I have every intention of urging him to turn back and wait."

"And ye and I both know that ye will try and fail. Brother, I know ye better than ye know yerself, if this prince once sets his eyes upon ye he will make ye do whatever he pleases. It is what he does! Yer beliefs — ones that belonged to our father and nae ye, I might add — and yer loyalty will blind ye to common sense and the disaster ye know this will be!"

"Ye have so little faith in me, John?"

"No, I know ye will try, but I have little faith in yer ability to overcome what was drummed into ye since birth."

Lochiel frowned. "His father is the rightful king, John. We are bound to serve the king, and that is what we have always done."

"Aye, we have, and look at where that has gotten us, hm? A father in exile, a clan still trying to recover from the *last* time we supported this mission. Use yer head, Donald! Hell, ask Euan!"

Euan blinked and looked at John, surprised to be pulled into this discussion at all, but as Euan opened his mouth to reply, Lochiel cut him off.

"Dinnae bring him into his!" Lochiel said in frustration. "He will do as I tell him, as he always does."

Euan's mouth settled into a thin line as he fought his desire to speak out and remind both men that he wasn't some simpleton waiting to be told what to do, where to go, or what he should think.

"Oh aye, he will, and ye will kill him along with the rest of us. I cannae support ye in this."

"What!"

"If ye do this, dinnae count on the support of the Camerons of Fassifern. I will nae condone this, and I can see what is coming even if ye refuse to. Ye know where yer room is."

Lochiel turned on his heel and left the room, Euan behind him, but John reached out and placed a hand on Euan's arm to stop him.

"Euan, I am sorry," John said when Euan looked at him with curiosity.

"For what, sir?"

"For what just happened there. I know ye; I know ye have thoughts and feelings on the matter, and I only wanted him to think about someone else for a moment. I am also sorry for what ye and I both know is coming."

"What I feel does nae matter. This is my job."

"Job or no, ye are nae some unfeeling lump. Ye are a young man with yer whole life ahead of ye who is watching yer chief walk ye right into a war with naught ye can do to stop it. Just know that, no matter what, ye and the other lads will be in our prayers."

"Thank ye, sir," Euan said, his appreciation genuine.

"Go on with ye before he gets into a temper at ye because ye are nae right behind him," John said, flashing a wry smile.

Euan chuckled despite himself. "Aye. Goodnight to ye."

There was no more talk that night, for there was nothing to say, and the party rose early the following morning to depart on the remainder of their journey. It was nearing dusk when they arrived at Lochailort where they would make camp for the night. They could easily make it the whole way, but Lochiel made it plain that he wanted to be rested before this meeting, knowing he'd need all his wits about him. Two-man watch shifts were assigned, and Euan volunteered to take the last shift, the only one where a man sat solo. It was often his choice when they traveled, as he rather appreciated the calm of the late night in those hours before dawn. The stars, the stillness, the time to think his way clear of things if he was troubled.

When they struck camp in the morning, Euan was given leave to take a quick nap while the others ate and made ready. When he rose, he ate a quick meal and helped to make sure everything was ready before they were on their way again. As they neared Borrodale House, which belonged to Clanranald, those clansmen guarding the road let them through as they approached.

"Lads, ye stay here," Lochiel said as he dismounted. "Except for ye, Euan. Ye come with me."

"Aye, Lochiel," all five said in unison as they dismounted their own horses.

Euan followed Lochiel to the house where the prince waited, and those who saw them moved out of their way, finding Euan's very presence intimidating. The French regulars all stared at Euan as he towered over them, and he had a feeling his appearance confirmed the tales they'd heard of Highlanders. Euan was more than happy to let them believe it, so they'd give him no reason to prove it to them. The walk was silent, and Euan could tell that Lochiel was going over his intended refusals in his mind.

"Lochiel, is it?"

Euan looked over at the man who had stepped out of the house and was looking expectantly at him as though *he* were Lochiel. His speech was Irish-accented, which Euan found curious.

"That would be me," Lochiel replied, correcting him. "This lad is one of my most trusted officers."

"I see," the man said, bowing. "Forgive my mistake. The prince is waiting on you and is glad to see you have finally come. He can wait outside," he said, gesturing to Euan.

"Nae a chance. He comes with me, and if ye try to push for it to be otherwise, I will be turning around, and the prince can figure out his rebellion on his own."

The man raised an eyebrow but nodded and opened the door to allow them entry. Lochiel stepped inside, followed by Euan, the two men directed to a large room where a young man sat in a chair. Both immediately offered deep bows, and he stood up. He wasn't as tall as Euan, but close, with brown eyes and reddish-brown hair. At Euan's best guess, he was no older than Euan himself and seemed almost delicate. His clothes were made of fine materials like silk, velvet, and gilt trims, and reminded Euan of all the courtiers he'd once known, though he was fairly certain that this man's shoes were worth more than Euan himself was.

"Do rise," he said. "It is good to see that you have decided to meet with us at last, Lochiel. I am sure you know why you are here."

"Aye, Yer Highness," Lochiel said as he straightened up. "Ye seek my support for a new rising against the Hanovers."

"Correct. You alone have sufficient authority to launch such a rising. If you come out in support, then the others will follow. I need you and your men."

"Yer Highness, there is little taste for a rising after the previous attempts, and many of us are still trying to recover from the last one. I urge ye to return to France and wait for us to send word when the time is right."

"The time is now, Lochiel."

"With all due respect, it is nae. Why do ye think the response to yer call for support has been slow? We have much to lose if we fail, and we have our clans to think of."

"Is that so? You would wish to remain to the side while the rest wage war for the fate of Scotland?" The prince's expression darkened. "Soon, with the friends that I have, I will erect the royal standard, and proclaim to the people of Britain that Charles Stuart is come over to claim the crown of his ancestors, to win it, or to perish in the attempt. Lochiel, who, my father has often told me, was our firmest friend, may stay at home and learn from the newspapers the fate of his prince."

Euan saw Lochiel wince at such a withering remark even as he saw the anger creep into the older man's eyes at such emotional manipulation. The prince was playing upon Lochiel's honor and doing so successfully. It was a shrewd move, to be sure, one that Euan could appreciate even if it angered him as well.

"Are ye insinuating I am a coward without honor, Yer Highness?"

"I would hope you were not and would do your duty to your true king by supplying the forces needed for us to go ahead."

Lochiel let go of a weary sigh, and it was clear he now knew that he was in a battle he had no chance of winning. "No, I shall share the fate of my prince, and so shall every man over whom nature or fortune has given me any power. If ye provide security for the full value of my estate should this rising prove abortive, then ye have the Camerons to support ye."

Euan stiffened as he heard his own fate sealed right before him.

The prince smiled. "You have it."

"Where and when do ye need us, Yer Highness?"

"The other supporting chiefs are meeting me at Glenfinnan on ninteenth August. Gather as many men as you can for our cause, Lochiel," he replied before then looking at Euan, sizing him up as if he'd just realized he was there. "Particularly if they are all as he is."

Euan fixed the prince with an impassive expression, unable to be impressed by royalty any longer, and Lochiel's own expression turned amused. "They are nae. Euan is the exception in my forces and nae the rule."

"How old are you?" the prince asked.

"Twenty and four, Yer Highness."

"And what is your position with Lochiel that you are here at his side for such an important moment?"

"I am one of his officers," Euan replied.

"Euan is one of my best, Yer Highness, a captain, and he will fight for ye until he can no longer do so. He has trained for this since he was just a wee boy, sent to France and well-schooled in strategy, tactics, and combat. He accompanies me everywhere I go."

The prince nodded. "Have you a wife and a family, Euan?"

"Non. Juste ma mère. Je n'ai pas eu envie de prendre une femme," Euan replied. *No. Just my mother. I have not had the inclination to take a wife.*

The prince raised an eyebrow. "Perfect French. You truly were educated in France as he said. As for not having a wife or family: good. That means you will fight harder when you have nothing to leave behind but legends of your bravery."

Lochiel frowned, the same expression Euan wanted to make, but which he kept smothered. "I will do as required of me, Yer Highness."

"I will return to begin raising men, Yer Highness," Lochiel

said in order to steer the conversation away from Euan before Euan told the prince what he really thought.

"Excellent. Please do stay as my guest for dinner and we shall speak more. I do, however, desire that your man step out for the rest of this discussion."

Lochiel nodded to Euan, who turned and departed, taking up a post outside of the door. Taking a deep breath, he exhaled and closed his eyes. It was war. Another war. God help them all.

After Lochiel dined with the prince, the two men returned to their own camp. Lochiel waited until they were a good distance from the prince's men before he spoke, though his voice was quiet when he did so. "So, it begins, lad."

"War, ye mean."

"Aye. Treason and the war it will bring with it," he said. "I admit I had rather hoped it would pass ye by, no matter what I trained ye for."

"He is young," Euan said.

"As are ye."

"Aye, but at least I know well enough nae to show up for a war with no army and try to lead a rising against the English."

Lochiel chuckled. "Aye, that is true, ye do have some sense in ye."

"Something does nae sit well with me about all of this, Lochiel."

"Oh?" he replied, stopping to look at Euan.

"It is what he said about my fighting harder with naught to leave behind but a legend. That is nae the way ye should see any man under ye. Ye should always treat the lives of the men below ye as if they were yer own. My life means naught to him, and no one else's will either."

"Aye, ye are right. We are all a means to an end, and it does nae sit well with me either. All we can do is take care of ourselves as best we can while serving him, and we are the power within our own ranks. It will be up to us to keep the men below us safe."

Euan nodded in agreement. "We should remain wary of him."

"Aye. Euan, I need ye to listen to me. Take note of who ye are in this very moment, because ye will never be this man again. War changes ye. Being the one to deliver so much death to others changes ye. The young man ye are is about to die, replaced by a man who has seen more than he should have."

Euan frowned, but he understood what Lochiel was saying. "I think that is true for all of us, but ye know I am well acquainted with both war and the dealing of death."

"Aye, but nae like this, Euan. Ye will nae be in some room plotting strategy with maps. No, ye will be on the front lines surrounded by men ye have known all yer life, and ye will watch them fall beside ye, hear them scream in agony. *That* is the difference. Ye have the education to know what is coming and what it all means when the others dinnae. Ye have skills far beyond a rifle and a blade, and that will make ye more in demand than the others. Ye will be called upon to do things no one else will be asked to do. Ye will see more. Do yer best to hold on to yer soul and to who ye are, even in the midst of all we are about to face."

These sorts of words from Lochiel made Euan uneasy, though he wouldn't say so. He knew very well that they were warnings rooted in experience, lessons learned from the rising that had banished Lochiel's own father to the Continent, never to return. It was true that this would be different. He would be fighting this time, not planning, and that meant he could die. If he didn't, he would see those he knew and cared for cut down in brutal ways. While he might have done a great many things during his time in France, he knew that whatever he did here would be far different with such personal stakes.

"Aye, Lochiel."

"Good. Come on, let us gather the others and let them know what has transpired. We have an army to raise."

The looks on the faces of the others as Lochiel broke the news were nearly the same as Euan's. There was concern, worry, unhappiness. It was what they all trained for while hoping they would never have to use it. Lochiel had them all back on the road as soon as possible, wanting to get as far from Borrodale as he could before dusk, his displeasure with the outcome as clear as his men's.

After passing the night at Fassifern once more, the trip back to Achnacarry was conducted almost in silence, each man pondering his own thoughts. Euan wondered how he would break this news to his mother and what her reaction to it would be. There would be many crying women in Achnacarry over the coming days as they readied their men to leave while knowing they may never return, and it made Euan glad he had no wife or children to worry about. Hearing his mother cry would be bad enough.

As soon as they arrived, the officers who were with Lochiel entered into conference with the junior officers who had remained behind. The faces in the hall were grim, but they knew their duty and would do it. Lochiel assigned them to different areas of Cameron land where they were to inform all those living there that their chief required them to gather for war, and the officers were then dismissed to their own homes if they had them, the barracks if they didn't. The five returning officers were given leave for the rest of the day and not sent on the errand of raising the Cameron regiment.

Euan returned home, his heart heavy. He wanted to see his mother but dreaded telling her what he knew would break her heart. As he stepped inside, he found her weaving and smiled. "I am returned, Mam, just as I told ye I would be."

"Oh, thank God!" Aileen cried out, getting up to hug her son.

When she released him, Euan went and sat down on his bed, back against the wall and gaze distant.

"Euan, what is the matter with ye?"

"It is war, Mam," he said in a near whisper as he looked up at her.

"What! No, Euan …" Aileen stammered, her face pale.

"We are to raise the regiment and meet the prince at Glenfinnan on nineteenth August."

"No! I forbid it! Ye are nae to go!"

"Ye cannae; ye know that. Ye can rail as ye will, but it will nae change things. When the Camerons ride for Glenfinnan, I will be with them."

Aileen covered her face, weeping, and Euan stood to gather her in his arms. "Ye are my only son! He cannae take ye from me! Ye only just returned to me after five years gone! What if ye never come home again?"

"If I never come home again, ye will know I died in service to my clan and my country. It is an honorable death, and I will be waiting for ye with father when yer day comes."

The words only made Aileen shift from weeping to outright sobbing as she clung to him, and Euan closed his eyes, fighting back his own tears. He'd known this would hurt, but he'd had no idea just how much.

"Mam, I am sorry. If I could change it, I would."

"Ye are being asked to fight for what ye dinnae even believe in!"

"What I do or dinnae believe is irrelevant, Mam. It is what Lochiel believes, and I follow him." Euan wouldn't tell her of the prince's words to him, for such a thing would only make it worse, as would the knowledge that even Lochiel didn't seem entirely behind the idea.

"It is to me, Euan! I may lose ye to something that yer heart is nae even in!"

He sighed and rubbed her back as he continued to hold her. "Everything will be all right, no matter what happens. Put yer trust in God to bring me safely home to ye."

Aileen said nothing, sobbing in her son's arms for a long

while as Euan did his best to comfort her. He hated that it needed to be this way, and he could only imagine what was happening in Malcolm's home right now as he told Catriona and the children that he was to go to war. He wished he could spare all of them this pain.

"What was he like?" Aileen asked when she finally had some control over herself, wanting to change the subject.

"Who?"

"The prince. Did ye see him?"

"Oh. Well, something like that."

"How do ye mean?"

"I spoke with him."

"What?" Aileen asked in shock.

"I went to the camp and inside with Lochiel. I was standing with him when he met with the prince, and the prince spoke to me, asking me about myself."

"Heavens! My son meeting a prince! I never would have thought it!"

Euan laughed. "Mam, have ye forgotten where I was all this time? Yer son has met a king and plenty of princes, enough to last him his lifetime."

"Ye never told me that!"

"No? Well, there ye have it. The prince is nae much older than I am, Mam, and he looks as though I could break him easily."

"He is nae a warrior like ye, Euan. He has others to do the fighting for him."

"Clearly," Euan replied with a hint of irritation. "I am nae sure he could do much fighting in the fancy clothing he wears."

"Tell me about them?" Aileen asked, desperate for a distraction.

"Almost entirely silk, from what I could tell. Embroidery everywhere. Fine shoes with gold buckles. Exactly as ye would expect a prince to have."

"An entire outfit made of silk. Can ye imagine?"

"I can, because I have worn them."

"Ye have!"

"Aye, I did sometimes, to do certain things that were asked of me, and it can make ye quite warm. Such things are nae for me."

"Of course nae, because that is nae the type of man ye are. Ye are far too active for something so impractical."

"I think I made him uncomfortable."

"Ye make a great many people uncomfortable when they first see ye."

Euan couldn't help but laugh. "Why do ye say that?"

"Ye have a commanding presence, son, and that makes people uncomfortable. I can imagine it makes people in power even more uncomfortable when ye are there, because it is clear ye can nae only outshine them, but also stand to steal their own people right from under them."

"I would nae do such even if I could."

"No, ye would nae because ye have honor, but ye could. Ye dinnae see it, but I do and so does Lochiel. People are willing to follow ye, Euan, and it is why Lochiel keeps ye so close."

"Keeps me close?"

"If ye are always in close service to him, then he does nae need to fear the men rallying around ye and nae him. He does nae need to fear mutiny. He may keep ye even closer while ye are out, when men may be unhappy."

"It will be my job, and the jobs of the others, to make sure they are nae so unhappy as that. I will nae stand for mutiny."

"Even if ye feel like doing it yerself?"

"I would nae —"

"Ye dinnae know what ye would do, Euan, for ye have never been in such a situation. Ye must watch yerself, for ye are the only one who will worry about yer safety. The others will be worried about themselves, no matter what they say."

Euan sighed but nodded. She wasn't wrong, and he knew that well enough, but it didn't mean it sat well with him. "This is what I have trained for nearly all of my life."

"I cannae tell ye how much I hate that ye have."

Euan frowned and looked at her. "What?"

"It is nae the life I ever wished for ye, Euan. I had always hoped ye would get yerself away from this place, away from the pull of the clan, and make yer own way. Then Lochiel took ye on after yer father died, and there was no prying ye from him. He gave ye what ye wanted. He gave ye a man to look up to, he gave ye the education ye craved, he promised ye importance. The life ye believed ye wanted was in his power to give, and he made sure ye knew that he was the only one who could give it to ye. Now ye have it, and I am nae sure ye truly want it."

Euan shook his head in confusion. Not truly want it? Of course he did! It was the culmination of all the hard work he'd put in for so long, all the suffering. Then again, perhaps she was right in a way. Did he truly want a life of war? Deep down, Euan had always desired the continuance of the education he'd begun, but it was never something he could have, so he always dismissed it.

"It will nae always be this way."

"Again, ye dinnae know that, none of us do. What happens if this fails? What happens to all of us? To ye, if ye survive the battles? Do ye think the English will give ye quarter as an officer?"

Euan pressed his lips together for a moment. "Then we had better nae fail."

Aileen sighed and shook her head. "Ye must go gather men then?"

"No," he replied. "Others have been sent while those of us who went to Borrodale have been dismissed to get some rest. The work begins when everyone returns."

"Then let us get some proper food into ye so ye can get some sleep. Ye look tired."

"There was nae much sleeping, but there never is."

"Well, there can be here. Get yerself down to the loch to bathe, then come have some stew so ye can sleep."

Euan chuckled and rose, making his way to the loch to do as he was asked. There was no use in fighting his mother on these sorts of things because she would always win. He wanted more than anything to give her the easy victories while he still could. It might be the last thing he ever did.

CHAPTER 9

SPECIALIST GEORGE SAT BACK in his chair, observing Euan's posture and expression as he lay on the couch, his eyes closed. It was clear they were drawing near things that were still fresh to him, and it was visible in the way he held himself, the way he spoke. Part of him was amazed the young man was being so candid, so willing to tell him things he'd not yet even told his wife. It showed his willingness, his desire, to try and make sense of all of it, as well as how to untangle himself from the strings that had so long been tied around him. At the same time, it showed his comfort, his trust, in the Specialist assigned to him. It would, however, be all too easy to shatter that trust now. The closer they got to Euan's recent past, the more emotionally taxing it would become, and pushing too hard or saying the wrong thing would see him slamming the door and refusing to continue.

"Let's start with something easy. You mentioned that you'd always felt there was someone waiting for you."

"Aye, but as we determined last time, I always knew in my heart it was Grace. She had come to me for so long, and while my waking mind did nae remember, my soul did."

"And you were upfront with the women you were previously intimate with?"

"Aye, I was. I told them nae to expect from me what I could nae give. I had nae the time nor the inclination for love or a serious courtship. I did nae want them hurt by it."

"You wanted them to go in with eyes wide open, so to speak."

"Aye."

"Did it work?"

"Most of the time. There were times when it did nae, when the lass found herself feeling more for me than she should. They would ask me for more, and I would always be kind in my refusal, reminding them of what I had said. I would never bed them again after that; such a thing would be cruel."

"What did you think when you were told you were going to meet the prince?"

"That I wished we would nae. It would mean naught but trouble, and I was right."

"How did it feel when Lochiel chastised you for stating you didn't think you could be an envoy?"

"Chafing, painful. I hated to displease him, and it hurt me when he would slap me down in such a way, especially when I was nae being entirely serious. I never knew where I truly stood with him."

"Could you have been an envoy, do you think?"

"I have been while working for The Council so, aye, I know now I could have. Well, I take that back, I could have if Grace were there to steady me. Dinnae know if I could do it on my own."

"It seems as though you could."

"Perhaps now, aye. She has changed me in so many ways. I can hear her in my head, and it snaps me back into line," he replied with a soft chuckle that made George smile. "Though, we would have been better off sending her as the envoy. Had we done so we probably would have seen the back of the prince soon enough, or we would have found far more support and won the war."

"Since you've mentioned him, let's talk about the prince."

"Must we?" Euan asked, making a slight face.

"Only a bit. What did you think of him?"

"Then?"

"Yes."

"I did nae trust him, nae a bit. I could nae trust anyone who held life so cheaply. It always amazed me how people could be so awed by him, so swayed."

"People, as a whole, are easily dazzled. You had a bit more experience with royalty than most."

"I suppose I did, but I did try to give him the benefit of a new look later, and that is something for a later time. Maybe I could read him then because I knew what to look for."

"Why did you speak French to him?"

"To let him know he was nae dealing with just some country lad. It would put him on notice, let him know I was watching him and could understand what he said."

"And when he challenged Lochiel?"

"He played on honor and it worked. Of course it did. Men cannae stand being made to feel as though they are cowardly or somehow shirking their duty, especially nae powerful men. Once the prince challenged his honor, Lochiel had no choice."

"I am sure it didn't sit well with you, the things he said about not having a family."

"Indeed nae, for it is nae true. Those who have something to return to will fight harder than anyone, precisely because they want to return to it. They have something to protect, ye know? Nae to mention it goes to show how little he thinks of human life if he was willing to so easily dismiss mine."

"You had your mother."

"Aye, I did. My mother, my friends, their children, their wives. All of that was on me."

"How so?"

"As an officer, I had to keep my men safe and return them to their families. It was my job to keep the war from the doorsteps of the defenseless, and it was always something I took seriously."

"Perhaps you could explain something to me that I don't understand."

"I can try."

"You spoke about honor and how the prince played on it in order to get Lochiel to do his bidding. I fail to understand such a concept, or how such words would force someone to put the fate of his entire clan at risk."

"Ah, I see what ye are asking. Aye, it would be a foreign concept for ye here, just as it is in the time I currently live in. Honor was often all ye had, yer most important asset. Yer honor served as yer credit; with it came money, allies, trust. Without it, ye would quickly find yerself with naught, and no one to help ye. It could be restored if lost, but nae quickly. For a man like Lochiel, the loss of his honor would mean everyone below him suffered. No one would ally with us, trade with us, lend money if needed. To risk the loss of such a thing because the prince called him out, to know he would make it public if Lochiel refused and thus brand him as untrustworthy and cowardly, well, he had no choice, did he? The prince backed Lochiel into a corner by playing on that, and it worked, as he knew it would. I hated him for it, but I understood it."

"I see, I think I understand now. If he said no, it would ruin you all, even more so if the rising succeeded and the prince came to power. He would remember and make all who worked against him pay dearly."

"Exactly."

"Do you feel Lochiel was right about remembering who you were in that moment?"

Euan was silent for a long moment and then sighed. "Aye and no. The man he thought I was did nae exist. He was already gone the day he got off that ship in France. In his place was a man who had already seen and done much and who could nae tell him about any of it. I did nae think it could get worse, but he was right there: it did. It is different when the ones dying beside ye are those ye have known yer whole life, when the ones on the other side of the field are the same. That changes ye in ways I cannae even describe."

"Was it painful to tell your mother?"

"Extremely. I can still hear her crying, and I will never forget it."

"What about the things she said to you about your potential?"

"It was nae something I had ever considered or noticed. No one followed me; I followed others. It is hard to explain, for I was so torn down by Jacques and the others that I did nae have any belief in myself. I could nae fathom that anyone would look to me for anything; why would they? I was naught, knew naught. Why would I believe that I had such power or such presence that the regiment would follow me if I mutinied? If that did nae occur to me, then neither would Lochiel keeping me close for any reason other than his protection, nor the reasoning behind him constantly pulling the floor from under me just when I seemed to feel sure."

"There are terms for such things now," George said.

"Are there?"

"Indeed. Emotional abuse and manipulation, coercive control, gaslighting. All recognized patterns, though I wouldn't say they all applied to Lochiel. Many of those would apply to Jacques and the others. I think, for him, I would say emotional manipulation and coercive control, though you could certainly argue that there was emotional abuse."

"I would nae call it abuse."

"No?"

"Abuse is intentional, and I dinnae think it was intentional."

George looked at him, brow furrowed in curiosity. "You don't think his denigrating your accomplishments, reminding you of your dependence upon him for the life you wanted, telling you that he alone could say what you were or were not, or destabilizing you by cutting you down and making you doubt yourself was intentional? All of that requires forethought, Euan. It doesn't just happen."

Euan opened his eyes, staring at the ceiling as the weight of those words settled on him. Forethought. It all required forethought. He'd had to have known what he was doing to Euan. George watched as the sharp and brutal pain the realization brought to him hit, and it was followed by intense anger. Euan had seen this on the French mission but had been able to dismiss it as being down to the interference of their new enemies; he'd said that himself. Now, here was someone shining a light on that ugliness so he could see that it had always been there and had nothing to do with Lochiel being controlled by others.

Euan closed his eyes again, and it forced the tears to roll down into his dark hair. "Why would anyone do that?" he whispered.

"It's hard to say. There are many different reasons. A desire for control, narcissism, abject cruelty, covering their own fears and insecurities. For you, it sounds most like the last one. He feared you, feared he wasn't good enough, feared what he'd created. He was insecure about his ability to lead, perhaps."

Euan shook his head, and it was obvious that he was doing his best to keep himself from fully losing his composure. "He did nae have to do that; I was no threat to him. I wanted to please him!"

"And he knew that. He used that desire against you by withholding praise when he knew it would bolster you, when he knew that withholding such a thing would only bring you down. He forced you to keep trying, harder and harder, to earn that praise because it was the thing you prized. It was his power over you."

Euan's breathing became ragged as he lost the battle for stoicism and began to cry.

"I'm so sorry, Euan. I know this hurts you, but that's why you're here, to pull yourself out of this web spun around you to hold you in one place. You want to see all of this, and now you do. You see your life through this new prism, see those interactions you once thought benign were anything but. Those moments are flashing through your mind even now, the malice and the intentions that always lurked in the shadows beneath are now thrust into the blinding light of truth."

Euan covered his face with his hands, openly sobbing in a way that broke George's heart for him. It was hard to stay emotionally distant from a young man who had worked so hard to secure the love of a father from the only man he could get it from, and to know that, in the end, he'd never gotten it. It made George want to comfort him, to find a way to give that care to him, even though it wasn't his place to do so.

"I think we should stop here for today. I'm not sure we can go further after this, and you'lll need some time to process it."

Euan nodded, wiping his eyes even though the tears were still coming. "Thank ye," he whispered.

"I wish I could make this easier."

"The truth is never easy."

"No, it's not, for if it was, then everyone would tell it. Come, let me see you out."

Euan stood, following the Specialist out, but feeling as though he were in a daze. When he reached Caia, she saw the look on his face and frowned, reaching out a hand but saying nothing. Upon arrival home, she squeezed his hand in an attempt at comfort and reassurance.

"Is there anything I can do? Do you need anything?" she asked.

Euan looked over at her, her worry for him written all over her face. "Would ye be so kind as to find my mam if she is here and tell her to meet me in the study? If she is nae here, come tell me."

"If she's not, did you want me to get Grace?"

"No need. She will find me."

Caia gave a nod and left the bedroom with Euan behind her. At the bottom of the stairs, she branched off to knock on Aileen's door, and Euan made his way to the study. He shut the door behind him and sighed.

"What happened?"

Grace's voice snapped the last vestiges of the control he was holding onto so tightly, and by the time he broke down and began sobbing again, she already had him in her arms. As he knew she would, she'd sensed something was wrong, had known where he'd go, and was waiting there for him. Euan clung to her, desperate for the peace her presence provided, even if it felt as though it may not be enough this time. He felt broken, raw, and it was more than he could take in her presence, she whose connection to him made him unable to hide.

Grace said nothing, holding him close and letting him cry. Euan knew she was intimately familiar with this feeling and knew that words would never suffice. There was nothing she could say or do in the face of this sort of hurt, particularly when the only one who could possibly set it right was long dead. He didn't need her apologies, placating words, or anything but her simple presence to let him know he wasn't alone in anything at all.

The door opened and Aileen entered, her expression of concern deepening when she heard Euan crying the way he was. "Euan, love, what is wrong? Ye sent Caia for me?"

He lifted his head and turned to look at her, eyes red and pained. "I need to speak with ye, and I know ye are the only person who can understand."

"Why is that?"

"I'll go," Grace said softly, kissing his hand and then squeezing it, taking no offense to his words.

"Thank ye," he said, stopping her for a moment to rest his forehead against hers and close his eyes. "And thank ye for always being my strength when I need ye most."

Grace smiled. "I always will be, just as you are for me. Do you want me to get you anything? A pot of tea to put your whisky in?"

Despite everything, the comment made Euan laugh a bit. She knew him well enough to know that whisky was his preferred method of easing raw nerves. "Aye, that would be grand."

"Be right back," she said, stepping away from him and leaving the room.

"Euan, what in God's name has happened?" Aileen asked.

"I discovered something today, during my session."

"All right."

"Everything I thought I understood was a lie."

"What? How do ye mean, son?"

Euan crossed the room to the settee, dropping onto it, and Aileen joined him there. "Do ye remember when I came home after that first meeting with the prince? When I told ye were to go to war?"

"Like it was yesterday. It was a horrible day."

"And do ye remember how ye told me Lochiel feared me and kept me close?"

"Of course."

"Ye were right. About everything."

Aileen sighed and shook her head. "I know, but I wish I was nae."

"How did I nae see it?"

"Ye did nae want to, Euan. Ye wanted to believe the best in everyone, especially him."

"I wanted to believe he wanted what was best for me."

"I think he often did, but he also had to keep ye under control. Ye did nae push back because ye so wanted a father and he was the closest ye had known."

"But it was intentional. Everything he did, everything he gave me, everything he took away, and every time shoved me off of the pedestal he built for me!" Euan said, angry now.

"And now ye finally see the truth and ye are angry."

"Aye, I am angry. I am angry at all of the times he re-minded me that my life was his to control, all of the times he reminded me of what he had given me and that I should be grateful for it!" Euan stood up and began to pace. "I am angry that I allowed it! Angry that I believed him and allowed him to define what I am worth!"

"Go on."

"I am furious I wasted so much of my life chasing something I would never have, something I would never earn from him no matter what I did or how hard I tried. I hate that I let him control me, let him convince me I was naught, let him shield my own power from me and seal it away to be used when *he* saw fit!" Euan shouted, slamming his hand down on the desk.

Aileen said nothing.

"I gave my life for this! I died for naught! I gave yer life for it, too, for ye died just as surely as I did, and all because I wanted to blindly follow. Because I did nae want to see it for what it was. I could have saved everyone with mutiny, but I was too damned *weak*!"

"Euan, no. Dinnae do that. Ye have no idea what would have happened at the end, and even if ye had managed to pull back from that battle, what then? How long would ye have gone on? What would ye have done when the chiefs came after ye? I know ye are angry, but dinnae put things such as that on yer shoulders."

Euan ran his hands through his hair, still pacing. "Even if that is so, the fact remains that I could have done it," he said, but then he stopped, his hands dropping to his sides. "I gave *her* life," Euan whispered.

"Who?"

"Grace. I forced her hand; I made her offer herself up like a sacrifice to *my* blindness and *his* pride. I sentenced her to death because I could nae see, because in that moment when I could have stood beside her, when I knew they were wrong,

I chose nae to. He said a word, and I backed down. I backed down and left her no other choice, and she died to save me from my own naïveté and reckless desire to please another."

"She had to, ye know that."

"Did she? Did she really, Mam? Or should I have seen the writing in the blood of thousands of Highlanders on the wall and walked away with her? Walked away and kept the both of us safe from that horror? Do ye think they would have said no if we did it that way? I doubt it."

"Euan —"

"No! Dinnae ye see it? She once wept in my arms because she felt that something she had done had cost me my life, but when I had the chance to save hers, I did nae! I knew how to stop it! I knew what was coming, and if I had only told him that night that I believed her, to look closely and see what she was saying was a possibility and we should do something else, at least she would nae have died! I *knew* she was right! I could see it with my own eyes! I knew it even then, and I did nae have the courage to break from him to save myself or her! I saw her face when I took his side and refused to hear her, heard the distress in her voice while she *begged* me to listen to her! She needed me to be strong for her, to make the hard choice and stand beside her instead of against her, and I refused! I blamed *her*! My wife and my mother suffered and died because I was a coward!"

"Ye were nae! Ye had been taught all along nae to trust yerself, that his word was the final one, and ye stuck to that as ye had been taught to do! Ye knew no other way, Euan! It is easy to look back at it now, with hindsight, and be angry at all ye think ye should have done, but in the end, yer training won out as it was always meant to do."

"And that is cowardice."

"No, it is what was done to ye. It was ye being made to never trust yer own judgment, so that when it really mattered, ye did nae have the confidence to push back even though ye saw the flaws in the plan. Stop blaming yerself for what some-one else did to ye! Ye are placing yer anger on yerself because ye still cannae bear to place it where it belongs! That is how deep this goes, son. Even now ye cannae do it. Ye would rather take the responsibility for actions that were nae yers than say the words ye know are true. Say them, Euan. Break those binds and speak the truth! Stop defending him!"

"No, I —"

"No!" Aileen shouted, standing up. "Say it, Euan! Ye did nae die because of what ye did or did nae do; ye died because of what *he* did! Those choices were his, and ye followed orders just like everyone else. He had his chances, and he made his choices, and those choices washed back on *all* of us! He made my son into an unflinching, unquestioning, soldier because that is what *he* wanted ye to be. Do ye really think he cared if that was what was best for ye? Do ye think he even thought about it? All those times he kicked ye down; do ye think he cared how it damaged ye? Had ye stood there that night and said no, do ye think he would have listened to ye? Do ye think he would have let ye just walk away? He would have killed ye before he let ye go, and in the end, that is *exactly* what he did! *He* killed Grace as sure as if he wielded that bayonet himself, and his power over ye is still strong enough that even from the grave, he has ye convinced that her death is yer fault, that her blood is on yer hands even when it is nae so. Admit it!"

The words hung heavy in the air between them, the truth so long unspoken. Euan turned and placed his hands on the desk to steady himself, dropping his head. "Ye are right," he whispered, "about all of it."

"Then say it. Say it yerself."

Euan squeezed his eyes shut, his body and his mind want-ing nothing more than to keep those words in and bury them deep beneath his own guilt and self-loathing. They sat heavy on his tongue, bitter and full of regret. "He did this. Nae me. He did this to me, and he did it to both of ye, to all of us."

"There. Now ye have said it, finally. Be angry, be hurt, but direct both of those to the root of it, and it is nae yerself."

"It is easier said than done."

"Of course it is, and it will take ye as much time to unlearn it as it did to learn it in the first place. The first step is always to speak the truth, and now ye have done that. Now ye have cut the strongest, thickest rope that has tied ye to those lies for so long, and ye can no longer defend him as ye have always done. As ye had to do from the day ye returned to Scotland. Protect him, defend him, trust him. Ye dinnae have to do it anymore, for his death absolved ye of that duty long ago. He is gone, Euan, and ye remain."

CHAPTER 10

OVER THE FOLLOWING WEEK, after their return from Borrodale, men began to arrive at Achnacarry, responding to their chief's summons. When all the men were assembled, they were divided up into companies of one hundred men, and each company came under the command of one of the officers. It was then up to the officers to drill the men and get them into some semblance of fighting shape. It was a task Euan took very seriously, because without organization and discipline, they wouldn't stand a chance. It also meant that all of his time was spent in the barracks at Achnacarry. If he wasn't training men, he was in conference with Lochiel and the others, leaving him unable to return home or spend time with anyone else. This lack of time upset Brenda, but that couldn't be a concern of his. He had work to do and, at the end of it, all he had the energy to do was fall into bed.

One night, as they neared the day of departure, he slipped away from supper to stand in the quiet darkness by the river. It was a moment to himself after what seemed far too long, a moment to take all of it in and remember it, just as he'd once done before leaving for France. Euan closed his eyes, listening to the sound of the water rolling over and around stones, found the familiar scent of the fields and the sound the breeze made as it rustled through the grass and the trees. Achnacarry was a beautiful place, and he said a silent prayer, hoping he would see it again.

"Euan."

The sound of a female voice whispering his name startled him, and he gasped, his eyes snapping open as he looked around and found no one there. It was a voice that was familiar, but he couldn't say why, and that confused him all the more. The sound set off a strange flutter in his stomach, and he listened intently, hoping he would hear the voice again. He wanted to hear it ... no ... he *needed* to hear it. Instead, there was nothing but the sounds of the night once more, and he shook his head before he turned to walk back across the field to the castle.

Before he could step inside, someone grabbed his arm, and he stopped to look back. "Brenda. Did ye just seek me out a moment ago by the river?"

"No?" she replied, the confusion on her face showing that she was speaking the truth. "But I am glad ye came. I wanted to speak to ye."

"About?"

She drew him away from the doorway into a space a bit more private. "Are ye unhappy with me?"

"No, of course nae."

"But ye have nae wanted to be near me."

"I have nae wanted to be near anyone. I have men to train, and that is my focus."

"Ye have nae even time in the night?"

Euan sighed. "I am exhausted by then. It has naught to do with ye, and I have told ye that."

Brenda looked at him, her sadness written on her face. "I just wanted to spend time with ye before ye go, in case ..."

Euan smiled, understanding her meaning. "I am flattered."

"I just dinnae want ye to go without me telling ye how much ye mean to me."

The smile on Euan's face faded. "Brenda —"

"Please, just listen. I know ye said ye were nae wanting such a thing, and I thought I did nae either, but I cannae help what I feel for ye."

Euan stepped back from her. "No. Please, dinnae do this."

"Why nae? Do ye plan on remaining unmarried the rest of yer life? If nae, ye will have to choose one of us eventually."

"Stop," Euan said. "I told ye that I cannae enter into such a thing, and I meant it, especially nae now. I cannae and will nae promise more than I can give, and I never have."

"Just consider it for when ye return."

"If I do."

"Dinnae say that!"

"It is a possibility, and a good one. Please, I care about ye, truly I do, but nae in the way ye want me to. I dinnae want to hurt ye, and I have been very clear from the start."

Brenda looked down for a long moment before she moved forward and threw her arms around him. Euan sighed as he embraced her, feeling her body shaking with sobs, and he wasn't sure if they were because he was saying no to a courtship, or because he was leaving. Perhaps it was both.

"It will be all right, lass. When all of this is over, ye will find a lad that will love ye as ye love him. That is what ye need to reach for, nae for me."

"Ye may feel differently when ye return."

"If I do, ye will be the first to know."

Despite her tears, she allowed herself a small laugh. "I dinnae suppose I could convince ye to find some time before ye go."

"Depends. Ye are nae planning on tying me up and hiding me away so I cannae leave, are ye?"

"No, though, it is usually ye who likes to do the tying," she said with a wink.

Euan laughed. "Aye, that is sometimes true, but ye have always been up for it."

"Hard nae to be when ye make it so appealing."

"Tying up women is a time-honored Scottish tradition."

Brenda joined him in his laughter and shook her head. "I suppose it is, aye."

"I will see what I can do, but I cannae promise anything. I dinnae know how things may go as far as time, but I will try."

Brenda nodded and cupped his cheek with her hand. "Ye stay safe and come home to us, Euan. It would nae be the same here without ye."

Euan looked after her as she dropped her hand from his cheek and walked away. Stepping back, he rested the back of his head against the stone of the wall and looked up. Thousands of stars sparkled in a clear sky, and as he studied them, he wondered why the duty he'd once relished had become so hard. There was a strange finality in all he did, a sense of needing to make sure those he cared about knew it, a need to remember all of these moments because they may never come again. He couldn't explain this feeling, this sense, that he wasn't going to be amongst those returning home. It sat within him, a constant companion, but instead of bringing him panic, it brought a sense of peace and acceptance. It was a strange thing to be so comfortable with the fact that he might very well die, comfortable with the feeling that it was a certainty, though he'd do all he could to prove it wrong. It was, perhaps, due to his earlier experiences and the moments when he'd not only faced death, but also welcomed it. It was, however, a premonition he'd never admit to his mother or to anyone else.

Euan pushed away from the wall, making his way inside and rejoining the other officers at the table. "What are we drilling tomorrow, lads?"

"Christ, Euan. Can ye nae even take a break from thoughts of war and training to enjoy some wine and food?" Iain asked.

Euan raised an eyebrow. "Do ye think war will take a break once we go, Iain?"

There was silence at the table as they all acknowledged what he'd said. "No, it will nae, but we are still at home and we should enjoy this while we can, because who knows when we will be home again," Malcolm replied. "Especially ye. Ye are the youngest of all of us Euan, but ye are also the most serious."

"Being the most serious is what will hopefully keep me alive to come home," Euan said before he took a drink of wine from the cup that had been set before him. "Ye must always be on yer guard."

"I think ye are plenty serious enough for that already and ye have some space to give yerself for a bit of enjoyment, lad."

Euan shrugged. "We will see how much time is left when my men are where I want them to be."

Malcolm and the others laughed. "They will never be where ye want them to be because there is nae enough time, but ye will get them as close as ye can because that is what ye do. I almost feel sorry for the poor bastards in yer company."

Euan grinned. "Ach, dinnae. I treat them fairly."

"Aye, ye do, that is true. Come on, lad. Loosen up," Malcolm said with a sly grin, elbowing him.

"Maybe he needs to go see one of the lasses," Iain offered, which brought laughter from the rest of the men.

Euan joined them in their joviality. Normally they'd be right, but even a tryst with Brenda or one of the others would do nothing to erase what he felt. "All right, fine. What would ye have?"

"Ye getting at least a wee bit drunk," Malcolm said as he slid Euan more wine.

Euan shook his head and chuckled. They were always the same. Lifting his cup, he took a long drink, but as he lowered it, something caught his eye. Near the doors to the hall stood a woman he'd never seen before. Her white dress seemed to shine due to the utter purity of the color, but the cut was unfamiliar. Golden hair tumbled over her shoulders in long curls, and it was pulled back away from her face, showing her almost inconceivable beauty. He stared at her in awe, unable to look away from her. She wasn't from here, he knew that. If she were a Cameron lass, he would've seen her before; there was no way she would've escaped his notice, but at the same time, he was aware that somewhere within himself he knew her.

Rising from his seat, he felt Malcolm reach out and touch his arm, but Euan shrugged it off, and any words spoken to him were so muffled as to be incomprehensible. Euan stepped over the bench and walked around the table toward her, the entire world slowing to a crawl. She stood still, watching him for a moment, before she turned and walked away from him, further into the castle. Euan's change in direction was immediate as if he were attached to her by some invisible cord that bid him follow wherever she might lead. No one else seemed to see her, or if they did, he didn't notice. Ahead of him, she walked into one of the smaller rooms they'd been using for planning. Following her inside, he stopped as she looked up from a map laid out upon the table she now stood behind. The smile that spread across her lips at the sight of him made his heart ache in a way that was unfamiliar as it touched a part of him he thought didn't exist.

"Hello, Euan."

That voice. He knew that voice. It was she who had called to him outside just a short time ago. "Grace," he whispered, the name coming to his lips unbidden from somewhere deep inside, as it always did. "I have been waiting for ye."

"Yes, you have. In many ways."

Euan walked forward, closer to her. "Why have ye come now?"

"You need me. You are so confused, so afraid. You called for me, and I have come, just as I always have, and as you always have for me."

"Aye," he said. "Aye, I have, I know that is true even if I dinnae remember how or when."

"Ever since we were children. When I was hurt so badly the once, do you remember? I came here, here to you, and we played together. We ran free in the woods, and you showed me your favorite places. We laughed and laughed, and you took care of me until it was time for me to return."

Euan smiled. "Aye, I do remember that. I remember how ye

122

shrieked when ye put yer feet in the water because it was so cold."

"Yes," she said, laughing.

"But that was nae the first time."

"You are right; it was not."

"Ye came to me when my father died."

"I did," she said, her expression becoming sad. "It was the first time you needed me."

"Aye, I remember now. I woke up, and ye were there beside me, holding my hand. I was nae frightened to find another child in my bed, no, I was comforted by the mere sight of ye."

"It was all I could really do."

"It was enough," he replied, stepping up to the table now and placing his hands upon it.

"You are never alone," she whispered, covering his hands with her own.

Euan closed his eyes and sighed at the touch of her hands, warm and soft against his skin. "No, nor are ye. We have always had each other."

"And we always will. There is no need to fear."

"I cannae when ye are here," he said, opening his eyes and smiling at her.

"You will be all right."

"Will I?"

"For as long as you need to be."

"I dinnae understand."

"Do not worry, it does not matter now. It will all make sense later."

"Ye are nae really here, are ye?"

"No, not yet, at least not in the way you wish I were or even the way I wish I were."

Euan leaned in across the table, bringing his face close to hers, desperate to be near her in any way he could be. "Aye, I wish ye were. Ye make everything right."

Grace placed one of her hands on his cheek and rested her forehead against his. "Soon, beloved," she whispered.

The intimacy of the gesture made him want to weep like a child. Lifting his hand, he covered hers on his cheek and pressed into the touch. "None of them are ye. None of them can compare, and that is why I feel as I do. It is ye, is it nae? Ye told me the last time we met that someone was coming for me, but ye could nae tell me who. It is ye. Ye are the one who is coming for me; at last, ye are coming for me. I have waited so long."

"Yes, it is me; you are right. And yes, you have, and if I could have made it a shorter wait, I would have, but your patience will soon be rewarded."

"I would wait for ye as long as it took."

"I know, and I would do the same."

"Ye have. How did I nae realize it was ye in those dreams all this time? It all makes sense now."

"Perhaps it would have made things more difficult as we got older. I cannot really say."

"Because ye are nae allowed?"

"Because I really do not know, I promise," she said, chuckling.

"This is the first time since we were bairns that ye have come when I have nae been asleep."

"I know, and I cannot begin to tell you how or why, but I am here so I do not care about the details. I am here with you, and that is what matters."

Euan turned his head and kissed her palm. "Aye, it is. I remember now; I remember last time. This is still yers," he whispered as he lifted her other hand and placed it over his heart.

"As mine is yours, always," she whispered before she looked alarmed. "He is coming."

"Who is?"

"Remember that I love you," she said, pressing her lips to his in a soft but fervent kiss.

Euan reveled in the stolen moment for as long as it lasted. "Aye, and I love ye. Be well, my own *leannan*, and I shall see ye again soon," he whispered.

"Euan?"

Malcolm's hand on his shoulder made him blink, and Euan turned to look at his friend in confusion. "Aye?"

"Are ye all right? What are ye doing in here?"

"I …" Euan began, standing up straight and looking around him in bewilderment. "I dinnae know. I dinnae remember coming in here."

"Ye just stood up and walked away from the table."

Euan shook his head, trying to remember why he was here or what had made him come here, but there was nothing. "I wanted to check something, a position, I think. Cannae remember what it was now."

Malcolm looked askance at him. "Right. Ye have nae had that much wine, have ye?"

"No, only the bit ye gave me."

"I think ye really do need some rest, lad. Come on, come back to the table. The food is out."

"Aye, of course," Euan replied, following Malcolm out after one last glance back at the map table. There *had* been something, and he wished he could remember just what that was.

CHAPTER 11

AS THE SCHEDULED DAY for the departure of the regiment to Glenfinnan neared, there was much to be done to pack up and make ready to march. The final tally of Cameron men was eight hundred, all of them drilled to within an inch of their lives. Two days before they were to leave, the officers were given the day to go home and make their farewells, as they were the only ones who hadn't yet done so. Euan was happy to take the opportunity, returning home with the intention of staying the whole day with his mother, talking and spending time with her. Though she was thrilled to see him, there was such a sadness in her eyes and her expression that it hurt and made his heart and head heavy with doubt, though he did his best to push it away.

"I wish I could keep ye from leaving," she said as he made ready to go later that evening.

"I know, Mam, but ye cannae. I have to go."

"I feel as though the young man who leaves here today will nae be the same one I get back, *if* I get him back."

Euan looked at her, his expression sad. "He will nae be, just as he was nae when last he left and returned to ye. To be so would be impossible."

"Then I will mourn this one as I mourned the first and wait to see who returns to me."

Euan stepped close to her and pulled her into a tight embrace. "Whoever comes back will still love ye the same, Mam. Dinnae mourn, for he is nae dying, just changing."

"Ah, love, it is yer belief that there is something good to be found in all people that will die. Such things cannae survive the horrors of war."

"Perhaps nae, but that is nae all of me, and I will do my best to return as much the same as I am able. I love ye, Mam, with all my heart."

"I know ye do, son. Wait ..." Aileen stepped away from him and went to her bed, pulling from under it the small box where she kept all of the things she prized most. She pulled two items out of it and returned to him. "I want ye to take these with ye as a token for bravery and safety, to help ye remember home and remember that ye are loved, to remember how much ye mean to me."

Euan held out his hand, and when she placed the two items in it, he looked up at her. "Mam," he whispered.

"Aye, that is my wedding ring and a piece of the tartan yer father wore the day we wed. Take them both and know we are with ye."

Euan slipped the tiny ring onto his smallest finger. It didn't go all the way down, but far enough to be snug and not fall off. He knew his father had borrowed money from Lochiel to buy it, a debt that was forgiven when he died. The piece of tartan he tucked inside his coat pocket; he would sew it in later so he didn't lose it. He pulled his mother close again, both of them holding each other for a long moment while both cried in silence, before Euan pulled back, kissed her forehead, and hurried out. If he didn't leave now, he might never do so. At the crest of the hill he turned back, once again bowing to her and placing his hand over his heart as he walked backward, before waving to her and disappearing from her sight.

Euan and the other officers milled about the yard, coming

and going as they assisted with the final load-ups in preparation for the morning's departure. The yard was a buzzing hive of activity as people delivered items to the loading areas and others called out instructions. Though they'd been working for weeks, it still felt as though there was too much left to do, and it left him wondering if it would all come together or if they'd simply make do with what they'd managed to accomplish in a short time.

"Euan!"

Euan turned away from his task of helping to tie supplies into a wagon to see one of the young men from the stables running toward him, and the expression on his face did nothing to set Euan at ease. "Aye? What is it, lad?"

"Lochiel wants ye immediately! Word has come back of a skirmish with shots fired at government men from Fort Augustus at High Bridge!"

"Get ye to the stables and start saddling horses. Do it now! Iain, Findlay, round up the other officers! Malcolm, come with me!" Euan called out before sprinting for the castle.

As the two men hurried through the doors, they almost collided with Lochiel coming out. Lochiel didn't bother to stop moving, the other two falling into step with him as they went out the same way they'd just come in.

"Aye, ye have the urgency right, lads," Lochiel said as they walked. "Keppoch and Glengarry sent a man back with word that they intercepted two companies coming down from Fort Augustus to bolster Fort William, just as we were suspecting they might. The force retreated under fire and are even now being pursued by Keppoch back toward Fort Augustus."

"And ye wish us to increase their numbers?" Malcolm asked.

"Aye, and to give them a bit of relief, but we need to move quickly."

"I have already called up the officers, Lochiel, and had the lad ye sent after us set to saddling the horses," Euan said.

"Brilliant, Euan," Lochiel said.

"Did nae think we were about anything else when the lad said there were shots fired."

"A very fair assumption," Lochiel said, "but then someone in yer position would nae think otherwise."

"Did they bring back word of casualties?"

"None on our side."

"Well, that is an excellent start."

Malcolm started to laugh and hid it in a slight cough while Euan shot him a wry smile. All merriment faded, however, once the horses were brought around. Lochiel and his officers mounted up and departed with all haste for the trip to Loch Oich and Invergarry Castle. By the time they arrived, hostilities had ceased, with the remaining Hanoverian soldiers having surrendered while Highland soldiers now surrounded them to prevent their escape.

As the Cameron men dismounted, Lochiel strode toward the chief of MacDonells of Glengarry. "John, well done to ye and yer men."

MacDonell shook Lochiel's hand with a nod and a smile. "I thank ye, but more credit goes to Major MacDonald, I would think, as he and his men are the ones who chased them here."

"They had only eleven men there!"

"Aye, and yet they succeeded."

Euan raised an eyebrow at the news of only eleven Keppoch men being part of this rout. "Lochiel, would ye excuse me?"

"Aye, go to," Lochiel said before he returned to talking to Chief MacDonell.

Euan made his way over to where Donald MacDonald stood with a few of his men. "I hear ye are owed a bit of congratulations."

"Did ye now?" MacDonald asked, smiling as he turned to look at Euan.

"I heard eleven men took on eighty-five and did nae lose a one of theirs."

"Ye heard right."

Euan laughed and reached out his hand. "Good to see ye, Donald."

"And ye, Euan," MacDonald said, shaking Euan's hand and grinning.

"How in the hell did ye pull this off?"

"A bit of trickery."

"Or a lot."

"Or both."

"Go on with ye," Euan said, chuckling. "Tell me, for I know ye are dying to."

"As much as ye are dying to hear it. We used the inn as cover, hopped rock to rock shouting, extended our plaids, whatever we could do to make us look larger in number than we were. Their leader, Captain Scott he said his name was, sent a couple of men to negotiate, but we took them prisoner instead. After that, he called a retreat, and we chased them here."

"Ye made him think ye had a larger force with all that!"

"Aye, worked a treat, too."

Euan laughed and shook his head. "Cannae believe that worked, but well done."

"Now to figure out what we are going to do with them."

"What terms did they surrender under?"

"They stood down with the understanding that if they gave any resistance, we would kill them. They are all exhausted after the march, battle, and retreat, so there is nae much else they could have done."

Euan nodded. "So ye have no reason to dispose of them unless they give ye one."

"Aye, unfortunately, but amazing how the threat works, is it nae?" MacDonald said as both he and Euan started laughing.

"Right lads," Lochiel said as he approached them. "We are taking this lot back to Achnacarry to treat their wounds. MacDonald, ye and yer men should come with us to keep things in order."

"What is the plan after that?" MacDonald asked.

"They will be marched to Glenfinnan with us and presented to the prince. Ye will join us on that march and be reunited with yer clan there."

MacDonald gave a nod of agreement and departed to give the instructions to the rest of his men and the Glengarry men holding the prisoners. Lochiel and his officers returned to their horses and the entire party moved out in short order. They didn't push their already exhausted prisoners too hard on the march, making sure to pause to let them rest along the way. There was a shocked silence by those present at Achnacarry as the group came into the yard, and the soldiers were taken right into the hall to have their wounds tended to while Euan and the others were released to return to provisioning. His unease about what was coming sat heavy within him, unabated by this small victory. He'd heard the others remarking about how this must be a sign that God was with them, but he wasn't so sure he believed it.

Though Euan managed to find time for Brenda that evening — attempting to ease his heart and mind — even that hadn't helped, as he'd known it wouldn't. He left her far sooner than he ordinarily would have to return to the barracks and sew the piece of his father's tartan into his coat. Once that was done, he tried to rest, though it was clear none of the men within seemed to be able to find any. All of them lay in the darkness in silence, lost in their own thoughts and worries, wondering what would become of them and if they would face whatever fate awaited them with bravery.

Before dawn, the Cameron officers rose to get their companies mustered and ready for the march to Glenfinnan. Euan waited on horseback for Lochiel to give the command to ride out, and he turned his horse to look behind him at the massed Cameron regiment. It gave him a small sense of pride to see so many Cameron men all standing at attention together in silence, banners waving in the morning breeze.

Lochiel surveyed his officers and nodded before he looked to Euan. "Are ye ready, lad?"

"Aye, Lochiel."

"Then let us away. Camerons! March!"

The order was repeated by each officer to his company, and they marched forward as one. The cries of women and children were drowned out by drums and pipes, something he was thankful for. His mother hadn't come to see them off, and he was thankful for that, too. Seeing her tears once had been enough.

The regiment was taking a different path taken to Glenfinnan, as the traditional route would take them too close to Fort William, and because of that change, they'd go through the hills instead. It would take them most of the day to reach the spot by this track, but they'd arrive by early evening. Lochiel rode at the head, with Euan and his company behind him. Behind Euan was Malcolm, and then Iain, and then the others.

By three in the afternoon, as the Cameron regiment neared their destination, the drums and pipes kicked in again to herald their arrival, with Euan leading them in song as they began their descent down the mountain and into Glenfinnan and the head of Loch Shiel. Ahead of them waited a regiment of MacDonalds of Glencoe, who cheered when they saw the Cameron standard and numbers. As they approached, Euan saw the prince sitting on horseback with seven men, smiling as he watched the Camerons pour into camp.

When they reached him, Lochiel bowed from his saddle, an action followed by his officers and their men. "The Cameron regiment, as promised, Yer Highness."

"We are pleased indeed to see you, Lochiel. We were beginning to think you had backed out."

"I would nae do such when my word is given, Yer Highness."

"I should hope not, or we would be in a bind before we had even begun."

"Aye, ye would be," Euan thought.

Lochiel nodded. "We await yer command, Yer Highness."

"Excellent. Let us see who else arrives."

"Camerons! Fall out and make camp!" Lochiel shouted, his officers turning to relay the order.

The men dispersed to greet old friends in the MacDonald regiment and to set up their own camp, and as Euan dismounted, Lochiel and Major MacDonald delivered their prisoners to the prince and his retinue. Euan joined the men in setting up tents and making the camp ready, more than happy to avoid being at Lochiel's side during further conversations with the prince, and it was not long before they were joined by the rest of the regiment of the MacDonalds of Keppoch.

Once camps were set, Lochiel returned to his men. "How are we, lads?"

"Well," Euan replied. "Everyone seems in good spirits. How many are we?"

"Twelve hundred now," Lochiel replied, "with more to come when we reach Perth. Lord George Murray awaits us there with his regiment."

Euan gave a small nod before something caught his eye and he turned to look at it. There, fluttering open in the wind, was the Stuart royal standard. Something knotted in the pit of his stomach to see it, and he turned away from the sight. There was no turning back now, for that flag signified the true launch of the rising and, with it, solidified their treason.

"Euan, I want ye, Iain, Malcolm, Findlay, and the others to ready yer men to follow me in the morning. We march with the prince after dawn."

"Aye, Lochiel, as ye wish."

Lochiel smiled at him. "Ye are welcome, lad."

Euan looked up from his task in confusion, raising an eyebrow, which brought a laugh from Lochiel.

"For nae asking ye to stay with me while I met with the prince. If I had, he might never make it out of Glenfinnan."

Euan gave a slight smile. "I did nae think it was that obvious."

"Nae to anyone who does nae know ye as well I do."

"I dinnae like the way he speaks to ye, or to any of us."

"He is a prince, Euan. He does nae think of us as equals and thinks God gave him the right to be where he is."

Euan scoffed. "If he does nae have us, then he will have no army and no one to fight his cause, and if he does nae have that, then he will have no throne upon which to sit his royal arse, now will he?"

Lochiel laughed and clapped Euan on the shoulder. "That is true enough. Lord, Euan, have ye no respect?" he asked even as he continued laughing.

"For him? No," Euan answered through his own laughter. "I will do as ye command me, but I will do it for ye and nae for him."

"That is fair. Just make sure ye hold yer tongue, lad, lest it earn ye a place in the ground before battle even begins."

"Aye, Lochiel. They can try, but I dinnae think it would go well for them."

"Dinnae give them a reason to try just because ye want to knock their heads, either. Ye are a good lad, Euan. I know yer feelings, I understand them, but this is where we are and what we must deal with. Our strength will make up for his weaknesses."

"We hope."

"More than. It has to, or we are all dead men," he replied before he walked away to his own tent.

Euan pulled a knot tight, his jaw clenched in irritation. "We already are," he whispered.

Once the work was complete and darkness fell, the men all gathered around fires to eat, drink, and talk. Drums came out, and while the songs started out lighthearted, they soon went a different direction. Before long, someone began one of Euan's favorites, a song about victorious warriors gathered in the hall to celebrate victory. The drumbeat was steady, almost warlike in itself. The man playing the drum sang the verses, with the rest of the men joining him to sing the choruses, and

Euan sang along from his perch on the ground. Resting on his side with one of his arms propping him up, he stared into the fire in front of him. He let his eyes become unfocused, and it was almost as if he could see the story happening in front of him, the players becoming the Cameron officers celebrating in Achnacarry. It made him smile, and he could only hope he would see it soon enough.

CHAPTER 12

AS ORDERED, THE CAMERON companies rose early to strike their camp and make ready to leave. As they marched out of Glenfinnan, each man settled himself in for the duration of what promised to be an extended campaign. It was a long march to Perth, a journey that would take them almost a month. The start took them very near home and around Fort William, and though they stopped for the night on Cameron land, there was no time for any Cameron man to return home. Once they got past Fort William, things became easier, and Euan alternated between riding and walking with his men. It was good to get out of the saddle and move, and it seemed unfair to him that he had the benefit of riding on horseback when they didn't. After a time, he noticed the prince doing the same while wearing Highland dress. He asked men questions about their families or the songs they were singing. It was a clever way to begin trying to earn the respect and loyalty of the men at his command, and Euan appreciated it for what it was.

When they camped at night, Euan slept with his company instead of taking refuge in the officer's tent because it made good sense to him to remain close to the men he was asking to fight and possibly die beside him. The prince had his own tent or would stay the night in a noble house if there was one. As each day passed, it seemed as though more men joined them, many of them deserters from the government army, bringing with them intelligence on the movements of the current regiments, their sizes, their command — all information that was very helpful to the Jacobites.

When they reached Moy after five days, they were joined by two hundred and sixty men from the Stewarts of Appin. Two days later they reached Abertarff, where the Grants of Glenmoriston and three hundred of the MacDonells of Glengarry were waiting for them, swelling their ranks to over eighteen hundred. That the Grants of Glenmoriston joined them was a shock to Euan, as he knew it was against the express wishes of Chief Grant, but he would never say no to more men, and that was between them and their chief.

"I need ye to come with me, lad, and be quick about it," Lochiel said, approaching Euan after camp was set at Abertarff.

Euan put down the things he was carrying and followed Lochiel without a moment's hesitation. "Is something amiss, Lochiel?"

"No, but I need ye in this council," Lochiel replied as he stepped inside a tent.

Euan realized as he followed behind him precisely what Lochiel meant. Gathered within were the chiefs or the representatives who were leading their men, along with the prince and his seven advisors. All of them turned to look at the pair as they entered.

"What is the meaning of this, Lochiel?" asked the head of the Appin Stewarts.

"Ye will want the lad here for this, trust me," Lochiel said. "Gentlemen, this is Captain Euan Cameron, one of my best officers. Trained in France for just this sort of thing, educated in tactics and strategy with experience from assisting with the same for the war in Austria. I believe he will prove invaluable to us as we plot our course."

Euan bowed but remained silent, doing his best to not look intimidating but knowing he was failing at it all the same.

The prince nodded. "Let him remain. I have met him before and know him to be trustworthy. If it is as Lochiel says, then his thoughts can only help us."

"What is the situation we face, Yer Highness?" Euan asked.

"It has come to our attention that Sir John Cope and his men are within two days' march of us. He counts three thousand men to our eighteen hundred, and the question before us is whether we engage him now with the men we have, or if we delay an engagement while we wait for reinforcements."

Euan made his way to the map, looking at where the troops were marked. "That he has nae made a direct line to engage us even though he clearly could, tells me he and his men are nae ready. They are buying time."

"The lad is right," one of the other chiefs said. "We should meet Cope head-on while he is weak."

The others nodded and voiced their agreement.

"What makes you think this, Captain Cameron?" the prince asked.

"If Cope felt well-prepared, he would have come straight to us, spoiling for a fight and the chance to put the rising down before it even started, making himself a hero in London. He has nae done so, and that tells me he does nae feel ready to engage."

"Do you agree with the others that we should go to meet him?"

All of them looked at Euan with expectant countenances, and he felt the weight of their stares fully. He wouldn't, however, let that affect his counsel. "Aye, I do, Yer Highness. We are ready even if they are nae, and if they are nae, that makes them an easier victory for us. It would get us off to a good beginning."

The prince was silent and then nodded. "I agree with all of you. We should engage General Cope at our earliest opportunity."

There were smiles amongst the chiefs that Euan wasn't sure were entirely prudent because it never paid to be over-confident when it came to battle, but it wasn't his place to correct them. Euan remained to help plot the course they would take and then returned to his men to inform them to ready themselves for battle in the morning. There was a cheer from the Camerons, and it spread across the camp as the chiefs reported the news to their own regiments.

That night was spent readying themselves and checking equipment instead of the normal singing and talk around the fires, and the Jacobite army was on the march by four in the morning, ready to take on Cope and his men. Reaching the mountain pass that the government army would need to come through, they disguised themselves to lie in wait. After a time, a rider wearing a government uniform approached on the road, a white cloth held high. Euan and several other Cameron officers stepped out onto the road to stop him, muskets aimed in his direction, causing the man to pull up on the reins of his horse sharply.

"Thank God, my kinsmen! I have found ye at last! I am here to join ye and tell ye that Cope has taken a different route."

"How did ye know we would be here?" Euan asked.

"They would have to pass this way if they were pursuing ye to their original plan."

"Cope is nae coming this way, ye say?"

"Aye. He and the regiments turned off toward Inverness at Blargie Beg."

Euan lowered his musket and nodded to Iain to take the soldier's weapons. The man did not fight them on it, adding another layer of truth to his statements.

"Cope is nae coming!" Euan called out.

From around them erupted sounds of disappointment mixed with a bit of amused jeering at what seemed to be government soldiers in fear of them. The other officers and chiefs came out of hiding to join them on the road.

"How many were ye?" Euan asked.

"Three thousand, but mostly new and untrained recruits. Only a few of us had training and were trying to teach the others."

Euan's lips spread into a small smile, and he glanced at Lochiel. It was just as he'd thought: Cope wasn't ready to face anyone.

The prince came out of the woods, grinning. "A dram for every man! Let us drink to the health of good Mr. Cope, and may every General in the Usurper's service prove himself as much our friend as he has done!"

This comment was met by much laughter, and even Euan joined in it. The drams were passed around and imbibed before they re-formed and continued onward to Perth. Camp was made at Aviemore that night, and the war council reconvened, this time without Euan, who went to meet with his company. As he was speaking with them, he noticed several of them glance over his shoulder and turned around to see Lochiel approaching.

"Euan," Lochiel said. "I need to speak with ye."

"Aye, Lochiel," Euan replied, bowing before he dismissed his men.

"Walk with me," Lochiel said, waiting for Euan to fall into step with him as he made his way to his tent. "They have decided nae to pursue Cope to Inverness, but to take advantage of his leaving the Lowlands unguarded," he said in a low voice. "We are to Dunkeld, Perth, and then to Edinburgh."

"Edinburgh?" Euan asked in surprise.

"Aye. Intelligence says the city shall be taken easily, and that is what they mean to do."

"There is no defense at all?"

"Nae enough to matter. We march south tomorrow."

"As ye say, Lochiel. The men will be ready."

"Aye, they will be. I know I can always count on ye, lad," Lochiel replied, patting Euan's shoulder before going inside.

Euan released a breath and shook his head before he

turned and made his way back to alert the men about the change of plans.

The decision made, the mass of men moved efficiently, and it took them only three days to reach Dalwhinnie, where they made camp. That evening, Euan and the others waited on some of the Cameron men to return from a raid at the nearby Ruthven Barracks. Euan heard the whistle they used as a signal and stood, walking toward the edge of camp and reaching it in time to see the men leading someone in. As they got closer, Euan recognized the prisoner in an instant.

"Cluny?" Lochiel said as he stepped up next to Euan.

The prisoner looked at the two of them and smiled in relief. "Hello to ye, cousin."

"Christ, man, what are ye doing here? Let him go," Lochiel said to the men.

"Taken prisoner, as ye can see."

"So few men took ye that easily? And yer Cameron kin, at that?"

A sly smile appeared on Cluny's lips, which spread to Lochiel.

"Jenny wanted ye to remain loyal, while ye wanted to come with us. So, ye had us 'take' ye, is that it?"

Cluny laughed and then nodded to Euan. "Euan! How are ye, lad?"

"Well, I thank ye, Chief Macpherson," Euan replied, bowing even though he was laughing.

"Good to see ye still have my cousin's protection in hand."

"Always," Euan said.

"Come on, Cluny, let us get ye to the prince," Lochiel said as he put his arm around his cousin's shoulders and walked off.

Euan smiled and shook his head as he watched them depart. If Cluny Macpherson was here, then his men wouldn't be that far behind him, and it would be good to see them again. After all, the Macphersons were like kin to the Camerons because Cluny was a first cousin to Lochiel; Cluny's mother was a Cameron. Euan liked the man a great deal and always found him to be amusing and good-natured.

After another three days' march, they arrived at Blair, where the Marquis of Tullibardine awaited them. The men camped on the grounds of Blair Castle, and the marquis held a supper to entertain both the prince and the Highland chiefs currently with him. Euan went in with Lochiel, as did an officer from each clan with their own chiefs. The officers were there to ostensibly stand guard, but it was almost certain there would be no need of them. The inside of Blair Castle was beautiful, and it was much larger than Achnacarry. Euan surveyed it appraisingly, appreciating the fine architecture and furnishings as the officers were led to another room once they were dismissed from service. They were to dine here, on the same food being served in the great hall to the prince and the chiefs, and would still be within easy distance if there was a disturbance. The fine meal set out before him made Euan uncomfortable, knowing his men would have nothing of the sort, but he also knew he couldn't refuse it and decided to let himself enjoy it. It was, quite possibly, the finest meal he'd eaten since leaving France, and he relished every bite. Many of the others were unfamiliar with such cuisine, and Euan spent time explaining what things were and how to eat some of them, much to everyone's great amusement.

On their second day at Blair, Lochiel approached Euan as he was drilling men.

"Hold!" Euan called out to his men before turning and bowing to his chief.

"Euan, I need ye to make yer men ready. Tell Iain, Findlay, and Malcolm I need their companies ready as well. We are to march ahead to Dunkeld and Perth to proclaim the king and the prince. We leave at dawn," he said.

"Aye, Lochiel," Euan replied before Lochiel departed, immediately calling a halt to the drill so they could switch to preparation.

As requested, Euan and the others had their men ready at dawn, and Lochiel rode out with four hundred of the Cameron men for Dunkeld. It was a day's march to get there, where the Camerons made camp as Lochiel proclaimed James VIII to be king. Euan kept his face placid as he stood beside Lochiel during the announcement, but he didn't feel as calm as he looked. To do as they had just done was one more charge of treason to add to the ever-growing list, and an incredibly serious one at that.

When they arrived in Perth the following morning, Lochiel made the same proclamation, and Perth was declared to be in possession of the Jacobites even though there'd been no fight against it. The prince arrived that afternoon with the rest of the army, and Euan watched the rather astonishing welcome he received. The people cheered him, and a public fair was held. The men were dismissed to go and enjoy themselves, including the officers, and Euan allowed himself to relax enough to go with the others — the first time in a month he felt like smiling.

The next day, a massive influx of men arrived. The Macphersons, with 300 men, were the first. They were followed by men from Nairn, Gask, Aldie, the Robertsons, and more Stewarts. The biggest arrival came from Lord George Murray and his Atholl Brigade, bringing their total force to 4,000. As soon as Murray arrived, he went into conference with the prince and emerged the Lieutenant General of the entire army. Euan and the other officers spent time drilling their men and making them ready for whatever might come next.

As Euan sat by the fire at the end of their fourth day in Perth, Lochiel joined him, but stopped him from getting up and bowing.

"Good evening, Lochiel."

"Euan, ye remember I told ye at Borrodale that yer particular skills would make ye more in demand and ye would be asked to do things others were nae?"

"Aye, Lochiel."

"That time has come. I need ye in Edinburgh immediately."

CHAPTER 13

"MILLER! ARE YOU DONE yet?"

"Just a minute! I only just got started!"

Andrew Miller stood before the tree as though he were urinating against it, but from his pocket he produced a piece of paper that he tucked into a hole in the tree, making sure it couldn't be seen. Once he was satisfied, he turned and walked back to the man waiting for him.

"About time."

Miller rolled his eyes. "I do not even think you could piss that fast, Jacobs."

Jacobs laughed. "I could if I knew those savage bastards were out here waiting to kill me. Come on, we have to get back," he said as he started to walk back from the patrol they'd been on. "Do you think the Jacobites are coming? They should have been here by now, right?"

Miller shrugged. "Who knows? Maybe they turned around and went back to the Highlands when Hamilton's dragoons met them."

"Maybe they did not have the numbers they hoped for."

"Possible."

"I mean, the Young Pretender sent those demands, and the city has not given in. You would think he would come by now if he really meant to."

"Maybe he did not really mean to, and it was an empty threat."

The two men stepped through the gate into the city, and it

closed behind them, locked by the sentry. Security in Edinburgh had been increased since word came of an impending invasion by the Jacobites, with all entries to the city sealed. They made their way to the guard post below Edinburgh Castle, and when the relief patrol arrived, Miller and Jacobs handed over the post and departed.

"Cover for me, would you Jacobs?" Miller asked.

"For what?"

Miller pulled a coin purse from his pocket and jingled it while grinning. "This is burning a hole in my pocket, and there are some lovely ladies to spend it on."

"You are insatiable. You will have no money left!" Jacobs replied, even as he shook his head and laughed. "Go on with you, then. You have an hour. I will not be able to hold anyone off longer than that."

Miller nodded and turned around, his smile fading as he threaded his way through the crowds at a brisk pace, having a particular place in mind and money to spend there. He turned down a narrow, darkened close, descending some steps located about halfway down it. Lifting his hand, he knocked on the door, and the woman who opened it smiled when she saw him.

"I was wonderin' if ye were comin' around again."

"Of course I was."

She stepped back to let him in and then closed the door behind him. "Did anyone follow ye?"

"No," he replied in a sigh of relief, his entire demeanor changing and relaxing behind the safety of the closed door.

"Good. Ye are as clever as they come, Euan Cameron."

Euan smiled at her. "I have heard that before."

"All true."

"Is everything ready?"

"Aye, it will be done as ye asked. Are ye sure it is ready from yer side?"

"It will be. Ye will need these," Euan replied as he handed her the bag of what Jacobs had thought were coins.

Taking the bag and opening it, she looked up at him in surprise. "Ye have the gate keys!"

"No, *ye* do, Davina," he replied, winking. "Use those to open the other gate. They will be waiting."

"At least have a drink before ye go, make them think ye came here for what they think ye came for," she said as she led him through the house.

"I will need some of ye, too."

Davina turned to look at him with interest, and he laughed. "Ye will need to give me a hug before I go, so I smell like perfume."

"Oh, and here I was thinkin' ye might have changed yer mind about enjoying some of our services."

"I appreciate the offer, and it is tempting, but I have work to do and cannae be distracted from it."

"Shame," she replied, her lips turning up in a wry smile.

"Maybe another time. Dinnae count me out yet."

"I will hold ye to it. Come on, have a dram and take a few moments to relax."

When Euan emerged onto the street again a short time later, it was as Andrew Miller once more. In his four days here, he'd seen enough to know that the city was ripe for seizure. There had never been a proper force here, and those few that *had* been here had left to intercept the Jacobites elsewhere. That left only old men, barely trained privates, and desperate citizens to defend the city, and Euan knew they didn't stand a chance. In all the confusion of changing defenses and panicked maneuvers, it had been easy to slip into the group of very inexperienced soldiers without anyone really noticing. The uniform he now wore had been procured from a laundress, and if he was asked who he was, he would say that he'd been sent to relieve someone else. Now the time had come for his plan to be set in motion, and after tonight there would be no more Andrew Miller.

There was only a short break before any man was put back

on the watch again because there weren't enough men to provide for proper relief. Euan was exhausted, but that was more from the constancy of his work. It had been four days of pretending to be English, not letting it slip even once, and the pressure of it was draining. Unlike normal, there weren't hours of downtime where he could relax. Instead, he had to remain focused, his mind whirling and making sure he was keeping his answers straight despite how tired he was.

Euan was able to take a quick nap before going back on the watch with Jacobs at the center of town, and it was near dawn when Euan saw the coach go by, headed for the lower gate. He hid his smile as it passed, for it meant the ladies had done their work, and he could only hope Lochiel and the Cameron men had done theirs. If they had, the coach leaving would open the gate for them to rush in without opposition, with a second unit entering through the gate he'd stolen the keys for. That question was soon answered when his clansmen came into sight, and when Jacobs got up to flee, Euan grabbed him while pulling out a sgian dubh.

"I suggest ye sit down, Jacobs. I would hate to kill ye; I quite like ye."

Jacobs looked at Euan in absolute astonishment as the man he'd known as Andrew Miller became Euan Cameron, the Highland officer. "But —"

"If ye stay pliable, ye will live, I promise ye."

The Cameron men entered the guardhouse and grinned when they saw Euan.

"About time ye got here, lads," Euan said.

Lochiel chuckled. "The others are already disarming the men at all the posts ye listed. The rest will be confined to the castle?"

"Aye," Euan said. "They dinnae have the numbers to come out against us and know the safest place to be is behind those walls. Ye and the council can debate whether ye want to take it."

"Excellent work, lad," Lochiel said before he looked at Jacobs. "Who is this?"

"Ah, this is Mr. Jacobs, and he has been my watch partner in my time here. He is harmless enough."

"Ye will wish to turn him loose then."

"Aye. We should send him up to the castle with the rest."

Lochiel nodded and then looked Euan up and down. "It pains me to see ye in those colors, lad, even if the uniform looks well on ye. Take it off."

"Thank Christ," Euan muttered in pure relief. More than happy to obey the order, Euan made quick work of stripping off the coat and throwing it to the ground before spitting on it. Someone tossed him a Cameron plaid, and he slipped it over his shoulder so they'd know he was one of them, no matter his state of dress.

"Ach, Euan, no. Here, put yer proper clothes on," Malcolm said, handing him a bundle. Euan laughed and took it from him, stepping aside to change the rest of his clothing.

"Much better," Iain said when Euan returned, handing Euan his broadsword.

"Andrew, you traitor!" Jacobs shouted as the Camerons around him laughed uproariously.

"I am nae Andrew Miller. I am Euan Cameron, of the Achnacarry Camerons. Sorry to have lied to ye but, well, needs must."

The men cheered, and Iain hauled Jacobs up, marching him off while the others were still laughing. Euan grinned and then stepped out into the street, feeling as though a massive weight had been lifted from him. No more lies, no more Miller, no more English uniform, no more watching his speech.

"Ye look exhausted, lad," Lochiel said.

"Aye, I am. Lying for so long takes a lot out of a man."

"Ye did far more than lie. If they would have caught ye, then ye would have been a dead man. Dressing up as a soldier was genius. It took balls the size of boulders, but it was genius."

"Then I suppose I should find something to wheel them

about in while I am here," Euan said, his cocky smile making Lochiel laugh.

"As soon as the city is taken, ye are dismissed to get some rest. Ye dinnae need to be here for the prince's entry. Ye have done more than enough."

Euan bowed, and as soon as the word came that all posts were secured, he departed for the only place he could think of. When the door opened, he greeted the mistress of the house with an exhausted smile as he leaned against the doorjamb.

"Success?" she asked, looking Euan over in appreciation now that he was dressed as a Highlander once more.

"Aye, success, and the city is now ours. May I trouble ye for a bed to sleep in? I dinnae think I have slept more than a few hours in the last four days."

"Aye, of course ye can, my sweet lad. Come in and take yer ease."

Grateful, Euan followed her toward the back of the house, collapsing into the bed in the room she gave him, and asleep before she'd even shut the door. He slept off and on throughout the rest of the day and night, his sleep now and then interrupted by female company in the form of the working women of the house, including the proprietress herself. He didn't mind a bit, even though he hadn't asked for them, happy for some sort of human connection with who he truly was and not who he'd been pretending to be.

As he prepared to leave the following morning, Davina entered the room, and Euan smiled up at her from the chair he was sitting in. "Thank ye for yer excellent hospitality, Davina; it was an absolute pleasure. How much do I owe ye?"

"Naught," she said, smiling.

"But —"

"They did it because they wanted to, nae because they wanted pay for it. There was nae a one of them who did nae want to get under ye the moment they saw ye, and when the first one reported back with glowing reviews, they all had to try."

"Even ye?"

"Oh, most definitely me."

Euan chuckled. "Well, thank ye, and please tell them I appreciate it."

"Oh, I think they owe *ye* some thanks from what I understand."

"Well, I could nae let them think badly of me. I have a reputation to uphold."

Davina laughed. "Insatiable *and* incorrigible, my favorite kind of man. Ye send yer men our way, would ye? That would be payment enough."

"Aye, of course," Euan replied. "More than happy to and I know they will be, too."

"But ye? Ye are welcome here anytime ye wish, and it is on the house. Even if it is just for a meal or sleep in a proper bed."

Euan grinned. "I appreciate that."

"Go on with ye. I am sure yer chief needs ye by now."

Euan stood, kissing her cheek before he swept past her and down the stairs, opening the door and exiting with a chorus of giggling goodbyes behind him from the women who had gathered for breakfast. He walked back toward the center of town to find Cameron men on guard in case anyone seeking refuge in Edinburgh Castle decided they should try to attack. To Euan it seemed unlikely, but people had done more ridiculous things.

"Where is Lochiel?" Euan asked one of them.

"Up at Holyrood with the prince and the others," he replied.

"Thank ye," Euan said as he turned and made his way up the street.

After a short walk, he entered the grounds of the palace and saw many men he knew on guard, including Malcolm and Iain, who directed him toward the Cameron camp. There was a cheer of recognition when he entered, which made him laugh.

"Lads! If ye are needing some lasses to entertain ye, there is a good house down by the castle. Ask for Davina's and tell them I sent ye," Euan announced, laughing as another cheer went up, this time for another reason entirely. Davina was sure to be getting some business this evening, and for as long as they were here.

"Ah, Euan! There ye are, lad. I was starting to wonder if there were some government men that got ye," Lochiel said, making his way out of a tent.

Euan bowed. "No. I was resting. And then nae resting. And then resting some more."

Lochiel got his meaning and laughed, shaking his head. "Fine. Are ye through?"

"For now."

"Right," he replied with a knowing smile. "Back to business: we have word that Cope is coming to engage us."

"Finally?"

"Aye, finally. Walk with me." Euan fell into step beside Lochiel. "There is more. Murray does nae trust the prince and cannae work with him. Their every meeting is a quarrel."

"Why?"

"I suspect Murray has the same issues ye do, along with a distrust of his military judgment. The prince is only here now because we have nae had to truly engage a force, and the one time we might have done, he was nae the one who led us or drafted the plans."

"He is focused on making the people want to come out for him," Euan said.

"Aye, and that is nae where his mind should truly be, at least nae fully. Instead, he listens to the counsel of men with no experience."

"I wish I could say that surprised me."

"O'Sullivan is sending a Cameron contingent to Tranent near Prestonpans, where they believe Cope will land, and I want ye to go with them. They will be looking out for Cope's arrival."

Euan bowed to Lochiel and departed to find the contingent being sent. With it being only a few men from each of the companies, they were quickly on the road. Once they reached Tranent ten miles away, they crept into the church-yard to keep watch, only to find that Cope had already landed. Swearing under his breath, Euan ordered one of the men back to inform the chiefs of what they'd seen, but before he could give another order, the boom of a cannon shook the ground, the ball striking near them.

"Back up!" Euan shouted. "Get out of range!"

They all scrambled backwards as another explosion sent a new cannonball their way, and the strike sent rubble from the churchyard wall flying in every direction. Euan felt a searing pain as sharp pieces of stone cut across his torso and arm before a larger piece collided with his side. His scream of pain was drowned out by the shouts of the other men. Another blast sent them running from the churchyard, around to the other side where they were hidden by the building.

"We need to stay here until we get orders to move or until we get reinforcements," Euan panted out.

"Christ! Euan, are ye all right?"

Euan nodded. It hurt like hell, but he knew he wasn't mortally damaged. "Might need some stitching though."

"Let me look," the young man said, then shook his head. "I dinnae know how, but ye dinnae even need stitching. It will sting a fair bit for a while, I imagine."

"It stings a fair bit now. Thank ye, Douglas."

Douglas nodded to him and took a seat next to Euan. "Ye are lucky."

"Aye, and likely nae for the last time."

Douglas laughed. "May it be so for all of us."

"Aye."

"Lochiel!" shouted the man who was sent back to Holy-rood as he ran up to him, panting.

"What is the meaning of this? Why are ye nae with Euan and the others?" Lochiel asked, wary.

"Cope has already landed, Lochiel, and we came under heavy fire from the cannons almost as soon as we arrived."

"WHAT!" Lochiel bellowed.

"The cannons were still firing on Euan and the other men when he ordered me back here!"

Lochiel, face reddening with rage, turned and stormed inside the palace. "Lord Murray!"

"What in the world are ye shouting about Lochiel?" Murray asked as he appeared from one of the rooms.

"I need authorization for an immediate withdrawal of my men from Tranent!"

"Whatever for?"

"Because Cope has already landed and my men have come under cannon fire, that is why!"

"Already landed? Christ! Form up the men. NOW!" Murray shouted. "Lochiel, ye have authorization to withdraw yer men to higher ground to await our coming."

Lochiel turned and stormed out, finding the man still waiting. "Ye get yerself back to Tranent and tell the men they have leave to withdraw to higher ground until we can get to them. GO!"

CHAPTER 14

AS THE MAN LATER came running back into the churchyard, shouting the order to move to higher ground, Douglas, Euan, and the others wasted no time in getting up and making a run for it. From their new position, they could both watch Cope and be out of the way of his guns. Euan now found it painful to take a deep breath, a familiar discomfort from his time in France that made him certain he'd broken a rib or two. When Lochiel, Murray, and the others arrived, it was just after noon, and Euan remained on his back on the ground with his eyes closed because it was easier.

"Captain Cameron, are you unwell?"

Euan's eyes fluttered open to find the prince kneeling beside him in concern, and John, the young nephew of Lord George Murray, watching in curiosity from behind the prince. "Yer Highness," he murmured, trying now to sit up.

"No, no, do not get up. You are clearly injured. Lochiel! Your man is injured!"

"Euan! What in the hell happened to ye?" Lochiel asked as he reached Euan's side.

"Cannon," Euan muttered. "That arsehole fired cannon shot on us. I got hit with some stone shrapnel and may have broken some ribs, but I think I will be fine."

Lochiel glared in the direction of O'Sullivan. "Ye would nae even *be* in this position if that idiot had nae put ye there and exposed ye needlessly."

"Lochiel, please," the prince said. "Now is really not the time. Are you able to stand, Captain? I think we have need of your talents in council."

Euan nodded and pushed himself up with a wince, taking Lochiel's extended hand and pulling himself up. "As ye wish, Yer Highness."

Euan followed Lochiel and the prince toward where the generals were meeting for a council on how to proceed, arriving to find the conversation well underway.

"We have the high ground, but he has natural advantages to his position. A full charge would break up in the marshy ground at the center, which will leave us open to cannon and musket fire. We have to attack his open left flank," Murray said. "That is the only thing that will work."

"Surprise has worked for us so far," Euan said, feeling no need this time to wait to be spoken to as everyone turned to look at him. "We took Edinburgh without a shot because they did nae expect what we were planning."

"What are ye suggesting, Euan?" Murray asked.

"If ye are going to attack the left flank, do it when they are nae expecting it. If we rest now and move before dawn, we can take them by surprise. Set up some of the regiments to make false moves to make them think we are up to something else entirely."

"He is right," a young man said. "I know this area well, and I know how ye can get through the marshes without them seeing ye. There is a defile to the east that will shield ye from view."

"Ye are sure about this, Lieutenant Anderson?"

"Aye, m'lord."

Murray nodded. "What say ye, gentlemen?"

"I dinnae think it will hurt," Cluny said. "I think attacking at dawn rather than at night will work well against such inexperience."

"Aye, I agree," Lochiel said as the other chiefs also murmured their agreement.

"Yer Highness?" Murray asked.

"Yes, I think so," the prince replied. "Surprise is always good if you can manage it."

"Then let it be done. Anderson, how long do ye think such a movement might take?" Murray asked.

"If we try to do it as quietly as possible? Two hours or so."

"Then let us have the men ready to move at four."

"You are dismissed, gentlemen," the prince said.

Euan bowed to the prince and the other chiefs and followed Lochiel out.

"Are ye truly all right, lad?" Lochiel asked.

"Well enough," Euan replied.

"That is nae what I asked ye."

"Aye, I should be ready to fight by the morning if I get rest now."

"Make sure ye do. We will need ye out there; yer men will need ye," Lochiel said as he patted Euan's shoulder and walked away from him.

"Captain Cameron, wait."

Euan stopped and turned at the unfamiliar voice to find John, the young page, hurrying toward him. Euan bowed to the young man, who was the nephew of the current Earl of Dunmore. "Master John. What may I do for ye?"

"I … well, are we …"

Euan took stock of the boy, who was, at most, fifteen. Though he was trying not to show it, Euan could see that he was nervous. "Are we going to battle?"

"Aye."

"Aye, we are." John paled and swallowed hard. "Dinnae fear, Master John, ye will be safe."

"I am nae afraid!"

"It is all right if ye are. Ye should be, as we all should be. Being afraid does nae make ye a coward, what makes ye a coward is what ye choose to do in the face of it."

John's gaze became curious. "Are ye afraid? Ye dinnae seem as though ye would be afraid of anything."

Euan gave a slight smile. "I have more practice at nae showing it."

"So, ye are, then?"

"A bit, aye. As I said, ye should be. To be so is normal, and the moment ye are no longer afraid before a battle is the moment ye become dangerous to yerself and everyone around ye."

"Ye said I would be safe?"

"Aye, of course. Ye are page to the prince, I dinnae think ye will be charging into battle with us. Ye will be sitting behind the lines if he is, and that is a far less dangerous place to be. If the worst happens, ye will either flee with him or ye will be captured."

"Captured!"

Euan chuckled. "Easy, lad. If they capture ye, they will nae kill ye. Ye are just a boy, but ye are also kin to a peer. Ye are far more valuable alive."

"Then what would happen?"

"They would likely try to get information out of ye. How many men we have, what our plans are, things of that nature."

"I will nae tell them."

"Of course ye will nae," Euan said, seeing no point in frightening him with the truth: that they'd resort to ever more painful methods to get information if they truly felt he had something they needed. "Ye are too clever for that. Ye will make something up."

"Aye, I would."

"Ye should get some rest, as I should, unless the prince has need of ye. Tomorrow will be a long day no matter what happens."

"Ye are right. Thank ye, Captain."

"Master John," he replied with another bow before watching the boy hurry back to command.

Euan felt for him, truly. He was about to learn a very bloody lesson in warfare, and he was about to learn it in the most up close and personal way imaginable. Euan understood why he hadn't asked those questions of his father or his uncle; he hadn't wanted to show them he was scared. He wanted them to think he was as brave as they were. It was something that bothered him, for a boy that young shouldn't be here, shouldn't be thrust into the middle of a war that would forever shape the way he saw the world, but it wasn't Euan's choice to make.

Euan made his way back to where his men and the other regiments were already setting up camp and spent the rest of that day trying to get some rest. As he lay on a cot in a tent that night, he could see Cope's men keeping fires burning on their front lines to prevent a night attack. Those fires would do them no good soon enough. They'd changed their positions in response to the false movements of the Jacobites, done as Euan had suggested, and that would harm them, too, though they didn't know it yet.

At the appointed time, long before dawn, Euan was in position with his men as the Jacobite forces began their silent march along the defile to the east. It was narrow so that only three men could walk together per line, but it served to mask their movements. When they emerged onto the plain, they found themselves altogether concealed by the mist that hung heavy in the air and on the ground, and they couldn't have asked for a better cover than this. Once they arrayed themselves in the lines they would attack from, Euan looked to his right to see who was placed where. Next to the Camerons were the Stewarts of Appin, MacGregor, Glengarry, Keppoch, and Clanranald. Atholl, Robertson, McLachlan, and Glencoe made up the second line, while the prince, accompanied by John, and his advisors took up the space between the two.

Closing his eyes, Euan breathed in as deeply as his injury would allow in order to steady his nerves. Battle, true battle, was finally here. He said a silent prayer before the sound of the pipes and the calls of the chiefs set the charges in motion at last. When Lochiel shouted the Cameron war cry, "Chlanna nan con thigibh a so's gheibh sibh feoil," *Sons of the hounds, come hither and get flesh*, Euan echoed the call to his company and ran forward, sword in hand, toward where he knew Cope's lines would be even if he couldn't see them.

Before Cope's men even knew what was happening, the screaming Cameron men materialized like demons from the mist, overrunning their cannons and killing every man within blade range as the luckier ones fled. The action succeeded in destroying the left flank, and Clanranald, Keppoch, and Glengarry took out the right in the same manner, thus exposing the government's center line where the more experienced men sat. Euan noticed that the middle of the Jacobite front line had somehow gotten bogged down, and the left and right wings of the Jacobites were now coming together to trap those unfortunate men in the middle. The center of the Jacobite line had now recovered, however, and were also closing in on them. As the three sides came together, the government center took heavy damage and fell apart in a near instant, sending what was left of Cope's men fleeing and ceding the field to the Jacobites, who let out a roar of victory.

The rest of the morning mist cleared away, the extent of the casualties becoming clear, with the government dead littering the marsh. Euan stood amongst the carnage, his breathing heavy, looking around him. Blood covered every inch of him, but none of it was his own, the metallic tang of it so thick that it drowned out even the scent of the sea. Grimacing, he placed his hand to his side when the pain of those broken ribs caught up with him in the next second. Now that he'd ceased moving, he could tell he'd worsened the injury with his participation, but there was nothing to be done about it either way. Euan found himself feeling strangely unmoved by the scene, at least in the way he thought perhaps he should be. It wasn't the first time he'd been in combat and needed to take a life, but it had never been this many at once, and there was an odd pleasure in the sheer scope of ruination he'd just been a more than willing agent of.

Euan smiled despite himself, letting the darkness such a victory brought take over for a moment before he staggered back toward where they'd formed up. The second line remained in place, staring and in awe of what had just happened. The entire action was over in ten minutes, and it took longer for the Jacobite men to reconvene than it had to defeat the enemy. Instead of following the first wave into bloody battle, the second line was sent out to make prisoners of any government men who remained alive. They wouldn't find many, as the front line had given no quarter, even though the prince had begged them to stop. His pleas had come far too late, and battle was never about mercy.

"Captain Cameron," Murray said as Euan walked past him, which made the young man stop and look at him. "Well done. *Very* well done."

Euan forced a small smile and a bow, noting young John sitting on his horse near his uncle, staring at Euan. His face was white as snow, he looked shocked and sick, and Euan knew he could smell the blood on the field and the blood that coated Euan — the reality of war. Euan nodded to him before he continued walking. As the rush of battle faded, he found that all he wanted was to get clean and try to drink the pain of his injuries away. That he'd emerged alive and victorious from this first battle, one that he helped to plan, would come to him later and he would be thankful for it.

A commotion drew his attention away from thoughts of drinking as much whisky as he could possibly manage, and he turned his head to see a group of men surrounding someone. Making his way toward them, he saw a Hanoverian officer on the ground, his foot stuck in one of the stirrups of his dead mount. The young man was doing his best to fight off eight men and had so far managed it, but the lack of honor being shown angered Euan. The man should have been let up and allowed a fair fight or the chance to surrender. As Euan was about to speak, however, a deep voice rang out.

"Devil take ye, ye paltry fellows, are ye nae ashamed eight of ye stand to the face of one man? What would that man do to ye if his foot were nae entangled? Stand aside and let me face him!"

Euan stopped and watched as Duncan Mackenzie, known as Big Duncan to all the men in the Cameron regiment where he served, strode toward the fray. Big Duncan was a stout, bear of a man and a fierce fighter, which had made Euan happy to have the man in the company he commanded. The group parted, and Euan remained silent and away from them, watching what might happen in case Big Duncan needed assistance.

"I am giving ye the chance to surrender now," Big Duncan said once the man was free of the stirrup.

"Stand back, you Scotch rogue!" the officer shouted in return.

Euan sighed, knowing that this was the absolute wrong answer to give at this particular moment, and he was proven right as Big Duncan drove his blade through the officer's shoulder and out through his armpit, killing him. Bravery was to be commended, but it was smart to know when one was outnumbered and outmatched and stand down, something this young officer should've considered. The sound of hoofbeats over the cheers of the watching men got Euan's attention, and he inhaled sharply as he saw a dragoon riding toward them.

"Be on yer guard Duncan," Euan shouted. "There is a dragoon making for ye!" he finished before he grimaced with pain, the effort of shouting aggravating his injury.

Big Duncan whirled around to face the rider, bringing his sword down onto the head of the man, but there was no give, and both Big Duncan and Euan realized that the dragoon must have been wearing a steel cap under his hat for protection. Big Duncan swore loudly and backed up toward a dyke, stepping back onto it and putting himself at the same height as the rider who came around for another charge. As the dragoon reached him, Duncan jumped forward and brought his sword down with so much force that it cut through the steel, cleaving the man's head through to his chin.

"Jesus Christ!" Euan shouted, too shocked to feel the pain of his own injury as he watched the rider fall from his horse and into a bloody heap on the ground.

Similar shouts rang out from the other Jacobite soldiers who witnessed it, all of them knowing the force and strength such a blow would take. Big Duncan stepped up to his dead opponent and picked the helmet up, blood dripping from it.

"It may be that this will cause talk yet," he said, almost to himself, before he looked up and caught Euan's wide-eyed stare. "Oh, hello Captain. Bit of a mess, aye?"

"Aye, a bit," Euan replied, unable to think of anything else to say. "Ye all right, Duncan?"

"Aye, well enough, thank ye. Ye dinnae look so, on the other hand. Dinnae worry, we will handle this."

"Right," Euan said in a bit of daze, "carry on then."

Turning around, he resumed his former path toward camp, shaking his head in astonishment while making sure he remembered to avoid facing off against Big Duncan if he could help it — not that he'd have a reason to anyway.

Cope's baggage train was captured by the second line, bringing in muskets, ammunition, and £5,000. Lochiel ordered the medicine chests found in the baggage to be used to treat the Hanoverian injured, and upon hearing the order, Euan started to make a move to go along and assist with sorting the munitions, but Lochiel immediately stopped him and sent him back to camp. It was clear Euan was injured and needed treatment, and Lochiel had no intention of letting this particular officer kill himself by volunteering for a task it was not necessary for him to participate in.

Euan began to clean himself off as best he could, looking up when Lochiel's brother, Dr. Archibald Cameron, came inside. Forcing himself to stand, Euan bowed but grimaced. "Dr. Cameron."

Archibald surveyed his movements and then nodded. "My brother sent me to take a look at yer injuries, Euan."

"It is well," Euan said, sitting back down. "Naught to worry about."

"I will be the one who determines that, as only one of us is a doctor, and it is nae ye, ye insolent whelp. Lie down," Archibald said with a chuckle.

Euan smiled and shook his head at the good-natured teasing but did as asked. "Ye are wasting yer time though, honestly. I am sure there are others who need ye more."

"And they are being seen to by others. Donald sent me explicitly to ye, so dinnae argue."

Euan sighed and then remained still as Archibald knelt beside him to check his injuries. The breath he sucked in was sharp, as first the cold of Archibald's hands and then the pain of the touch hit him, and Archibald immediately pulled back.

"Those are broken then."

"Aye."

"Will nae touch them for now," he said as he returned to looking at the other wounds caused by the cannon blast from the day before and nodded. "Ye were lucky; none of this requires stitching, but we will have to clean it out. The bits of rock and dirt need to come out. Wait here."

Euan nodded and Archibald left, returning with a basin of water, some cloth, and a small brush. Surveying it with a wary eye, Euan had a feeling he knew what was about to happen, and Archibald nodded.

"Aye, ye are thinking correctly. This is nae going to be pleasant, but it must be done."

Cursing in his head, Euan closed his eyes and waited. The water was warm, which was pleasant because he was freezing, but then the brushing began. Back and forth over the already raw skin, the pain of it made him cry out and brought him to tears almost immediately. His hands gripped the sides of the cot, and he clenched his teeth, the next scream strangled between them as he fought his urge to pull away from the pain.

"Aye, I know, and I am sorry. I am trying to be as quick as I can."

When he was done, Euan lay there panting and in tears while Archibald smoothed some salve over the bleeding wounds and then bandaged them.

"Try to get some rest, Euan," Archibald said. "Ye have earned it."

When Archibald was gone, Euan covered his face with his hands and allowed himself to cry for a few moments as the pain radiated over his skin in stinging waves. He knew the ribs were worse, he could feel it through the scrubbing, but he had no intention of saying so. There was nothing to be done for it anyway, and he wouldn't shirk his duty because of it. Removing his hands and opening his eyes, he stared at the ceiling of the tent and tried to calm his breathing. It wasn't long before exhaustion pulled him down into a sleep so deep the pain couldn't find him.

When he woke again, it was dark, but as he tried to move, all he could do was groan in pain. Every part of him hurt and made him not want to even think of moving again, but he forced himself to sit up as his training shoved the thought away. The pain of the movement shut his eyes once more, and he sat still, breathing through it and the nausea it brought with it. When it passed, he opened his eyes and saw the fires burning outside, but there was no real movement or noise beyond. Euan suspected it was because everyone was asleep and rose from the cot, clenching his teeth against the pain of more movement, compelling himself to dress. When he stepped outside, he could hear the sounds of the sea, of the wind moving through tents, and the crackle of the fires, but all else was still and silent, with no hint of the bloodshed that had occurred only hours before. Euan closed his eyes again and focused on that, wanting to bring himself back from the edges of wherever the battle had taken him, still feeling the darkness pulling at him.

"Trouble sleeping, lad?"

The sound of Lochiel's voice opened his eyes, and Euan turned around to face him, attempting to bow as best he could. "I only just woke."

"It is good ye are getting some rest when ye can find it."

"I wish I had stayed asleep. I dinnae think there is a part of me that does nae hurt in some way."

Lochiel chuckled. "Aye, I am there with ye, though probably more so, as there are twenty-six years between us. Archibald says ye have broken ribs, but ye already knew that. He did say ye likely made them worse when ye charged in with the rest of us."

Euan nodded. "I am lucky it was nae worse than that."

"Ye were. I still want to strangle that idiot for putting the lot of ye out there needlessly. The man has no sense or experience."

"All ye can do is try to counter him as best as ye are able."

"And I shall, believe me, but so shall ye."

Euan looked at him with curiosity. "How?"

"Ye will keep giving counsel when asked, but I also will be sending ye out on things I request of ye at my own discretion."

"Like Edinburgh."

"Just like."

"I will nae put the uniform on again."

"Never say never, lad."

Euan sighed, irritated at the very thought. "What happens now?"

"We go back to Edinburgh for now until the prince decides what he wants to do next."

"The winter will be here soon," Euan said, his voice quiet.

"Aye, but I am nae sure we are going anywhere anytime soon."

"That is good to hear. It will give me a bit of time to heal before we move on."

"There is talk of England being next," Lochiel said.

Euan turned his head to stare at his chief in shock at both the suggestion and the nonchalance with which the man said it. "No …"

"Ye think it is a bad idea too, I see."

"We have nae the men for that, and we never agreed to take England!"

"We go where he bids us, remember that," Lochiel replied, sighing.

"How would four thousand men stand a chance against thirty thousand on their home ground?"

Lochiel said nothing.

"His advisors are foolishly urging it in spite of the numbers," Euan said, his tone flat as he realized what Lochiel's silence meant.

Lochiel nodded. "Men with no real military sense."

"I could try to speak with him," Euan offered.

"No, ye will nae. Nae unless ye are asked. Remember yer place, Euan."

Euan pressed his lips together tightly at the blunt reminder that he was not an equal here and never would be, no matter what he did, what his counsel provided, or how successful he was. "Aye, Lochiel," he said, keeping his voice as quiet as he could, almost unable to mask the anger he felt.

"As ye are awake, ye can take the watch," Lochiel said before he turned and left Euan standing there alone.

Euan closed his eyes and tried to shove down what he felt. One thing he could not abide was someone being dismissive of him. He hated it more than he had words to express, and it was all because he'd faced it almost his entire life. If he felt he was gaining something, some new achievement, someone was always there to shove him back down and remind him of who and what he was. Most often, it was Lochiel himself, though the others in France had done the same. Lochiel would build Euan up only to rip away what he'd built and remind him to whom he owed his allegiance and all of his accomplishments. It was moments like these when he seriously considered walking away from all of it. He could take his mother and move to the Continent or to the Colonies. Away from this place and the clan, able to be their own bodies for once. He had plenty of skills he could make use of to survive, so he knew he'd be fine. He couldn't leave now, of course, as he had men under him who depended on him and desertion was never something he would countenance. After the war was done, perhaps.

Euan walked back into his tent and picked up his baldric, grimacing as he slung it over his head and into place across his body, then hissing in pain as the weight of his broadsword pulled the leather taut across his chest and against some of the wounds on his torso. After a few attempts at deep breathing to let the pain pass, he realized it was only bringing more pain and abandoned it. Opening his eyes, he pushed himself back outside to begin the watch.

"Ye are nae looking much better, Captain."

Euan looked to his left and saw Big Duncan come out of the darkness with a silence of step that was surprising in a man as large as he was. "Nae feeling it, either," Euan replied.

"Aye, I can tell, and that is unusual for ye."

"I am still human, and even I cannae mask the pain of multiple injuries for long," Euan said, his half-smile adding to the sarcasm that dripped from his words.

Big Duncan gave a quiet chuckle in response. "Aye, fair enough."

"Ye did well today, Duncan."

"Thank ye, Captain … which part do ye mean, exactly?"

Euan smiled despite his pain. "All of it, but the last was a thing of beauty, I must admit. Terrifying, but still a thing of beauty."

Big Duncan grinned. "Aye, it was, was it nae? Thank ye for the warning, by the way."

"Well, I certainly was nae going to let him run one of my best men through."

"No, of course ye would nae," Big Duncan replied, going silent for a moment as he stared into the darkness before them. "Ye did well, too."

"How do ye mean?" Euan asked, raising an eyebrow.

"Come on, Euan," he replied, dropping the formality for a moment. "Ye dinnae think no one has heard by now what ye have done, do ye?"

"Here?"

"Aye here, and in Edinburgh. Ye were fair injured after the cannon and ye charged in with us anyway, injuring yerself further. Ye did it to protect us, as ye always do."

"I could nae do anything else."

"Aye, ye could. Ye could have stayed here."

"Why in the hell would I do that?"

"Because ye value yer own life?"

Euan scoffed. "I dinnae value it more than any of yers."

"That makes ye rarer than ye realize, I think. Of course, that is aside from what ye did in Edinburgh. Ye are a madman."

Euan chuckled. "I have been called worse."

"I dinnae doubt it."

"I did what needed to be done," Euan said, looking over at Big Duncan, "what I was trained to do. Nothing more."

"There is nae one in a thousand of us could do what ye did there. We admire ye for it, admire the massive stones ye must heft about to even consider such a plan. Any man can swing a blade, but very few have the ability to become another human being entirely and have no one be the wiser. Nae only that, but with nae a tremor of fear to be seen."

"I think they could if they were trained to do it, as I was."

"Ye can think that if ye wish, but ye and I both know that is a lie. It is frightening how good at it ye are."

"Are ye saying the men fear me?"

"Christ, no! Nae a bit. Well, at least nae in any way they should nae. We know what ye expect of us and know that ye respect us as men. Because of that, we respect ye tenfold and are with ye to the last drop of blood and breath. We are nae loyal to ye out of fear, Euan; we are loyal to ye out of respect. I promise ye there is nae a man in our company who would betray ye or cross ye, and if we found one that tried, he would nae live long enough to go through with it."

Euan smiled. "Thank ye for that, Duncan. I dinnae think ye realize how much I needed to hear such a thing just now. Know that I feel the same about every one of ye, and I would give my life for any of yers if required."

"We know that, and that is why we never want to give ye cause to do so. Ye are a good man, an honorable man, the kind of man the rest of us look up to and strive to be like. Ye dinnae belong dead on a battlefield because one of us failed ye."

Euan was silent, not knowing what to say, and knowing that if he spoke now, his voice would betray the emotion dredged up by Big Duncan's words. Respect meant everything, and this was respect he'd more than earned, but not purposefully.

"Nae that I think ye would anyway. Ye are a terror with a blade, so I would nae wish to fight ye."

"I was thinking the same about ye earlier," Euan said, laughing now.

Big Duncan joined him in his laughter. "Well, let us call it a draw then, aye?"

"I can agree to that."

"Ye on the watch, then?"

"Aye."

"Would ye care for company?"

"Would never say no to yers, Duncan," Euan said, his smile becoming a grin.

Big Duncan returned the grin. "I will be right back then. Let me fetch my blade so ye are nae the only armed man on."

Euan gave him a nod and watched as Big Duncan turned and faded back into the darkness. Having a friend partner up on the watch always made the time pass more quickly and helped to keep him awake. At the same time, it would also distract him from the intensity of the pain he was in and help him shake off the mood Lochiel's words had put him in.

Camp was struck early the next morning, with Euan doing his best to assist with it and his men pushing him away from doing so, knowing he was injured. The respect for Euan that Duncan had spoken of the previous night wasn't confined to his own company; it came from all the others too. All of them knew that if Euan was sitting something out, it was because he was physically unable and not because he thought the work beneath his position, and even then, he was still trying. Prevented from physical tasks by his own men, something he couldn't be upset about knowing their reasons, he instead turned his mind to helping organize the strike and where things should go.

When the time came to mount their horses for the ride back, it took Euan several moments to force himself to do so, knowing how painful it was going to be. Though he clenched his teeth, the scream that got through was unable to be stopped, and he gripped the reins so tightly his knuckles turned white. The men near him winced, well aware that for such a thing to come from him the pain had to be excruciating. He tried to breathe through it but couldn't take anything more than a shallow breath without further pain, and he felt as though he might be sick.

"Euan," Malcolm said as he saw the tears the pain had caused hit the leather of the saddle. "Are ye all right, lad?"

Euan gave a faint shake of his head, the only thing he was able to do.

"Christ, I am sorry for it."

Euan said nothing in reply, sending his horse forward so he could get into position for the ride back. He was in no mood for conversation, particularly with Lochiel, so he let Iain's company take the lead behind Lochiel, followed by himself, and then Malcolm. What Euan didn't see through the haze of his own pain were the dark looks on the faces of the men at the lack of care shown to him. It wasn't something missed by any of them, and while Lochiel would hope that, as their chief, they would support him in such a situation, they didn't. There was, instead, a quiet anger at the disrespect shown for the young man who led them so capably and whose counsel had helped them to their first victory.

The ten-mile ride itself was jarring and painful, even with a slow pace. Euan kept silent for the entirety, doing his best to focus on just staying upright. The movement of the horse jostling his body made it impossible to hide that he bore some quite serious injuries, and by the time they arrived back in Edinburgh, Euan's face was ashen, and he was fighting to remain conscious. The army was welcomed back into the city like conquering heroes, proceeding to Holyrood as they were cheered by people who had come out into the street, and once they arrived the companies were dismissed to their rest or to duty stations. Each one of Euan's men stopped to touch their hat in salute to their young leader, who remained on his horse for the moment. He was touched by the gesture and nodded to each one as they went by, thanking them by name. It was then not just his men, but many of the men of the other Cameron companies as well. If Lochiel wouldn't show the man respect, then *they* would. When they'd all passed him, Euan closed his eyes and lowered his head for a moment as he tried to fight the pain before he heard them shout all together.

"Go mbeannaí Dia duit, gaisgeil Euan! Chlanna nan con thigibh a so's gheibh sibh feoil! Fàilte!" *May God bless you, brave Euan! Sons of the hounds, come hither and get flesh! Salute!*

Euan's eyes snapped open, and he looked up, his expression unguarded for a brief moment and making his shock at the words plain while he watched them all hold their weapons up to their faces in a salute before they dispersed. Euan didn't know what to make of such a gesture, but he didn't dare look for Lochiel to see what he might think of it.

Behind him, Lochiel's expression darkened for a moment as it was made clear that his own treatment of Euan in front of his men had spurred the display of respect toward him. Though he'd earned it, deserved it, and shouldn't be begrudged such an honor, it proved what Lochiel already knew: if Euan Cameron turned against him, he would take the entire regiment with him. It was a mutiny he could ill afford and showed that treating Euan in the same way he once had would only spur ill will toward him. Such sharp checks on the young man might work in private, but aside from that it was unwise.

Still sitting in the saddle, Euan didn't want to move, but he knew he'd have to because he couldn't stay there forever. Forcing himself off in a swift move, a jolt of searing pain burned through him the moment his feet hit the ground, and his legs ceased to support him. Euan cried out in shock as well as pain as he fell onto his hands and knees but catching himself with his hands sent yet another spike of anguish through him, and this time he screamed, feeling as though he were drowning in pain with no escape.

Malcolm and Iain ran to him to help him, but as soon as they put their hands on him, he shouted at them in anger. "NO! DINNAE TOUCH ME!" Forcing himself up, he staggered forward despite the pain, feeling as though he could hardly see. The world seemed to narrow and then shift, leaving him unable to fend off help this time as Malcolm and Iain were there to support him as he stumbled and nearly fell. "Leave me ... leave me ... alo ... alone ..." Euan panted, finding it difficult to speak, much less think.

"Come on, lad, easy," Iain said, in a quiet, gentle tone to avoid agitating Euan further. "Ye will be all right."

"No ... stop. I can ... I can do ... can do this."

"Do what?" Malcolm asked.

"Get to the —"

"To the tent? Nae likely, because ye cannae even think straight and yer face is as white as the snow. We will help ye," Malcolm said.

"No," Euan said, his voice now as weak as the fight he was trying to put up.

"Damn ye, lad, stop!" Iain shouted at him. "Ye can only be so strong, and ye have reached the limit. Ye have naught to prove!"

"Weak … I am weak …" Euan replied, able to hear the voices of Alain and the others in his head, taunting him, shouting at him about how feeble he was, even as delirium began to seep in.

"Ye are full of shite is what ye are. If this is weak, then I am no better than a new bairn every day of my life," Malcolm shot back.

"Euan, ye are to let these men help ye to yer tent, and Archibald will see ye. I dinnae want to hear nor see ye fighting them. That is an order, are we clear?" Lochiel said as he approached them, having seen the whole thing and knowing Euan wouldn't give in unless his commanding officer ordered him to do so.

Euan looked at him for a moment as though he were trying to figure out who he was, before he nodded. "Aye, Lochiel," he said in a near whisper as he struggled to keep his eyes open.

"Malcolm, Iain, go on with ye," Lochiel said.

Both men nodded. "Aye, Lochiel," they said in unison before they half-dragged Euan, who was now no longer resisting them, away.

Once the two men got Euan to his tent, they heaved him onto the cot and covered him with his plaid to remove the chill. They stepped out as Archibald stepped in and, moments later, the sound of Euan's blood-curdling scream rang through the camp. Heads turned in an instant toward the sound before it stopped. Malcolm and Iain looked at each other, shaken and with concern etched on their faces, as Lochiel came up beside them looking just as rattled.

Archibald stepped out a few moments later and shook his head. "The lad is hurt far worse than we thought, Donald," he said to Lochiel.

"How do ye mean?"

"More of those ribs are broken than I previously thought. Either he made them worse during the battle and the ride, or they were always that bad and he hid it. I assume it was all the former because he would nae have been able to hide that, as ye just saw and heard. There is also some serious bruising that was nae there yesterday morning. It is dark and seems deep."

Lochiel cursed under his breath. He never should've made Euan do the watch last night, but the battle was in all probability more responsible for the worsened injury than that was, and the ride back hadn't done him any favors either. "What do ye suggest?"

"Rest. It is all ye can do. He needs to stay off a horse for at least two weeks and away from actual combat for longer than that. He will be able to help ye and the council, help the watch, and anything that does nae require too much physical work. It will be a task to keep him down, I know, but he will nae improve otherwise. I gave him some laudanum; that should help for now."

"Ye might want to keep that up for a day or two, Archibald, just to make sure he stays down for a time. We will work on the rest when he comes around."

"Aye, I agree. In the meantime, we should see if we can find the lad a proper blanket to keep him warm," Archibald said.

"I will find one," Lochiel replied. "That bastard O'Sullivan owes me that much. Euan would nae be injured if he had nae been so foolish as to put them where there was no cover."

"What is done is done and the lad will live. That is the best outcome ye could have gotten other than him nae being injured at all."

"Nae at all would have been preferable."

"I will keep an eye on him, but ye may want to post at least one of his men on duty outside of his tent to make sure he remains there. Ye know how Euan can be."

"Aye, I do." He knew only too well because he'd made him that way. "Malcolm, speak to his men and see who will volunteer."

"I dinnae think volunteers will be a problem, Lochiel," Malcolm said.

"Likely nae. Go." Malcolm turned and walked off to fulfill the order as Archibald returned to the tent with Euan, and Lochiel shook his head in irritation.

"I really should do all of us a favor and make O'Sullivan simply disappear," Lochiel thought as he headed back to the palace to inform the prince and the other chiefs about Euan. "It might save us from more idiocy before the man gets us all killed."

CHAPTER 15

"THERE IS MUCH TO go over after all of that," Specialist George said after his customary moment of silence to make sure Euan had said all he intended to.

"Aye," Euan replied. "Much happened in a short amount of time."

"Let us start at the beginning. You threw yourself into training your men. Other than the obvious reason, was there another reason you became so focused?"

"Such as?"

"Well, did you do it to avoid feelings or situations?"

"Nae really, no. It was my job, and I did it. Perhaps I could get lost for a bit and ignore the feelings I had that I would nae return, but it was nae intentional. We had so little time to accomplish what was needed."

"Keeping you so busy that you neglected other things."

"Aye, but again, nae intentionally. The only way any of us would make it was if we were as prepared as possible. That alone had to be my focus."

"When you were standing by the river, you heard a voice."

"I did," he said, his voice softening. "I thought it was in my head, but I know better now."

"Oh?"

"She was calling me. Wherever she was, her soul could feel the distress in mine and let me know she was with me always."

"Watcher Cameron?"

"Indeed. I would recognize that voice anywhere now."

"Intriguing."

"I wish I could tell ye how it works, but I cannae."

"And what of Brenda?"

Euan's brow knitted for a moment. "She was … I liked her well enough, dinnae misunderstand me. I cared for her and about her welfare, but it was nae love and never was. I was as honest with her as I was with the others; there would be naught like that from me."

"Did it upset you when she confessed such feelings to you?"

"Upset is the wrong word. I did nae want her to speak them because I did nae want to hurt her when I reminded her of what I had said. I was hurting enough people already and did nae wish to add another to it. She was also doing it after I had heard the voice saying my name, while the feelings it stirred in me were still fresh."

"You said you were already starting to regret what you knew you had to do."

"Who does nae when it comes time to go to war? Ye dinnae think it will be as hard on ye as it actually is until the time comes."

"You mentioned feeling as though you wouldn't return."

"It was such a strong feeling, too," Euan replied, his brow furrowing again. "I was at peace with it, and at the time I assumed it was a premonition that I would die in the war. Now, however, I wonder if it was something different."

"Something different?"

"Aye. It feels now as though I somehow knew what was coming. I knew I was nae going to return, and that part proved correct, but I was nae going to return because I came here, nae because I died. My soul knew what I did nae; she was coming for me and I would be leaving all of it behind."

"What a fascinating observation, and quite possibly entirely correct. Did you ever remember what led you into the map room, where Malcolm found you?"

"Aye," Euan said, his smile returning for a brief moment. "But nae until very recently, after our last session."

"What was it?"

"My beloved one, my Grace. She came to me there, the night before we departed. Her voice had nae done enough to calm me, so she came instead. I dinnae remember it fully, but I do know she was there somehow."

"What an extraordinary thing to have happen. The bond between you is so very strong and seems to have existed long before anyone else was aware of it, even you."

"Aye, it is strange to think about yet nae at the same time. It is as though I have always known it, but my mind buried it to protect me from the pain of being in a world where she was nae yet living. To know it, to admit it, to speak of it to another living being makes it real, and it feels right to say it, to let my soul release the memories my mind had long suppressed."

"Indeed. Let's talk about your mother."

"If we must," Euan said, frowning.

"Why don't you wish to?"

"It was all so painful, those last moments. I did nae know if I would see her again, or if I came home if I would be the same person. Perhaps I would be crippled in some way physically or mentally; who knew? I did nae have any wish to cause her pain, but that is exactly what I was doing, and I had no control over it."

"She wanted to protect you."

"Of course, and what mother would nae? But we both knew that I would nae be the same no matter what happened. Such a thing was impossible."

"She said she would mourn the loss of the young man who was leaving."

"Aye," Euan said, his voice softening to a near whisper. "She knew that, once again, the son she had known would leave, never to return."

"And she gave you talismans for protection."

"In the form of her wedding ring, aye, and the piece of tartan. To keep them both with me, ye see. She lived and would pray for me, and I would carry those prayers with her ring, and the soul of my father would guide and protect me from harm, a piece of him carried with me in fabric."

"What happened to those pieces?"

Euan held up his left hand, smiling. The ring was still visible on his smallest finger. "I still have it, as ye can see. The tartan was moved to the new coat she made me after we returned from Stirling, and it resides there even now."

"On your uniform?"

Euan nodded. "My uniform that came here with me and now sits safely stored in the closet of my home. So, both of my parents are still with me in this future."

George smiled. "That's very sentimental."

"No one could ever accuse me of nae being such," Euan said, chuckling.

"What was it like to ride out at the head of an army?"

"Terrifying," Euan replied before he gave a gentle laugh. "But ye get past it. I was nae truly at the head of it anyway."

"Close enough."

"If ye say so," Euan said, laughing a little harder now. "At the head of my company, at least."

George laughed with him. "I suppose it's painfully obvious that I know nothing of military things."

"Why would ye need to?"

"Could you explain it to me?"

"The entirety of the men at our disposal is a regiment. We started with eight hundred. Those eight hundred were divided into companies of about eighty men, and each company had an officer in charge. The officer's job was to train them, get them ready, and then keep them together. The men in each company trained together, marched together, ate together, slept together. The head of our regiment was Lochiel, who had no specific company but oversaw the officers, who got their orders from him and then passed them on to their companies. On the march, the officers would ride alongside their companies, often somewhere toward the middle of the line."

"Was there a pride of place in that lineup?"

"There could be, but it was often set in stone. The strongest companies in the front and rear, protecting everyone else in case of attack."

"Very interesting. Did you know the men in your company?"

"I did nae before they came, but I did afterward. I did things a bit differently than everyone else. I got to know them, understand them, and let them get to know me. I wanted them to know I respected them, was looking out for them, and did nae see myself as any better than they were. When we marched, I walked with them at times to show I was nae above it. I stayed with them instead of with the other officers because I was nae above them in that way either. I would never ask any of them to do what I was nae willing to do myself."

"I'm sure that made you well-liked and respected."

"Seeing them and treating them as people did that."

"When you arrived in Glenfinnan, you were not happy to see the prince."

Euan scoffed. "No."

"Because you didn't wish to be there at all?"

"Precisely."

"Were people optimistic?"

"Aye, somewhat at least."

"Let us jump ahead a bit to the moment you were first called in to advise the war council."

"At Abertarff?"

"Yes. Were you nervous?"

"Nae at all. I knew perfectly well what I was doing. The concern I had was whether or nae they were going to listen to me or dismiss me outright because I was someone of no rank."

"You said you were an officer?"

"I was. By no rank I mean I had no title. I was nae a chief or anyone like that."

"I see. Was it thrilling for you when they did listen?"

"I dinnae know if thrilling is the right word for it. Relieved, perhaps, though it was nae really that difficult a call to make. If the person who is supposed to be coming to challenge ye suddenly turns away, it is clearly because he does nae yet feel ready to do so. Ye have a chance to catch yer enemy unprepared, and ye should take it."

"Then, of course, Cope didn't come."

"Of course nae."

"And this proved you correct."

"Aye."

"Tell me about Cluny Macpherson's kidnapping."

The laugh that escaped Euan was loud, and it was obvious the memory was still amusing to him. "Nae sure ye can really call it such when the entire 'raiding party' consisted of his own kin."

"Really?" George asked, joining him in laughter.

"Oh, aye. We all knew it was a ruse so he could say he was forced to join if his wife got after him for it. His wife was the daughter of Simon the Fox, well known for playing both sides. She was nae a stupid woman."

"I see," George said, still laughing. "You mentioned you were uncomfortable once you reached Blair Castle. Why? You were used to such things, weren't you?"

"Aye, I was, and it was nae for that reason. My discomfort was for a meal and surroundings my men did nae get to share."

"That wasn't your fault."

"No, it was nae, that is true, and there was naught I could do about it, so I went with it. I will admit it was rather nice to eat such a fine meal again. Had nae had such a thing since France."

"You ate well there?"

"After the first year. When ye work for a king, ye dine like a king."

"How were you feeling when you went ahead to proclaim the prince?"

"Wishing we were nae, but what choice did we have? We had already committed treason, aye, but this just seemed more egregious for some reason. A slap in the face, daring the Hanovers to come for us. It seemed unwise."

"Do you still think so?"

"I understand why it was done, to drum up support, but I still feel uneasy about it for reasons I cannae explain."

"Now, we come to more difficult matters. Let's start with Edinburgh. Did Lochiel tell you what to do?"

"No," Euan replied. "He told me only that he wanted me to go to Edinburgh and find a way in and then help them do so. They would have a man watching for me to leave messages to alert them to my discoveries. The way I made those discoveries and plans was up to me."

"So, it was your idea to dress up as an English soldier?"

"Best way to do it."

"Were you worried about being caught?"

"Nae at all," Euan said, amused. "I had excuses and plans if I did, but never feared I would have to use them."

"Why is that?

"Things were in such disarray. No one knew who was coming or going, what little defense they had marched off to supposedly meet us, and I already knew from the messages that the movements were false in order to draw them out."

"It still seemed as though it was difficult for you when you were discussing it."

"The difficult part, really, is to keep any game up for that long. Ye must always be mindful of what ye say and how ye say it, every move ye make, the expressions of others to see if they seem suspicious. At the same time, ye are making mental notes of everything they do and say so ye can either use it to get to something or relay it back. It can be exhausting work. It was nae the first time I had gone so long, but the first time I had gone so long in such a high stakes game. There was a very, very short window, and I had to get what I needed quickly."

"You have, of course, gone longer now."

"Ach, aye, far longer than I ever had in my old life. Going on missions with Grace, I might work several weeks at a time, as ye know, but in a way that makes it easier. Ye have time to settle in, to become the person ye must, to build bridges and relationships. She, of course, makes it look ridiculously easy. I think Jacques and the others might have wept with joy and kissed her feet after watching her work."

George chuckled. "As they do here in some ways."

"*That* is a whole session unto itself and nae for me."

The comment made George laugh. It was nice to see Euan loosening up enough to joke around with him, and he found he quite liked Euan's company. "So, you were in, you had the information you needed, and you enlisted the help of prostitutes?"

"Ah, ye see, ye must never doubt the ability of working lasses in my time to get things done. They held the keys, the secrets, for there was nae a man who did nae pass through their doors at some point. They could tell me who supported the prince, who might be able to help me procure things, who might be able to tell me where weaknesses might be because I did nae have time to really scout them on my own. Davina and the ladies were gems."

"Did you feel bad about deceiving the young man you partnered with?"

"Jacobs? No, nae really. I knew his affiliation with me would save him, in the end. I dinnae know what became of him after we left Edinburgh, but for the time we were there, he was safe. I am sure he was either sent to England, to the Continent, or faced us in another battle."

"Do you feel like you used him?"

"No, because I did nae. He was assigned to me as a partner, but he had as much information as I did. He gave me naught."

"Were you happy to see your clansmen?"

"More than."

"And happy to get out of the uniform?"

"Definitely, but also happy my plan had worked."

"As well as happy that Lochiel was pleased."

"Oh, he certainly was, and *I* was pleased to be able to finally get some rest."

"Well, at least a little bit of rest."

Euan laughed. "I would say it was equal. It is hard to explain how such work sometimes makes ye desperate for a human connection in the midst of all of it."

"I can understand why it would. You don't feel real, but such things remind you that you are."

"Aye! Exactly!" Euan said.

"Then came Tranent."

Euan sighed. "Aye, Tranent and then Prestonpans."

"Once again you are called in to give counsel."

"Aye, and once again they listen."

"But you're already injured, aren't you?"

"I was. Nae as badly as I would become, but aye."

"You were lucky."

"Very, and the first of many times in this campaign."

"So, now you and the army are lined up and ready to attack, provided cover by heavy mist. Are you nervous?"

"Of course. If ye are nae nervous in such a situation, there is something wrong with ye. Ye are facing yer own death and the deaths of those around ye and in front of ye. Ye should be more than nervous; ye should feel some sort of fear even if ye are well trained. It is yer ability to overcome that and go forward anyway that makes ye a warrior, and perhaps whether ye live or die."

"Were your men afraid?"

"They were about to run headlong toward a line of cannons. What do ye think?"

"Fair enough. Once the charge is called, what's in your mind?"

"Naught but focusing on going forward, nae dying, and

killing as many of them as I can. There is no time for fear then, or doubt, or anything else. Survival is all that exists, because I promise ye that yer enemy is only thinking of their own."

"Was there any sort of reticence to kill?"

"From me? None. It was nae the first time or the last. For the others, I doubt it. If ye dinnae kill them, then they will kill ye, so ye best make sure ye are on the winning end."

"When it was all over, what were you feeling? Was there horror at the carnage?"

"As horrible as this sounds, no. I was alive, and there was elation in that. The injuries to the dead were horrific, as injuries from broadswords tend to be, but to see it did nae bother me. I was covered in blood, but none of it was mine. Have ye ever been in a place where a lot of blood has been spilled?"

"I can honestly say I haven't."

"Ye can smell it. There is a metallic bite to it, and it surrounds ye. It is so strong ye can taste it. This was the first time I had been in a situation where so many lives had been lost at once, and that is the thing I remember most — the smell of blood. I will never forget it, and I dinnae think ye can once that smell has etched itself onto yer memory. I should have been disgusted, but I was nae. Instead, I felt almost ..." Euan said, then paused to think about it, "almost happy. Proud of the damage, the death. There is a dark pleasure that overtakes yer senses and yer thoughts, urges ye to do more, feeds on the rush of such a victory. To me, that is the horror."

"That pride and pleasure seems unlike you, at least what I know of you."

Euan made a small sound of amusement. "Ye dinnae know me that well, nae yet. It is nae something I am proud of, but it is something that is also nae abnormal in such situations. I saw it in everyone. I see it in Grace when she outsmarts or outmaneuvers someone during a mission, or when we are successful. Warfare, whether mental or physical, can generate strange things in a person."

"That may be true, but you don't seem like a person who would normally revel in death and destruction."

"Aye, that is true. I dinnae want to do it, but I will if I must, and if I must, I will show no mercy because it means I have no other choice."

"Did it make you happy that Lord Murray and Lochiel were pleased?"

"In the moment it did nae matter. I honestly cannae remember if I thought about it later or nae."

"Tell me what you thought when you saw young John Murray."

Euan shook his head. "I felt badly for him. The lad was obviously terrified, but I saw myself in him, too. I saw the young me, who felt the same fear at nearly the same age when I was dragged off of a ship. He never should have been there."

"You wanted to look out for him. Where would you have had him be?"

"If he had to be on campaign, he should have remained back at the command tent where he was safe, where he did nae have to see it, hear it, smell it. His life changed in that moment, and nae necessarily for the better."

"Do you think it informed his later dealings in the war with the Colonies?"

"I dinnae see how it could nae, but I dinnae know what sort of campaigns he led, so I cannae say how much."

"When you woke that evening and had the conversation with Lochiel, were you angry when he told you to remember your place?"

"Christ, yes. I hated it when he did that. I see now, after last time, how that was just another piece in the game."

"I'd say so, yes. Do you think the prince would've listened to you?"

"Hard to say. He may have if I spoke to him the right way. We were the same age, and at that point I might have been able to talk some sense into him, but we will never know."

"Did you often stand alone after a battle?"

"Always. I needed time to focus and bring my true self back from the dark place I am forced to go in order to kill without thinking."

"Are you always able to do it?"

"Aye, I have never found it impossible. Sometimes it may have taken longer, but I always got there."

"What of Big Duncan?"

Euan grinned. "Ach, Big Dunc. I really *was* fond of him. He was a good man, a good soldier, and a good friend."

"You mentioned your shock at his killing the dragoon."

"We were *all* shocked. That was nae normal and was quite impressive. From what I understand, when the men sat around talking about who had done the best that day, Big Duncan was mentioned. No one believed it, and they sought him out so they could see his sword. Well, when they saw the damage to the blade, then they believed him, and he was offered a pretty penny to sell the sword, but he ended up refusing. Later he was captured, and as part of the conditions of his release, he had to surrender the sword. It was, apparently, lost for a time but recently found in the Duke of Argyll's collection at Inveraray by a Macdonald, of all people. He took it back, laid it on Big Duncan's grave, and held a small ceremony there before returning it to the Duke. A beautiful thing to have done."

"That's a very touching thing for him to have done, I agree. When you spoke with Big Duncan later that night, how did that conversation make you feel?"

"Better. It was good to hear that I was valued even if it was nae by the person I wanted it from. To know my men respected me so much was an incredible feeling."

"Let's talk about the next day and the ride back to Edinburgh."

Euan winced, and it was obvious he was still able to remember the pain.

"Is there a reason you didn't ask for assistance?"

"Proving a point, I suppose, nae to mention I felt that if

Lochiel wanted me to ride in a cart, he would have told me to do so."

"But he ignored you."

"Aye, he did."

"And so, you were forced to make the ride back as injured as you were."

"Aye, and it was excruciating. Every move, every bump, it all just made the pain stronger. Mounting the horse was bad; getting off of it was worse."

"Do you think you lost consciousness on the ride back?"

"No, but almost a few times."

"How did it feel when your men saluted you?"

"I felt honored by it, that they thought so much of me that they would do so."

"And you knew each one's name."

"It was my job to do so, and I made sure I did."

"What did you feel when that salute became the whole regiment?"

"I was shocked. I had no idea they would do such a thing, nor did I feel I deserved it. To do so in front of Lochiel was —"

"Was a push-back."

"What do ye mean?"

"They put him on notice with their actions that they wouldn't tolerate such disrespect toward you. It's clear the men all respected you a great deal, and they saw the way you were treated. They took what power they had and used it. Did he ever treat you that way again in front of the men?"

Euan paused, thinking about it. "No," he said, his voice quiet as he realized it. "He did nae. Ye are right."

"It just further proves the theory that your sway over the regiment was great, and he had to play the game carefully to ensure you never knew that."

"I never would have used that power even if I knew I had it."

"You know that, but clearly he didn't. I think that's enough for today."

CHAPTER 16

THE FEELING OF SUDDENLY coming back to himself and to consciousness was jarring. There was no subtle drifting from the darkness of a drugged sleep, but instead, a hard shove back into the world of the living, with all of its sounds and smells. The sudden roar of a military tent city was almost deafening, the air filled with the sounds of conversation, horses, weapons, footsteps, shouting, and all other manner of things. Euan tried to open his eyes, but the light was sharp and felt like daggers shoved into his skull, so he quickly shut them again. The groan of pain that escaped him was involuntary and immediate.

"Steady, lad."

The voice of Archibald Cameron cut through the haze, and Euan recognized it at once.

"Keep yer eyes closed awhile; it will help."

"What is going on?"

"Ye have come off the laudanum, that is all."

"Why was —"

"Because it was the only thing to make sure ye felt no pain and could rest," Archibald replied, cutting him off. "Ye are quite badly injured, Euan."

"No, I am fine," he replied, trying to sit up, but the excruciating pain the movement sent through his side took his breath away, and he went right back down again with another loud groan.

"As ye can feel, ye are nae. Ye have a few broken ribs and some fairly nasty bruising. Ye are nae going to be fine for quite some time."

Euan sighed, though even that was painful. "How long?"

"Until ye are fully healed? At least six to eight weeks. Ye will likely still have some lingering pain after that, but it will fade."

"That long?" Six to eight weeks was far too long. They were in the middle of a war, and his men needed him. Lochiel needed him.

"I dinnae have a way to make broken bones heal faster, lad. That is how long it will likely take ye. Longer if ye dinnae listen to me and push yerself too hard too soon. Ye are off a horse for at least two weeks, and dinnae even try to swing a sword until ye are entirely healed. Ye are on light duty until then, and the watch will be about all ye do, along with helping the council if they need ye. And dinnae think ye can just do as ye feel either, because there is nae a man here who does nae know what yer restrictions are and will make sure ye keep to them, my brother included, since he is the one who ordered them."

Euan kept still in silent irritation. His being down this way meant extra work for others, and he hated the mere thought of it. What he couldn't do, however, was go against what Archibald was prescribing and make himself worse so that he'd be entirely useless whenever they returned to battle. If he did that, extra work for others would mean nothing if they were dead.

"Thank ye, sir," he finally replied, sullen.

"I know ye are frustrated, Euan. Any young lad like ye would be aggrieved to be restricted in such a way. Nae to mention my brother training ye all yer life to chafe against anything restricting ye from the duty ye feel compelled to."

"The fact that I cannae even breathe without pain ensures that I will nae be trying to disobey ye. At least nae right now." It was true, however. Anything that kept him from his duty was something he had no time for.

"Do ye remember anything from when ye arrived back here?"

"I remember the salute from the men," Euan replied, the memory touching his heart once more.

"But naught else?"

"No."

"Probably a good thing. Ye went down as soon as ye dismounted and screamed in pain. We all knew then that something was very wrong with ye. Let me help ye sit up, and we can get some small ale into ye, though it will hurt, I warn ye."

Knowing that would at least let Euan expect it and brace for it. Nodding, he clenched his teeth as Archibald helped him to sit up, but it didn't keep in the pained shout of doing so. Archibald draped the plaid over Euan's head and shoulders to block as much of the light as possible so that Euan might be able to open his eyes and begin to adjust to the light. The pain of sitting up left Euan panting for a few moments, and when it eased, he opened his eyes again. The shade of his plaid helped, though the light it let in was still painful, but he forced himself to keep them open anyway. Archibald pressed a cup into his hands and Euan lifted it to his lips and drank deeply, not having realized how thirsty he was until the cool liquid hit his tongue.

"Careful, lad. Ye dinnae want to choke. I assure ye that coughing in yer condition would nae be pleasant. I would like ye to stay abed until tomorrow but, as I know ye will nae, I just ask that ye dinnae wear yer baldric or weapons. Ye dinnae need the weight or pressure against the bruises on yer chest."

"Aye, sir."

When Euan emerged from his tent a couple of hours later, he was fully dressed, but it was obvious that he was unwell. He'd let himself adjust as much as he could until it reached a point where he knew it wouldn't get any better, then rose to clean up and dress with Archibald's assistance. He wanted to be outside instead of on a cot, needed to be. To be down and injured that way brought back unpleasant memories that would only be banished by no longer being there. The man posted outside called out his emergence, and any of his men nearby stopped and saluted him. Euan offered a weak smile, nodding his thanks before continuing on his way, his arm resting across his chest and his hand on his side as he walked.

"Euan, wait!" Malcolm called out as he hurried to catch up once Euan stopped and turned around. "Good to see ye upright."

"Thank ye, Malcolm. Have I missed anything?"

"No. Everything has been fairly quiet here. Men have been taking shifts in the Cornmarket outside of Edinburgh Castle in case any of those within have the bright idea to come out, but otherwise it is the usual."

Euan turned and kept walking, keeping his pace slow. "I apologize for making more work for ye while I am like this."

Malcolm scoffed. "Ye are nae doing anything of the sort. It is nae as if we dinnae know ye are injured and instead think ye are doing it out of laziness. Ye would be in full form if ye could."

"Aye," Euan admitted. "But it does nae make me feel better about it."

"Unless ye got in the way of that cannonball on purpose, ye should just accept it and concentrate on getting well before the next battle."

"Is there anything new on that front?"

"No. The prince and council meet daily, but we dinnae know what about or what they plan to do next."

For a brief moment, Euan considered telling Malcolm about England but quickly decided against it. It wasn't his place to give such information, and the plan very well could have changed by now. "I am sure they are trying to decide what to do during the winter."

"I rather hope retiring home for the winter is an option. I am nae particularly enamored of the idea of marching about in the snow."

Euan smiled but was careful not to laugh. "Nor I, but who knows."

"Ach, come now, ye have to be missing Brenda at least a bit."

"No," Euan said with a gentle shake of his head. "We did nae have that sort of an understanding. I dinnae want such a thing."

"A woman?"

"A permanent one. At least nae yet. I cannae explain it."

"Ye are young yet. Perhaps that is what keeps ye from it."

"Perhaps, but I feel as though it is something more than that. I cannae say what that is, but it has always been there. All the same, Brenda tried to tell me she felt a bit more for me before we left, but I asked her nae to."

"Was she aware ye did nae want a courtship?"

"Aye, from the start, for it is something I have always been open and honest about. She was well aware."

"Sometimes emotion will do what it will no matter what we do or say."

"It has nae changed for me and will nae."

Malcolm shrugged. "I am sure it will all sort itself out eventually. She may find a different lad if she knows ye dinnae feel the same for her."

"Maybe. I am sure my mam would be happy to have me home though," Euan said.

"Oh aye, I am sure she would. Ye, Iain, and Duncan, 'her boys' as she calls ye. I am sure all of the women will be happy for us to be home again. I know Catriona will be happy to see me, and the bairns, and I long to see them."

Euan was silent for a long moment before he spoke again, lowering the volume of his voice. "Do ye believe in this?"

"In what?"

"In this rising. In the right of the Stuarts. Do ye believe it?"

Euan watched Malcolm look around to make sure they were alone before he shook his head. "Aye and no. Do ye?"

"I am nae sure, honestly, but the more I see, the more I want to say no entirely."

"Oh?"

"He cannae yet lead, Malcolm. At least he cannae lead an army. If ye cannae do that, how will ye lead a country?"

"Well, his father would do it, nae him."

"He would still be king someday."

Malcolm gave a nod in concession. "True, but ye would hope he would have time to grow into it a bit more. He was sent here with naught and told to overthrow the English, so I can understand he is still trying to get his bearings and figure out what he wants to do. I have nae had as much experience with him as ye have, however."

"As far as I am concerned, one king is the same as any other, no matter what name they bear."

"But at least it would be a Scottish king."

"No, it would nae," Euan replied. "The king has been abroad all this time and lived in England before that. The prince has never set foot in this country until now. The Stuarts have nae been Scots since before Queen Elizabeth died. Do ye ever wonder why we do this? Why we fight for what we may nae even believe in?"

"Because it is our duty as officers. Ye know that as well as I do. It is nae up to us."

"Aye, and I will do it as I must, but it does nae help me stop questioning it or feeling as though we are a means to an end who will be forgotten once they have gotten what they want."

"It should nae stop ye. Ye are far too clever for that."

"Lochiel does nae think so."

"Ah, ye are wrong there, little brother. He knows ye are, and *that* is why he treats ye as he does. If ye feel yerself too high, ye can ask questions; ye can rebel."

"Why would I do that?"

"Ye would nae, but that does nae mean ye could nae."

"Perhaps I deserve such treatment for trying to think above where I have been placed. Maybe he is right to do it. The night before, I offered to speak to the prince myself."

"Why is that bad?"

"Because I am no one. I am nae Lochiel or Lord Murray, I dinnae get to make that decision and would only do so if he asked me to."

"I dinnae think it is a terrible idea. The two of ye are the same age, ye might be able to find some commonality with him and open up communication with him in ways others could nae. He might listen to ye."

"Lochiel disagrees, and that is all I need to know to realize I stepped out of my place in suggesting it."

"Euan," Malcolm said as he stopped walking. "Listen to me: ye have more power than ye know. Ye seem to be the only one who does nae see it, and that is because ye are loyal to a fault. Dinnae let him make ye think ye are less, because ye are nae. They are none of them better than ye, and all the titles and money and learning in the world will nae change that. We all saw what he did to ye. He is partly responsible for yer condition right now because he should have had ye riding in a cart instead of on a horse. It was his duty to look after ye as yer commanding officer and yer chief, and he did nae because he wanted to put ye in yer place unnecessarily. It was foolish, nae only because he could have and did cause ye graver injury, but because it caused ill feeling amongst the men."

"I could have asked to ride in a cart but did nae."

"Ye see? Ye are taking responsibility even now for what was nae yer fault. Ye should nae have had to ask, Euan. It should have been done without question, but instead, we all watched ye damned near kill yerself so ye could prove to him that ye were worthy of his respect and to atone for doing something wrong when ye did nae. Respect he still refused to give ye, I might add. That salute from the men was genuine, and it was them giving ye the respect they feel ye deserve even if he will nae."

Euan sat down on a wall, needing to take a break. "As appreciative as I am of it, they should nae have done that."

"Why?"

"I am sure he saw it and it only made it worse."

"He *should* see it!" Malcolm said in exasperation as he sat down beside Euan. "He should know how the men feel about ye and treat ye accordingly, because if he does nae, they will nae follow him."

Euan looked up quickly, his expression alarmed and unhappy. "No, they cannae do that. They must follow him no matter what he says or does to me, and ye must tell them that. I will nae be the cause of anyone's disloyalty."

"I am sure Lochiel is smart enough to see what happened. He is no fool. Ye have let him do this to ye all yer life, Euan, so much that ye dinnae even believe in yerself. Ye feel ye cannae be anything without his approval; ye dinnae know who ye are without him telling ye."

Euan opened his mouth to protest, but found he could not, and sighed. Malcolm wasn't wrong, but it was more than just Lochiel, and there was no way he could really explain such a thing.

"Aye, ye cannae argue that, can ye? I have watched it happen; we all have. He has molded ye into the soldier ye are, but he cannae change what is truly inside of ye. Ye are a natural leader, and ye always have been. He made ye dependent on him so he could harness that without caring what that might do to ye."

Euan shook his head. "He does have a care for me, and I owe him much."

"Ach, Euan, ye are brilliant and stupid all at once. The only care he has for ye is whether or nae ye are willing to do what he tells ye. He took a wee lad with no father, convinced that boy that he was the father he was seeking, and used that need to make that wee lad into a man who would never cross him. He schooled ye, but only in what he wanted ye to know. He forced ye to look to him as yer only source of approval. He is nae yer father, Euan, and he never was. He does nae truly care about ye, nae the way ye want him to, and maybe it is time ye finally see it as we all do."

Euan's chest ached, and it was not because of his injury. Malcolm's words hit home and touched a truth he'd always known was there. He was right, of course he was, and deep down, Euan knew it even if he didn't want to admit it. His mother had said the same thing to him many times, but he'd never wanted to hear it.

"I hate to hurt ye, lad; ye are one of my closest friends, and I have always considered ye my little brother. But I cannae sit back and continue to watch this. I cannae watch ye grovel for approval ye will never get, for the expression of pride ye will never hear or see. I have watched ye do it from the time ye were small, and I have always hated it."

"How do ye stop feeling and thinking what ye have done for so long? How do ye change it?"

"By seeing things as they truly are and nae how ye wish them to be. By refusing to fish for that tiny grain of possible praise to hold onto. Ye will soon see that everything he does with ye is for his own benefit and nae yers."

"I will try, but I am sure it will be harder than it sounds."

"Of course it will. He has had twenty years to build this cage around ye. Ye will nae be rid of it overnight."

"Thank ye, Malcolm, for yer honesty."

"I could nae be otherwise with ye. Just know that even if he is nae proud of ye, *we* are."

"What?"

Malcolm smiled. "I am proud of ye, and the other officers are just as proud of ye and what ye have become. We have all watched ye grow. Ye are the best of any of us, Euan, and we could nae be prouder of ye. Ye dinnae need to seek it anywhere else but from those who actually love ye, from yer brothers, nae someone who pretends to love ye when it suits him."

Euan said nothing, pressing his lips together and looking

away from Malcolm. He'd never heard those words from anyone but his mother, and to hear it from those he loved and considered brothers was something altogether deeper. It was respect as well as pride, things he'd earned from them.

"Did ye wish to keep walking?" Malcolm asked as he saw Euan struggle to contain what he felt.

"I probably should nae."

"When has *that* ever stopped ye from doing anything?"

Euan smiled and shook his head. "True."

"Come on, I will be with ye to keep eyes on ye. Let us find an inn, eh? Ye look like ye could use a good drink."

"Ye are nae wrong."

Malcolm chuckled and patted Euan's back before helping him up, starting them toward town.

As the weeks passed and the weather grew colder by the day, the men continued to train while holding the city. Supplies were gathered and stored, repairs were made to equipment, and all made ready for whenever the order came to depart. Euan, to everyone's surprise, kept to the restrictions set for him and did so without complaint. He was given leave as an officer to sleep inside of the palace but refused it, for if his men couldn't go inside to sleep, then neither would he. This led to Malcolm, Iain, and others choosing the same path and following Euan's example on how to keep their men loyal.

At the end of six weeks, Euan felt almost entirely better. There was still some pain with certain movements, but otherwise he could breathe again, ride a horse, and drill his men. He still took things easy, knowing he wasn't out of the woods yet, and could very easily reinjure himself if he pushed too hard before he was ready. The longer the army remained in Edinburgh, the more they all began to feel a sense of security, that perhaps they may remain in Edinburgh for the winter. Those hopes were dashed when Lochiel ordered his officers to meet with him in his tent on the last day of October.

"We depart for England in a few days," he said. "I can see the concern in yer faces, but this is what the council has decided. There is a promise of a French landing in England and the rising of the English supporters. I need ye to prepare yer men, make sure we are well-supplied and ready for a long march through England to London."

"London! But —" Findlay began before Euan caught his eye and shook his head to tell him to stop.

"Aye, London. With the promised supporters, the prince and the council believe we can take the city and oust the Hanover king. Are the orders clear, men?"

All the men seemed to sigh together, but they saluted Lochiel and departed to inform their men that there were new orders. There was some protest, but many of them were too stricken to speak. None of them wanted to go to England, the officers included, and there was a palpable sense of betrayal amongst them. England had never been agreed upon; this was supposed to be a battle for Scotland. Nonetheless, preparations for departure began immediately. It was decided that a force would not be left behind to hold on to Edinburgh, though Euan wasn't sure why. It made him feel as though his work and the work of the Camerons to capture the city would all be wasted. As soon as they left, the government would retake the city, and it angered him to think of it.

On the watch that night, Euan continued to turn all of it over in his mind, the feeling that leaving Edinburgh without a garrison was a mistake sitting strong in his gut. He wondered who had made this decision and how. Who was consulted? Euan knew full well that Lochiel wouldn't have sanctioned such a move, so who had? Lord Murray? Lord Elcho? Chief Macpherson? Or had it been one of the prince's men whispering into his ear as they always seemed to be.

Something stirred in the darkness and Euan drew his blade. "Identify yerself."

"I think you know me quite well."

As the figure of Colonel Francis Strickland came into the light of the torches, Euan looked at him in curiosity, but bowed to a superior officer. "What may I help ye with, Colonel?"

"Quite a bit, I think. You seem to have a way with the enlisted men, Captain."

"I have done my utmost to earn their respect."

Strickland looked at him for a long moment. "You are a smart young man, so I will not insult your intelligence with small talk. I will get straight to my reason for coming here: when we take London, I think I should like to see you on the king's council."

Euan blinked in shock. "Me? Why? I have nae the experience for such a position."

"You do, you just do not realize it. He would need a man like you, a man willing to be honest in spite of risking displeasure."

"It would be an honor I would never dream of, but I serve Lochiel."

"When the time comes, I will deal with him. And, when the time comes, I would like you to deliver the Cameron regiment to us."

Euan's mouth opened in slight shock, and then he frowned, unsure he'd heard the man correctly. "What?"

"Your regiment is bold and well-trained. They will follow you wherever you lead them, and I would like you to hand the command of them over to the Crown once the throne is ours again. We would fold them into the regulars, make them a royal regiment of their own. Even better, I truly believe the regiments of Murray, Glengarry, Appin, Macpherson and the others would also follow you, and you could deliver them to us as well."

"I could nae do such. We are the only defense of Cameron lands, and if all the men go to ye, there will be none left to defend it or our women and bairns," Euan explained, still frowning. "The others are much the same and dinnae belong to me to lead."

"We could station soldiers from Fort William to defend the Camerons in the absence of the regiment."

"The soldiers at Fort William have a great many Campbells amongst them, and those that are nae with them run sorties from there and are protected. It is Campbell land, and they are our sworn enemies. Ye could nae trust them to defend our families because they would slaughter them without a second thought and take our lands for themselves."

"You seem to believe this is a request instead of an order, Captain Cameron."

"Ye are ordering me to commit mutiny and betray my chief and my clan? To incite other regiments to mutiny and get them to betray *their* chiefs and *their* clans? Their wives and their bairns? Has the prince sent ye to ask me to do this?"

"*We* decide what things constitute mutiny and who commits it. You would be very handsomely rewarded, I assure you. Money, position in court, command of these new Highland regiments, perhaps a title. The prince has no knowledge of my request at present, but I know it would please him to have those men who have been so loyal to him around him at the start."

"He will have the entirety of the Crown forces at his disposal! What need would he have of us!"

"There would surely be defections from the Crown forces, but until everything is well and truly settled, we could make sure he was fully protected by those absolutely steadfast in his service."

Euan remained silent, seething with rage he was somehow managing to conceal.

"That, however, is a long way from now given our present course, and that is what we must focus on. Thank you for speaking with me, Captain Cameron."

Strickland turned and departed, fading into the darkness

again before Euan could even say a word. Turning away, Euan let the wind cool his burning fury. This man couldn't be trusted, just as he and many others had long believed. He was commanding Euan to do something that was against every instinct, something akin to treason, and he would hang for a traitor's death before he would ever comply with such an order. Worse, he was being commanded to do all of this even when Strickland knew the slaughter that would await those left behind. Pacing, Euan wondered if he should tell Lochiel what he'd been asked to do, but decided against it. No, things were tense enough as it was; there was no need to mention something he knew he'd never do and make it worse. What he could and would do was keep himself alert for anyone else who may have been asked to do the same so he could stop them.

The snow had already begun to fall when the army of five thousand men started its march out of Edinburgh on November 4th. They left in two columns in order to hide their true destination in case General Wade, stationed in Newcastle, might send a force out to meet them and prevent their crossing. Conversation was quiet, as were the camps at night, as they all worked to keep themselves warm. All were grateful for the warm wool of their plaids, and at least for the officers like Euan and the chiefs themselves, the trews to cover their legs. Though they normally weren't worn together, it didn't matter when they were trying to keep from freezing. The mood amongst the men became increasingly somber as they neared the end of the four-day march from Edinburgh to the border with England, and Euan felt no better about it than his men did.

In the bitter, icy wind that whipped across the moor, the varying regiments waited for their turn to cross the River Esk and thus the border into England. From the banks, Euan watched as the regiments of the prince, Lord Murray, and Lord Elcho crossed into England in silence. As it neared the time for the Cameron regiment to cross, Euan swung down from his saddle and turned to face his men, some of whom shook his hand. When their turn came, he would do it on the ground with them, not atop a horse. Taking a deep breath and releasing it, he closed his eyes, listening to the sound of the river and the wind, easily heard in the shocking silence present amongst so many men. It unnerved him, and he did the only thing he could think of: sing. It wasn't a song of happiness to lighten the mood, but instead reflected what they all felt, almost like a dirge.

The men listened to him sing the first verse on his own before they joined him, a thousand voices strong. Lochiel and the other officers left their saddles as well, joining their men on the ground and in song. Wanting to lead by example, Euan turned and forced himself to walk forward, leading his horse toward the river even as he and the men continued singing. The first step into the water made Euan's heart ache, for he was leaving home while everything in him was screaming to turn back, and the cold of the water was biting as it soaked through his clothing to freeze the skin of his legs. Shaking it off, he pressed forward. He had no choice in this; none of them did, no matter how much they might hate it. As he reached the other side, he turned and pulled his broadsword from its sheath, lifting it before his face and saluting his homeland.

As each man crossed, they did the same, turning and saluting Scotland — a gesture of respect for a home they all prayed they would return to, because they had no idea what awaited them or if they would survive it. It was one thing to fight British regulars on ground they were familiar with, but entirely another to fight those same regulars on their home ground where they were far stronger in number. The Scots who formed the other regiments that had already crossed joined the Camerons in song, pulling their broadswords or muskets and holding them before their faces in a salute, holding it until every man had crossed.

Lochiel was the last man to cross and, upon reaching the English side, followed the rest and drew his sword to salute his homeland. Euan saw him cut his hand on the blade as he drew it and looked at his chief even as he heard the sharp intake of breath from the men behind him who had also seen it. Cameron blood already shed on English soil: a bad omen, indeed.

Lochiel turned to his men. "Form up, lads! We still have a long way to go before we are through."

Euan returned to horseback along with the other men as the Cameron companies reformed their lines and took their place amongst those of Lord Elcho and Lord Murray.

A long way to go before they were through.

CHAPTER 17

WHEN THE ARMY REACHED Carlisle two days later, a message was sent, requesting that the city surrender peacefully, as they were now surrounded on all sides by the prince's army. The order was refused, with the mayor firing a cannon instead but hitting no one. Soon after, the prince received a letter stating that General Wade was on his way to relieve Carlisle, and the council pressed him to advance to meet the General and his forces. The prince agreed, and the army marched to Warwick and Brampton, only to find that the information was false, and Wade wasn't marching to Carlisle. The Atholl Brigade was then sent back to lay siege to Carlisle in revenge, a siege completed in two days. Much to Euan's annoyance, the Camerons weren't included in the force sent for the siege, instead being tasked with guarding the prince. When they rejoined with the Atholl Brigade in Carlisle, the men were glad of a longer rest and the ability to switch out of the royal watch. Intelligence soon reached them that ten thousand British soldiers were returned from Flanders, landing in London before they were massed in Staffordshire to oppose the Jacobite army. The council was swiftly called to discuss what should be done, taking the decision to continue on toward London while leaving a small garrison in Carlisle.

The weather became ever more brutal as they made progress further into England, with the English citizens far less willing to be of any assistance than they should've been based on reports from the prince and his advisors. When they reached Preston on the 26th of November, the men were thankful for the chance to find quarter wherever they could in order to get out of the bitter cold. As Lochiel entered the lodging that had been assigned to him with Malcolm and Euan at his side, all three were taken aback when the landlady threw herself at Lochiel's feet.

"Please! You may take my life, but please spare those of my two young children!" she wailed as she knelt at his feet and cried.

"Are ye out of yer senses, woman? What is the matter with ye? Explain yerself!" Lochiel shot back.

"Everybody says the Highlanders eat children as a matter of common occurrence!"

"Ye are absolutely mad!" Euan said in shock.

Lochiel held out a hand to silence his young officer. "I assure ye, we have no intention of injuring ye or yer children, or anyone else for that matter. We are just here to rest and get out of the cold, naught more, naught less, and I dinnae know any one of us who has ever eaten anything resembling a person."

"Well, there is the tale about Sawney Bean," Malcolm said.

"He was from the Lowlands though," Euan countered.

"Both of ye shut up," Lochiel said, though he was trying as hard as the other two were not to smile or laugh, and both Malcolm and Euan hid their laughter in sudden coughing fits.

The woman looked at them in surprise. "You can come out, children! The gentleman will not eat you," she called out.

The children came out of hiding and knelt in thanks before Lochiel, who looked even more shocked at this display. "Get ye up off the ground, all of ye, and show me and my men where we might rest for the night."

The woman nodded, getting up and showing them to a room. All three men availed themselves of hot water and rags, happy to get clean and be out of the wind that seemed to sink the cold into their very bones. Lochiel took the bed while

Euan and Malcolm were more than happy to sleep on the floor before the fire, warm for the first time in weeks.

Though they all hated to leave the warmth of shelter, they pressed forward to Manchester, arriving there two days later. Here, they received the first influx of English recruits, some three hundred men who were formed into the Manchester regiment. Euan and several others were sent forward as an advanced party to Newcastle-under-Lyme to distract Cumberland's council by making them think the Jacobites were on their way to engage them. The English remained where they were to prepare for the false engagement while the rest of the army slipped past them on the road to London. Upon reaching Derby on the 4th of December, the men were grateful for what promised to be a longer rest. It had been a month of near-constant movement since they'd left Edinburgh, and they were now within four days' march of London. Euan and many of the others took the chance to get a proper bath and a shave, both of which felt wonderful after so long. The prince convened the council the next day while the men, knowing that they were separated from Cumberland's army by only a few miles, immediately set to making sure their weapons were sharpened and prepared for the battle that was sure to come.

The following day, Euan found himself called into the council for only the third time since the campaign had begun, and that alone made him wary. He stood alongside Lochiel, silent, as the council debated the next steps, and he knew by the looks on their faces that this wasn't going to be a pleasant conversation. John Murray stood against the wall behind the prince, trying to keep his face neutral, but not doing a very good job of it.

"We have gone as far as we can, Yer Highness," Lord Murray said. "There is now a great possibility of being caught between Wade's men in the north and Cumberland's men in the southwest. Both armies are twice the size of ours, and if we are between them, we would have no hope of victory."

"A regiment of Royal Scots and Irish Piquets have landed in Montrose," added Chevalier Johnstone, who had joined them in Perth and was the aide-de-camp to both Lord Murray and the prince. "Together they are three thousand strong and even now come forward to reinforce us with men, weapons, ammunition, and silver."

"It would seem wise to fall back to meet them," Lord Murray continued. "It would grow our number to eight thousand and make an attack against either Wade or Cumberland a more likely success."

"I feel we should press on," the prince replied. "London is within our reach."

"But what will ye take it *with*, Yer Highness?" Lord Murray asked in exasperation. "We have five thousand men, and there is no chance the capital has nae prepared for us all of this time."

"I will not be denied my prize!" the prince shouted. "We have come this far, and I will *not* yield now!"

"Then ye would condemn us all to death here instead of thinking of tactical advantage?" Lord Murray asked, incredulous. "Ye can return to England, we know it can be done now and how, but we dinnae have the forces needed!"

"Lord Murray, please! Do not stand in my way! I must do this for my father, my family!"

"If ye do this now, ye will get nowhere but in the Tower for yer trouble and the rest of us in a grave! We are nae saying ye should never take London; what we *are* saying is nae now! We are nae ready!"

"God has blessed our expedition and shall continue to do so. Look at the victories we have so far attained!"

"Nae one of the conditions ye promised us in Edinburgh has been met. Where is the French landing in England that d'Eguilles promised? There is no sign of it. Where are the English supporters ye said would come out in the thousands? They have nae appeared."

"I have not heard from them since I left France, but I was assured of their rising once we got into England!"

All of the air in the room seemed to be sucked out when those words left the prince's lips. Euan was sure he'd never actually intended to say them, but it was too late now. There had been no word from the English Jacobites since July, in spite of the prince's repeated assurances to the contrary. The faces of all the chiefs darkened, and behind the prince, young John's face fell before shifting into utter dismay.

"Ye mean to tell me ye lied to us at Edinburgh?" Lord Murray said, his voice laced with quiet rage.

"No, I —"

"Ye *lied*!" Lord Murray shouted, which caused his nephew to jump. "Ye told us ye had heard from them only weeks before with assurances they would come out for us when we reached England! No wonder we have seen no one! They have no interest in risking treason for ye the way *we* have!"

The prince stood up and slammed his hand on the table. "Remember who you are speaking to, sir!"

"Aye, I know who I am speaking to. I am speaking to a lad who had no real idea of what awaited him and none of the support he believed he had. When he realized it, he knew the only way to get those loyal to him to follow was to lie. We have all committed treason for a lie!"

There were now tears of anger in the eyes of the prince at seeing his only support crumbling from beneath him. "It is not so! You did this because you support my father and the Stuarts. I will do what I must to achieve my aims, and you will not stop me!"

"Then ye can do it without my men," Lord Murray said.

"What?" the prince gasped, staring at him in astonishment. "You cannot leave!"

"I will nae send my men to die when I can see them home to regroup for a better chance at battle when the winter is over. Their lives may nae matter to *ye*, but they matter to me, and I promise ye any of these men here will tell ye the same. These are our kin, our tenants, and we have a duty to see to them as best we can."

"No!" the prince shouted before breaking down into tears, slumping back into the chair. "Please, Murray, I beg you …"

"Ye will nae sway me, Yer Highness. We can continue this war for several years if we remain in Scotland and force the Crown to come to terms because they need their men back on the Continent. Do ye nae see how much better such a thing might be? Back in Scotland where we have the upper hand?"

"You would not all leave," he said through his tears.

Seeing the young man this way startled Euan. It wasn't that he thought princes and kings couldn't feel or cry, but that he would do so in front of so many. Euan understood the keen disappointment of seeing a long-held goal within reach and being pulled back from it, but he didn't understand the desire to override common sense. The prince would never achieve his aim if he and his army were dead from an ill-advised engagement with troops they stood no chance of defeating. These were not Cope's men; these were battle-hardened men fresh from the front at Flanders, men brought home to defend their country. *They* wouldn't flee.

"How many of ye wish to continue on to London?" Lord Murray asked as he turned to face the assembled council. The room was silent, and Lord Murray nodded. "I thought so. And those of ye who wish to return to Scotland to regroup?"

"Aye," all the chiefs answered unanimously, with not a one of them whose eyes didn't still hold fury at discovering they'd been lied to.

Murray turned back to look at the prince. "There ye have it. We have no interest in going forward, and if ye insist on doing so, ye will do so alone."

"This is blackmail! You leave me no choice!" the prince shouted through angry tears.

Lord Murray's expression was unapologetic. "Ye have the

choice to think of yer men and be a proper leader, Yer Highness. I suggest ye take it."

All of the fight seemed to go out of the prince, and he sighed. "Very well."

"We fall back in the morning," Murray said before he turned and swept from the room without bothering to wait to be dismissed, the other chiefs following him.

Before he left the room, Euan turned to look back at the prince, watching him fall onto the table and cry into his arms. John looked positively lost as well as angry, torn between duty to his family and his clan, and duty to the prince he now served. Euan shook his head and sighed before he left, shutting the door behind him. There was nothing to say in such a situation, though he felt as though the council had made the correct choice. In light of the truths spoken in that room, Euan knew full well that a fracture had just opened up within the command that might doom them all. As he stepped into the anteroom where the chiefs now stood, the fury was no longer contained.

"I cannae believe he lied to us!" Lord Murray said.

"I can," replied Lord Elcho. "I have long been concerned with his autocratic ways, and ye know I have always felt he was too influenced by his Irish advisors. He is single-minded and will stop at naught to get what he wants even if it means lying and letting us die for it. He no longer trusts ye, George, and has nae since Broughton tried to tell him ye were nae loyal."

"We all know it is Broughton who is nae loyal; he just has nae had a chance to prove it yet. But he will."

"Ye spoke for all of us, George, when ye urged caution," Lochiel said. "I will nae send my clansmen into the jaws of certain death just because he believes God will somehow guide us to win. We have already suffered desertions due to men nae wanting to come into England. I dinnae know how he thinks they would fight when faced with twenty thousand Hanover men."

"Aye," Lord Murray agreed. "The question is, what do we tell our men?"

"I say we dinnae," Lord Elcho replied. "Let them believe they are to face Cumberland in the morning. They will realize soon enough that we have turned back. It seems less likely that any will try to remain here."

The others nodded and then dispersed, and Lochiel turned to Euan. "Say naught."

Euan nodded in acknowledgment of the order. "I will admit I feel no disappointment in this."

"Because ye have sense and dinnae wish to die."

"At least nae in England," Euan replied, his mouth twisting into a small smile.

"Hopefully old in yer bed, lad, home in Scotland where ye belong. Ye are dismissed," Lochiel said as he walked away.

"Aye, hopefully," Euan whispered, the feeling that it would not be so still lurking deep within.

As discussed, none of the men were informed of the retreat, and they began their march in the early morning by moonlight, as they'd done since they'd crossed into England. All of them believed they were going to fight Cumberland, and there was some excitement about finally facing this long-feared foe. Euan knew otherwise and waited for the sun to rise and show them the truth. When it did, and the men saw their own marks on the road and familiar landmarks from only two days ago, the entirety erupted with anger. Lord Murray rode down the lines and told them they were welcome to stay in England if they wished and face Cumberland and Wade alone, or they could go home and meet up with a larger force so that they might return stronger. This silenced the men, and they fell in with the march north. Euan understood the frustration at feeling they'd come all this way for nothing — he felt the same — but he was satisfied with not facing either Wade or Cumberland without more men.

The prince himself looked so dejected as to be nearly unrecognizable. Where once he'd ridden at their head, he now reluctantly followed behind them. Gone was the Highland dress he'd worn, and in its place was the clothing expected of a prince, as if he sought to remind them of who he was and of their supposed betrayal. He rode at the back of the army with a rear guard who seemed to always be waiting for him to catch up and endangering everyone by doing so. They could only go as fast as they could say together, and he slowed them down with his antics, leaving them more open to attack. The prince would slink from his lodgings each morning, the very picture of dejection, and it grated on the men who saw it. He'd mount his horse and ride on, no longer speaking with or walking with the men the way he once had.

"If he considers this some sort of punishment, this rebuke of our dress and the chance to lead us, then he is fooling himself," Euan thought ruefully.

His petulant, childish behavior served only to alienate him even further from the chiefs and the men they commanded, and Euan was surprised that he seemed to take no notice of the ill will he was bringing upon himself with each passing day. He couldn't imagine doing this, being this way; then again, he couldn't imagine waging a war based on lies either. That the prince should be surprised to find anger when his manipulations were revealed, that he believed he could still force them onward once they knew, and that he seemed to feel not an ounce of remorse, boggled Euan's mind.

In spite of the prince's behavior, the entire retreat was conducted with such secrecy of movement and expedition that they were two days ahead of Cumberland before he realized they were retreating. Not to be outdone, Cumberland rallied his dragoons and rode after them, but the Jacobites never gave them the opportunity to gain any sort of advantage over them. They moved quickly and kept ahead of him for twelve days, including two full days of rest at Preston and then at Lancaster. Wade had reinforced Cumberland by the time

Cumberland reached Preston, giving Cumberland a force of four thousand horse to pursue them. Though the order was given to the country residents to break down bridges, destroy roads, and do all they could to impede the retreating army, this proved to be a mistake, as it didn't hamper the Jacobites but made the roads nearly impassable for Cumberland's dragoons when it was combined with the terrible weather.

When the Jacobites reached Penrith on the 17th of December, it was only the main body of the army, with the regiments of Murray, Macpherson, Lochiel, MacDonald, Glengarry, and Stewart of Appin having shifted from vanguard to rear guard when the army left Lancaster. The entire body was forced to slow due to broken ammunitions wagons, only making it as far as Shap, and the decision was immediately taken to leave the rear guard and have the rest press on. The current make-up of the rear were the best regiments of the army, able to put up a competent defense of their munitions if needed. This delay meant that the first companies of Cumberland's dragoons were able to overtake the rear and were spotted by the Jacobites when they began to finally make the march from Shap to rejoin the rest of the army. At Clifton Moor, a body of Cumberland's men appeared to be watching them from a bluff.

"Glengarry!" Lord Murray called out.

"Aye, sir!" the Glengarry officers called out.

"Forward! Advance on the light horse!"

"Aye, sir!" the Glengarry officers shouted as they and their men immediately ran forward to engage the body that seemed to be massing for an attack.

The body of dragoons immediately retreated before the Glengarry men could even engage, causing them to stop and look at each other in confusion, as did everyone in the other regiments.

"What do ye suppose that is about?" Lochiel mused.

"I dinnae know," Euan replied. "Ye would think they had

enough men. Perhaps it is an advance guard, but it does nae sit well with me. Something is nae right."

"Aye, I agree," Lord Murray said as he rode up beside them. "Colonel Stuart!"

"Aye, Lord Murray!"

"Ride ye ahead to Penrith. Tell the prince that Cumberland has caught up with us and have him send a thousand men from the main body to reinforce us!"

"Aye!" Stuart said as he turned his horse and sped off for Penrith, only ten miles ahead of them.

"The rest of us need to prepare for battle," Lord Murray said to Lochiel, who nodded, as did Cluny Macpherson and the others who had joined them. The order was passed down, the regiments beginning to set up for the engagement that was sure to come, and it was nearing dusk by the time Colonel Stuart returned.

"Stuart, what news? Are the men behind ye?" Murray asked.

"No, m'lord. The prince requires us to march with all haste to Penrith and nae engage."

Lord Murray's face was grim, as were the faces of the others. "Dinnae engage? So they can feel free to slaughter us before we get to Penrith? No. Men! Draw up on the moor to the right side of the road. Do it now!"

The regiments obeyed the order the instant it was called out by their chiefs and officers, just as the entirety of the Duke of Cumberland's pursuing force arrived and formed up opposite them. Though they were outnumbered, the Scots were almost desperate for a battle after doing nothing but marching for so long and found themselves unconcerned with numbers. They stood in the darkness, swords drawn, muskets and pistols loaded and primed, bodies tense, awaiting the attack order. By the light of the moon, they could see a body of Cumberland's men on foot coming toward the road to engage them.

"Glengarry! Appin! Advance!" Murray called out, now on foot at the head of the Macphersons with Cluny. The dragoons immediately fired upon them the moment the two regiments moved, which was just what Murray wanted them to do because it gave him leave to attack in defense. "Glengarry and Appin, fall back to the right! Left wing! Claymore!"

The order to attack now given, Euan grinned before he shouted and charged forward with the others. As they collided with the dismounted dragoons, the attack from the Highlanders was fierce and unrelenting. It pushed the dragoons back toward their main body with absolute bloodshed and slaughter, the dragoons attempting to fight back but finding themselves overwhelmed in an instant wave of broadswords. There was a savagery in the way Euan and the others cut the dragoons down, taking out weeks of pent up anger and frustration on them. He knew he'd taken cuts but could barely feel them and didn't care. As he cut down one man, he saw a figure fast approaching him on the other side and pulled the pistol he carried. He took quick aim and pulled the trigger, but it misfired. Euan swore, and the man immediately stumbled back to escape him.

"Left wing! Fall back!" Lord Murray called and the three regiments of Murray, Macpherson, and Cameron backed away to their original position. "Right wing! Advance!"

The Glengarry, Appin, and MacDonald regiments now charged the body to the right with a ferocity equal to that of the left wing, and a slaughter just as savage, before Lord Murray drew them off. There was an immediate order to disengage and quick march for Penrith, with Lord Murray knowing the enemy wouldn't engage them now, having to regroup and see to their dead, which Euan estimated to be at least one hundred and fifty.

Euan could only imagine the sight they made, riding into Penrith blood-soaked, wild with the rush of victory, and toting a prisoner. The darkness had returned for him, but this time he was far less eager to be rid of it. The release of rage and frustration felt too good, too intoxicating, to let go of it just yet. The main body welcomed them back with a rousing cheer, drawing the prince himself out of his lodgings.

When he saw the state of the arriving men, his face darkened. "Lord Murray! I told you not to engage! Explain this!"

"They fired on us, Yer Highness, we had no choice but to engage," Murray replied coolly, and Euan looked away to hide a smile. "We did, however, bring a prisoner."

The man was pulled from a horse and shoved to his knees in front of the prince, who surveyed him curiously. "And who are you?"

"The Duke of Cumberland's footman, my lord."

"I am not a lord; I am a prince."

"I am sorry, Your Highness," he said, though the words dripped with disdain. To this man, the one standing before him was nothing, for to him the true prince was his master. "I know nothing of help to you and ask that you return me to my master immediately. He was almost killed, but the pistol the man used misfired!"

There was a loud gasp from everyone able to hear him, with all the men from the left-wing regiments looking at Euan with wide eyes. They knew full well that it was Euan who'd used his pistol, the only one to fire a shot.

"Christ, lad! Ye almost killed Cumberland!" Lochiel said to him.

"Shame it misfired," Euan muttered. "The whole war might be over."

"Nae quite, but that would have been a severe blow. Well done, lad. Even if ye did nae kill him, I bet he had to change his breeches!" Lord Murray said before he started to laugh. It was not Euan's fault the pistol misfired, after all. It was one of those rather unfortunate and unavoidable things that happened with muskets and pistols.

Euan joined Lord Murray in that laughter, as did everyone else, breaking the tension, but the footman glared at him. "I will tell His Highness that you laugh at him."

Euan stopped laughing, but his smile did not fade, becoming cold and causing the footman to shrink back. "Will ye? I would be incredibly obliged to ye. Tell him Captain Euan Cameron, an officer in Lochiel's regiment, sends his regards. Tell him that next time, I will nae miss."

A flicker of a smile made its way across the prince's face, the first one in days, even as the other men resumed their laughter at Euan's comments.

"Leave here and return to your master. I suggest you do not look back or tarry," the prince said as he cut the rope binding the footman's hands.

The man immediately stood and ran, and the prince looked at Euan. "Captain Cameron, see yourself to a bath and then come to see me. I wish a word."

Euan bowed. "Aye, Yer Highness."

As the prince returned inside, Murray nodded. "Men, well done! Ye have given a severe check to the forces of the son of the usurper! Ye are dismissed for rest and refreshment!"

Euan dismounted and one of his men led Absalon away to be fed and watered so Euan could fulfill the prince's order without delay. He and the others were swiftly directed toward their lodgings so they could bathe and rid themselves of the blood and gore that now covered them. Euan made sure to wash the blood from his kilt and trews, hanging both before the fire to dry as best they could. He wrapped his plaid around himself, the one item of clothing that had remained clean because he'd stuffed it away before battle, and belted it so he was not entirely unclothed before making his way to where the prince lodged. As he stepped inside, he was surprised to find Archibald waiting for him.

"I hope you do not mind, Captain, but I sent for your physician so he might tend to your needs before we talk."

Euan turned and bowed to the prince. "Thank ye, Yer Highness."

"Sit ye down, Euan," Archibald said.

Once Euan was seated, the plaid was pulled down to give Archibald an open view of his chest and back. He lifted each arm and examined it, nodding. "Legs?"

Euan pulled it away from his legs to show they were undamaged. "Naught but a few mild cuts on yer torso, arms, and hands. No stitching needed, but I will clean it."

Euan nodded but inhaled sharply as the first dab of alcohol made its way into the open wound, though he remained otherwise still. Once Archibald finished, he turned and bowed to the prince before he departed, and Euan sat before the fire, waiting for him to speak.

"You intrigue me, Captain Cameron," the prince said after a moment of silence.

"Do I, Yer Highness? I dinnae know why someone such as myself would be intriguing to someone like ye."

"Indeed, and for many reasons, though there is no need for titles in this current conversation. I wish to speak to you as one man to another."

"As it pleases ye," Euan replied with a small nod.

"How old are you again, Mr. Cameron?" The prince asked, dropping Euan's rank.

"Twenty and four. I will be twenty and five in January."

"We are nearly the same age then. You see, what I find intriguing is your bravery as well as your acumen for battle and strategy. How did you come by it?"

"I have been training in it since I was just a wee lad. After my father died, Lochiel took my care in hand and educated me."

"Educated you? In war, I assume?"

"Oui, ainsi que dans les formes plus traditionnelles d'éducation et d'étiquette, il a jugé bon que je les possède." *Yes, as well as in the more traditional forms of education and etiquette he saw fit for me to have.*

The prince stared at him, wide-eyed. "I had forgotten you speak French! And quite excellent French as well."

"Aye, I do. Ye never know when ye might need it," Euan

said, his smile becoming sly. He wasn't about to reveal the truth of how he came by it.

"Your bravery comes from the surety of your knowledge, then."

"Aye, though it is nae bravery to do what ye have trained for and do it without thinking. Such things are etched into yer memory by repetition until yer body and mind do it without prompting from ye."

"I am sure some would argue otherwise."

"Nae any of us. If ye asked any of the officers here, they would say the same. Constant training is key."

"I am also struck by your command and leadership amongst your men. They are fiercely loyal to you."

"I have nae given them reason nae to be."

"That is the secret? Somehow I doubt it."

"Part of it. They have to trust me, or they will nae follow me."

"What is the other part?"

"Treating them as equals. I am nae better than they are, no matter my station. In the end, we are all men; we will all die and end up in the ground where station does nae matter. I will nae put them through anything I would nae be willing to go through myself."

"I did try that."

"In a way ye did. Ye tried to get to know the men, which was good, but ye were never their equal and there was no way for them to forget ye were nae. Some of that is down to ye, much of it is nae."

"But I am not their equal. How could I be? I am a prince."

Euan fought the urge to laugh at such a statement. "Ye just showed yerself the reason yer efforts did nae accomplish all ye wished with them. Ye dinnae think of them as men just like ye, men who can think and feel as ye do. No amount of education or birth to a title changes those essential facts. It also does nae change the fact that ye are, indeed, a prince and thus cannae truly understand the lives we lead and we cannae forget who ye are."

"It cannot be that Lochiel and the others treat their men as their equals."

"Did ye nae see them tonight? Covered in the same blood as the men they led? They were on foot with the rest of us, nae too good to die at our sides the way we would die at theirs. In battle we are all equal. We all bleed and die the same."

"Do you believe we should be retreating? You were there at the council meeting," the prince said.

"Aye, I do. The men are tired and had no wish to invade England in the first place. They dinnae wish to die here, no matter how they may act, and they *would* die if we sent five thousand against twenty thousand with the weapons and supplies we currently have."

The prince sighed. "We were so close."

"Nae as close as it seems, or as close as ye wish to believe. Ye have the chance to come back; London is nae going anywhere."

"You do not believe we could have taken it?"

"No. Ye are confident because of our victories, but ye fail to see the truth in them. Cope's men were new, easy to strike fear into and break apart. The men waiting in London? Those are men who have been fighting a long war on the Continent. They are battle-hardened, and there is naught we could throw at them that would bring even a flinch. Lord Murray was right when he said it is best to return to where we can draw the battle out long enough to make them come to ye. They need those men in Flanders, nae here, and if ye stretch this out, they will pull them back because they have to. There is naught to say ye cannae sack London when they have sailed away."

"Clever," the prince said, smiling. "We could, could we not?"

"Anything is possible."

"Do the men need rallying?"

"No, but it seems ye do."

"What do you mean?"

"Ye have shrunk from the men, and they can see ye are demoralized. It angers them, causes them to lose faith in ye. Why should they fight for ye if yer response to seeing sense and thinking of their lives is petulance? They are yer subjects, yet ye dinnae seem to care if they die as long as it suits ye and gets ye what ye want. If ye want them to follow ye, ye need to be a leader again, true and steadfast. Ye need to be able to take setbacks, for there will always be setbacks in war, and ye need to take them with stoicism and renewed determination to find another way to achieve yer aims."

"You have no fear of saying this to me."

"Should I? Ye asked to speak with me as one man to another, and if ye ask me to discard titles, I will speak truth to ye as I would any other man."

The prince stood and, as Euan moved to do the same, gestured for him to remain seated. Going to a sideboard, he took a decanter and poured whisky into two glasses before crossing the room and handing one to Euan.

"Thank ye," Euan said.

"You have earned it after tonight, I should think," the prince said. "Nearly killing Cumberland is quite the feat."

"Nae as much as actually killing him would have been," Euan replied, showing a wry smile before taking a drink of the whisky.

The prince chuckled. "That is certainly true, but you are not at fault either," he said, falling silent for a moment before sighing. "You are wrong, you know."

"About what?"

"I do care if they live or die even if it seems as though I do not. I was taught that it is best for a military commander to not be sentimental about those he is leading."

"There is a difference between sentimental and dismissive. Ye told me the first time we met that it was good I was nae married, for I would fight all the harder with naught to leave behind but a legend. How do ye think that sounded to me?"

223

The prince winced. "Terrible, I am afraid. I should not have said it. I wanted to seem strong so that Lochiel would respect me."

"Ye are a prince; he respected ye already. All that did was make him concerned for his clansmen because it seemed as though ye cared naught about them."

"Though I do not know what it is like to live as these common men do, I did spend some time in poverty in France while hiding there. I shopped for my own food, endeavored to learn how to cook for myself."

"Endeavored?"

"I was not always successful, let us just say that."

Euan laughed and then cleared his throat. "Sorry."

"Do not be," the prince said, laughing. "It is rather comical. The point is that I do know that there is suffering, I do know what it is to be considered worthless, but no matter what I do, I cannot adequately convey such a thing to the men."

"Perhaps nae, and it does nae matter now, I dinnae think. What ye *can* do is show up as their leader again. Ride at the head, inspire them. Ye can do that. Go amongst them in camp in the evenings. Eat with them, make yerself human."

"All good pieces of advice," he admitted.

"As I told ye, there will be mistakes, setbacks, but ye must accept them with strength and move on to the next battle with new lessons learned."

"Would you help me if I needed it?"

"In what way?"

"It is interesting to speak to someone my own age, someone who has no fear of being honest with me and tells me what I need to hear instead of what he thinks I want to hear. Someone who has more experience of the world than I do."

"Nae more, just different."

"Would you?"

Euan was quiet for a long moment before nodding. "Aye."

"Because you want to or because I order you to."

"If ye would have asked me at Glenfinnan or after Derby, I would have said it was the latter."

"And now?"

"Now it would be because I want to if ye call on me for such a thing."

"I may just do that," the prince said, finishing his drink. "You, however, have earned yourself a rest."

Euan nodded and finished his drink, standing and placing the glass on the bench beside him before bowing. "Yer Highness."

"Goodnight, Captain."

When Euan departed, the prince sighed, placing his hands on the table as he closed his eyes and let his head drop for a moment. All the advice the young captain had given him was good advice, solid advice, perhaps the most practical he'd ever gotten from anyone. There was no question as to whether he'd take it, he certainly would, but he only wished it had come sooner. In a way, he wished he could pluck Euan Cameron from Lochiel's control and place the young man within his own council. It would never happen, but he couldn't help but wonder what it would be like if he could. What would it be like to be around someone his own age who was honest, wise with his counsel, and kind in its delivery? What would it be like to have a friend like Euan, a man with whom he'd instantly felt comfortable, a man he knew he could trust and who would be loyal because he was a true friend, not because he had to be or because it would serve his ambitions? Perhaps, when this war was won, he could convince Lochiel to allow Euan to serve on his council. The sound of the door opening brought his head up to find Lord Elcho.

"My Lord Elcho, good evening," the prince said.

"Yer Highness," Lord Elcho replied with a bow. "Ye sent for me?"

"Yes. I wanted to speak to you about someone."

"Very well. Who?"

"I want to speak to you about the man who just left here."

"Captain Cameron, Yer Highness?" Elcho asked, raising an eyebrow.

"Indeed. I have been watching him, and I have seen how he inspires a great deal of loyalty from the men in not only his own regiment, but also others."

"Aye," Lord Elcho replied. "For he is one of them, from amongst them, nae born to privilege like ye or me. He does nae assign his men to do anything he would nae do himself. In fact, he will take on more so they may do less. He does nae consider himself above them and they love him for it."

"They certainly followed Captain Cameron across the border into England without hesitation, despite whatever they may have felt."

"Of course they did. Every one of them would follow that lad into hell to face the devil himself if he asked them to, and if I am honest, I am certain a fair few of mine, as well as a majority of the men from other regiments, would join them. *That* is how respected he is."

"Lochiel should be proud to have such a man to command his troops," the prince said.

"Oh, he is, but he is also nae a fool. Lochiel knows that if Euan were to turn against him, he would find himself in the midst of an unmitigated disaster, something he is well aware of. He keeps the lad close to him for a reason: keeping him tethered allows Lochiel to use Euan's influence to his own advantage. As long as Euan is loyal, so will the others be."

"I do not think Lochiel needs to fear such a thing. The captain is loyal to a fault and would never betray his master."

"It is nae a chance Lochiel wishes to take, and I dinnae blame him for it."

"Thank you, Lord Elcho," the prince said. "You have given me much to think about."

"Good night, Yer Highness," Lord Elcho said, bowing before he left the room.

The prince picked up his glass, leaning against the table and watching the fire dance through the crystal's prisms. Elcho had confirmed that everything Euan had said to him moments ago had been truthful. The things he did to inspire loyalty and respect were simple, and he commanded a sort of loyalty amongst his men that the prince had found himself unable to inspire as of yet. It was a loyalty he'd expected but hadn't been able to earn because he'd assumed it would come due to his station, but that seemed not to be the case. Perhaps he *could* learn something from the young officer after all.

Euan left the meeting with the prince, stopping to bow to Lord Elcho as the man passed, confused about his own feelings. While he still didn't believe in the cause, it turned out that the prince was human after all. The prior dislike Euan held for him now eased to almost nothing, though he knew it was likely the man would do something to raise it again. Whether or not that would be the prince's own fault remained to be seen.

When he arrived at his lodgings, Malcolm was already asleep. After setting out his own bedding, Euan rested on the floor, looking into the fire. It was strange to see someone who should have everything seem, for a moment, to be just as lost as Euan himself was. What was it like, he wondered, to always need to suspect that those around him only wanted his company or friendship for their own gain and not for himself? The prince's own words had made it clear to Euan that this was something the young royal encountered often, and it made Euan sad for him. Did he know true friendship? Did he know love or care or family? He had a father, of course, but how close were they? Did he see his son as anything more than a means to an end? The last thought brought a frown to Euan's face. Perhaps they were more alike in that regard than either of them had realized.

In the morning, the army left Penrith for Carlisle, arriving by early evening to find they still had possession of the city. It was decided that when they departed the following morning, they'd leave a garrison of three hundred soldiers in place, to be made up of men from the Manchester regiment, the Lowland regiments, the Irish, and the French. Euan watched as the prince promised to relieve them as soon as he could, though he was sure they all knew relief would not be coming soon enough, if at all. Those three hundred would die there under Cumberland's orders, Euan was certain of it, and the last sound they heard from the city was the three hundred singing their farewells from the walls.

As they finally approached the Esk once more on the 26th of December, Euan felt a palpable sense of relief. The river itself was swollen from several days of rain and was fast-moving, but there was no intention of letting such a thing stop them from crossing back into their homeland. Several of the officers on horseback were stationed both above and below the intended crossing. Those above would break the force of the current, and those below would catch any who might be carried away. The infantry lined up on the shore, twelve across and arms linked, before they progressed into the water. This allowed them to support each other against the rush of the water, and once there was sufficient space for the water to pass between them and not back up with a crush of men, another twelve went forward. After an hour, the entirety of the army had passed through the river and found themselves once again on Scottish soil. As they sat before the fires to dry themselves, there was joy and an infectious laughter that spread through the men like a wildfire.

They were home.

CHAPTER 18

"YOU WERE QUITE LUCKY to survive after Prestonpans."

"I was, that is true, and nae the last time, either."

"I'm surprised you took your restrictions so well."

"What else could I do?" Euan said, smiling. "I knew perfectly well that I was badly injured, and if I wanted to keep my men safe in what was to come, then I had to do what I was told. I did it for them."

"Not for yourself?"

"No. They were what mattered."

"Tell me about Malcolm."

George noted that Euan couldn't hide the pain on his face at the mention of the name. "What do ye want to know?"

"What would you want me to know?"

"He was … Malcolm was always like an older brother to me. He took care of me, looked after me, because he was several years older than I was. I think, of all of them, he was the closest to really understanding me. One of the best men I have ever known or ever will, he was always kind and always generous with his time. He would stop everything he was doing if ye needed him, and it always felt as though whatever ye were going through was the most important thing there was. He could make ye laugh and always loved a good joke. I loved him dearly, and there will never be a day I dinnae miss him."

"And Iain?"

Euan closed his eyes, unable or unwilling to stop the silent tears as he was asked about his dearest friends, his brothers. "Iain was a brother, too. The jester amongst us, but always there for ye. Loyal to a fault, ye dared nae harm someone in his presence. He was a fine tailor, too, though his specialty was waistcoats. He made them for all of us, and when I came home, he made me an embroidered one to wear if I had to attend Lochiel at formal functions. He was empathetic and kind. Iain once made a beautiful pair of doe skin gloves for a lass in thanks for her care of his father, but he took that doe himself. He made sure to kill it cleanly, nae letting it feel a moment of suffering, because he knew the lass could nae abide the suffering of animals. He did nae wish to taint her gift with such a thing."

"Findlay?"

"Finn took a while to warm up to people, but once he knew ye, he always had yer back. Underneath it all, he had a big heart that held such a surprising depth of feeling. He could also be melancholy often, or lost inside his own thoughts, and easily hurt, though he would deny it. He was a fine horseman and an excellent shot with a bow."

"How about Duncan?"

"Duncan was … we were the same age, where the others were all a few years older than I was. We grew up together, the pair of us, friends from our earliest days. When his mam died, my mam filled that role for him and loved him like her own. Still does. Iain, too. I found out later that when I was away, they were at my home often, looking after her or keeping her company, allowing her to fuss over them because it made her feel better," Euan said, pausing to smile. "Duncan was a big man with a bigger heart. Creative, he was quite a woodworker. My fondest memories of him are seemingly endless walks under the guise of hunting, or sitting at his table drinking, laughing, and talking."

"They all sound like wonderful men."

"They were," Euan replied, his voice soft and sad. "But they are gone now."

"Are they? Or do they live on in your memories?"

"They may be in my memories, but that is all. They are memories no one else has, and when I am gone, they will be too. Everything that made them what they were is gone, buried with them."

"Perhaps you could share it so that someone else knows."

"With whom?"

"You don't feel you could tell Watcher Cameron?"

"No," he said. "She suffers enough guilt for what she feels was her role in my death. I will nae add to it by making them more real to her than they already are and watching her heart break because she couldn't save them, too."

"Have you spoken with her about any of this?"

"No. I cannae, for I fear the horror and disgust I know will be in her eyes if I do. She does nae know any of this, does nae know the monster her husband truly is, and when she finds out, I know I will lose her. It is nae a thought I can stomach, and I am nae sure I could ever tell her."

George shifted the topic, wanting to avoid upsetting him when there was still much to discuss. "Malcolm tried to warn you, as your mother did, about what was happening to you."

"Aye, and I did hear him, but it was nae that easy. I could nae just walk away. As my mam pointed out, he would have killed me before he let me go."

George raised an eyebrow. "That seems a bit extreme."

"I was too valuable for him to risk my falling into the hands of another. Believe me when I say that death would have come for me at some point. It would have been seen as a massive betrayal."

"What did you feel when you learned you were going to England?"

"Angry. It was stupid, a waste of time we could have spent building our forces or resting at Edinburgh. And then we leave Edinburgh to be taken back by the English once we leave. What was the point of taking it?"

"Were the others angry?"

"The officers were, the chiefs were, but none said it out loud."

"Let's discuss the crossing. What made you do what you did?"

"Which part?"

"All of it."

"I walked amongst them because they were my men, and if they had to cross the river on foot, then so would I. I knew they did nae wish to go, so I led by example and went first. Singing the song helped, gave us something to focus on, and put words to our emotions."

"And the salute?"

"My own farewell, but I was nae sad to see the rest follow suit."

"You mentioned that Lochiel cutting his hand was seen as a bad omen."

"Aye, it was, but thankfully naught came of it on our journey through England."

"What were you thinking when the woman begged you not to eat her children?"

Euan started to laugh. "Ach, it was infuriating then, but now it is just funny and ridiculous. Bairns as common food for Highlanders, what nonsense," Euan said, then paused. "Though, there was that group in the 16th century robbing and murdering travelers and then eating them."

"You're kidding."

"No, I am nae, I swear it. Sawney Bean is the name."

"The one Malcolm mentioned!"

"Aye! That is the one," Euan said, laughing. "But as I said then, they were Lowlanders, so Highlanders still dinnae eat children, or anyone for that matter."

"That brings us to Derby."

Euan rolled his eyes. "Derby," he groused. "What a bloody mess that was when the truth finally came out."

"Were you surprised?"

"We all were. It was quite the lie, quite the betrayal, and then he had the nerve to rail and weep about it!"

"Would you have felt a bit differently if you didn't already dislike him?"

"I think it would have been worse if I had nae. I would have felt angrier, far more deeply betrayed. It only further proved what I just told ye about leaving Edinburgh. It was a waste of time and resources, and we gained naught from it."

"And the men lost faith in him?"

"Oh aye, they did, especially when they watched him essentially abandon them in order to pout about being caught out and forced to listen to reason."

"And then comes Clifton Moor."

Euan couldn't help his smile when George mentioned it. "Aye, Clifton Moor. A good battle, something we needed to put Cumberland on his heels."

"You relished the battle this time."

"Aye, I did, and I was nae sorry. Still am nae. Everything I had felt in those last weeks came to the surface, and I vented it on every red coat I could reach."

"And then you found out that you almost killed Cumberland and bragged about it?"

"I did," Euan said, chuckling. "Could nae help it. It would have been quite an accomplishment and would have significantly changed the war itself, and the arrogance of the man grated on me. I am still sad my pistol misfired and can only wonder how different things might have been had it nae."

"What were you expecting when you met with the prince that night?"

"I honestly cannae say. Perhaps a dressing down for my comment, or some question about the upcoming crossing back into Scotland, but most certainly nae what I got."

"I'm sure it was surprising to have him ask you to speak informally."

"Actually, it was nae. Nobility are human, and sometimes the formality can be exhausting. They just wish to speak to another person as though there was nae this gulf created by birth looming between."

"Has that happened to you before?"

"A few times, but nae with a prince or a king."

"You were honest with him in your counsel, frank."

"I could nae be otherwise. He asked for it, and I gave it."

"You mentioned that he seemed more human to you after that meeting, that you understood him in a way that surprised you."

"Aye, that was strange, and I still dinnae know what to make of it. Knowing what I do now of his life, of what happened to him afterward, I actually feel quite badly for him. He did nae have what I had, did nae have true friends or a family who loved him for just himself instead of what he represented. I think he was lonely, surrounded by people but still feeling alone."

"Just like you did."

"Aye, and that made me uncomfortable. Maybe he sensed it in me as I did in him. Still, it was why I was honest. Deep down, I knew it was what he needed."

"He could've reacted poorly to it."

"Could have but did nae. I was nae cruel in what I said. Though, had he taken it poorly and ordered me arrested, I would have liked to have seen whether or nae that order would be obeyed."

"You don't think they would've?"

"If I am honest? No. Nae at that time, anyway. They were fed up with him, and I have a feeling that the chiefs would nae take kindly to such an order after all I had done. The rift that would have caused, us against him, would have put him in a precarious position, and he was nae a stupid man, no matter what the English try to say."

"Precarious in what way?"

"It is very possible he would have been deposed, marched

back to Clifton Moor, and handed over to Cumberland. He and his advisors."

"Mutiny then?"

"Oh aye, mutiny on a scale grander than he could have overcome, and there is no way he would nae have known that."

"What about the mutiny Strickland asked you to commit?"

"The mutiny *he* asked of me would have killed an untold number of innocents, while the other would have killed only the prince and his seven men," Euan said, his expression darkening.

"It still angers you."

"Always will. He looked me in the face and all but said he did nae care about our lives or the lives of our families. We were only important as long as we were useful, and the Scottish people were nae useful to him outside of the soldiers we could provide. What did it matter if our families died as long as he had the men?"

"And to ask it not only for your men, but also for others. Do you think he was right? Would those men follow you?"

"For that? No. I know they would nae have. They would have had the same concerns as I did and never would have done it for that reason alone. They would have strung me up for a traitor before they did that, my own clan first among them."

"Did you even consider it for a second? With the promises he made?"

Euan's laugh was bitter. "Absolutely nae. I knew perfectly well he would give me none of it once I delivered, for it was nae in his power to give. Dinnae forget, I had been at court; I saw how those games were played. He did nae know that, of course, but I was nae that naïve, a country lad blinded by promises of power and wealth. That is nae the first and only time I was offered such."

"Oh?"

"People would try to bribe me all the time in order to save themselves. Then, on our last mission, Lochiel offered something similar, and I did nae want it then either."

"Do you think Watcher Cameron would've been, as you say, 'blinded' by it?"

Euan laughed harder now. "Christ, no. She would be the last person on earth who would want anything to do with any of it, and she meets nobility all the time. That lass would even do her work as a Watcher in anonymity if she could. She does nae like being the center of attention in such a way, and dealing with duplicitous people all day would both exhaust and anger her. People might end up heading for the gallows by midday because she was that irritated."

"A bit Queen of Hearts there."

"Aye," Euan said, still laughing.

"You recognize the reference?"

"I have read the book, aye. Grace has it."

"Interesting! Are you a prolific reader?"

"It is my favorite thing to do."

"I like to read as well."

"I am sure ye have read things nae even written yet, at least for me."

"I most definitely have. Let's get back to that moment with Strickland. Why did you decide not to tell Lochiel or the others?"

"It was safer nae to. No need to make the situation worse when I had no intention of doing it. I think it would have made them suspicious of me, and that was nae what was needed."

"A fair observation, I think. Did those left at Carlisle die?"

"Aye, most of them, just as I knew they would, but they held it as best they could and put up a hell of a fight. Those that did nae die were held in prisons and transported as slaves to the Caribbean. They were singing songs of farewell from the ramparts as we marched out."

"Yes, you mentioned that. So, they knew."

"They did. Ye could see it in their faces, and it only served to make me angrier, for it was a waste of three hundred lives. Ye leave them there to defend Carlisle, for what? Three hundred men against thousands? What would they do? I still dinnae understand it. Ye abandon Edinburgh, but ye leave a garrison for Carlisle?"

"It was a foothold in England."

"It was a foothold ye could retake, and to me it was wiser to let it go because ye could nae be sure how long it would be until ye could return."

"I see your point."

"In the meantime, we lost the capital and the advantage it provided us."

"A bad plan, hm?"

"Of course it was. This campaign often felt like it was a series of bad plans, and look where it got us."

"But you all finally made it back to Scotland."

"Aye, we did, and I cannae tell ye the relief it was."

"What happened afterward?"

"From there we moved on to Glasgow, but that almost went terribly wrong."

"In what way?"

"There was anger amongst the men that the city had raised troops for Hanover, and many wanted to sack the city in revenge. Somehow, Lochiel managed to stop them from doing so and put us on patrol to keep the peace. The city rang the bells in gratitude … did ye know the bells of Glasgow still ring out whenever a Lochiel is there?"

"I didn't, how fascinating!"

"After we rested and resupplied at Glasgow, the Frasers, Mackenzies, and Gordons showed up, as did the Scottish and Irish drafts the French had promised. That alone grew our numbers to nine thousand. It was grand to see the Frasers, who have always been allies and kin, and a bit of a relief to see friendly faces at home."

"How long did that relief last?

"Nae long enough."

CHAPTER 19

THE SOUND OF THE cannon boomed across the moor, part of yet another bombardment of the walls of Stirling Castle, and the sound could be heard for miles. The town of Stirling had surrendered to the Jacobite army on the 8th of January, allowing them to bring cannons in to begin the work of bringing the castle under their command. It wasn't a task any of the officers or chiefs felt particularly inclined to, though there were strategic advantages to it. If they took control of Stirling Castle, it would allow them to maintain control along the coasts to ensure their supplies from the Continent. It was also the key to Scottish communications, as all passed through Stirling, central as it was. It would be quite a jewel for them, but they all knew it wouldn't be easy and wondered if it was the best use of both their time and artillery. The job of laying the locations for the siege was trusted to a man named Mirabel de Gordon, who then picked a questionable location, but the prince wouldn't hear otherwise.

When they'd arrived in Bannockburn on the 4th, the prince immediately ceased to hold councils with the chiefs, deciding to rely only on his Irish advisors. This was a cause of major resentment within the Highland ranks, who now felt cut off from the decisions that affected their lives and their country and felt the snub of their leader keenly. All observed that the prince was now drinking more often than he previously had, which disappointed Euan even though he also understood why he might be doing so.

When word came from the south that General Hawley was coming from Edinburgh with seven thousand men to relieve Stirling, the chiefs met in spite of the prince's refusal to see them. This mass of incoming men was a source of extreme concern to them even if the prince didn't seem to think so. The decision was taken to dispatch the Highland regiments to prepare for battle with Hawley at Plean Muir on the 15th, but Hawley, his men, and the attack never materialized. Euan and others were sent to ascertain what Hawley seemed to be planning and to gather what intelligence they could.

"Euan, what news?" Lochiel asked as the small group rode back into camp at Plean in the late afternoon, almost before Euan was off of his horse.

"Plenty," Euan replied.

"Come into the council, lad, and make yer report."

Euan nodded and followed Lochiel into the tent where the other chiefs were meeting, bowing as he entered. "Gentlemen."

"Good to see ye have returned, Euan. What have ye found, for I know ye will nae have returned empty handed." Lord Murray said.

"Hawley's men are camped at Falkirk moor near Callendar House, where Hawley has made his lodging. There seems to be no intention of advancing, as they are being entertained there by Lady Kilmarnock. The number we heard seems to be correct, with several regiments of dragoons and infantry."

"They have no desire to engage? Then why are they here?" Lord Murray mused.

"If their only wish is to relieve Stirling, it is my guess they have no wish to do battle with us first in order to relieve it. They would rather wait us out," Euan said before looking to Lochiel. "There are Campbells within their ranks."

"Of course there are," Lochiel grumbled.

"If they dinnae want to engage us, then I say we go to them," Lord Elcho said. "They cannae be allowed to relieve Stirling."

"Aye," Lord Murray said. "I agree."

"There is a chance to surprise them," Euan said. "If we stay off the main road and head for Falkirk Hill, they will be below us, and we will have the high ground. The terrain there is better suited to us than to them."

Lord Murray smiled. "Well done, lad. Ye never fail us and never fail to have a plan already in yer mind. I like the idea, so if we are in agreement, let us inform the prince. Lord Elcho, ye should go; he still seems to listen to ye."

Lord Elcho nodded and departed, and Euan followed him out.

"Euan," Lochiel said as he came out behind Euan.

"Aye, Lochiel."

"I want ye to lead the men."

Euan's eyes widened. "Why? Are ye ill?"

Lochiel chuckled. "No. I will be there, but I think ye have more than earned yer chance to lead the Cameron regiment into battle. I want ye to call the commands for us."

Euan couldn't imagine a bigger honor and bowed gratefully. "Thank ye for yer confidence. It would be my honor to lead our men."

"Good. I have faith in ye, lad," he said as he departed.

Euan took a deep breath and shook his head. Part of him wondered if Lochiel was finally able to see his value, how hard he was working, and might actually be proud of him for once. Turning to go back to his own tent, he was lost in thought. He was due a rest and he should take it, particularly since he was leading the Camerons tomorrow. He hadn't made it far before he ran into one of the Fraser officers, who happened to be his cousin, Murdoch.

"We are to battle then?" Murdoch asked.

"Aye, in the morning," Euan replied. "I will be leading the Camerons."

Murdoch grinned. "About bloody time. I will tell the others. Know that the Frasers are with ye. We will follow whatever orders ye give and pass them to our own men."

"Why would ye do that?" Euan asked, surprised.

"Because ye know what ye are doing, Euan. We all know that, and now it seems the chiefs do, too. We are behind ye."

Euan smiled. "Thank ye for that, Murdoch."

The young man nodded, patted Euan on the back, and hurried off to spread the word.

The following morning, the regiments massed to set off for Falkirk moor. The march was silent, avoiding the main roads to keep the element of surprise as Euan had suggested. They met no resistance, and Euan wondered for a moment if they were being led into a trap in spite of what he'd seen, but by the time they appeared on the ridge and began organizing near the English encampment, it was clear there was no trap and the Hanoverians weren't expecting their arrival. He watched as the dragoon regiments hurriedly rode into position, followed by the infantry, but it was far more disorganized an ordering than he'd ever seen. The total disarray made it even clearer that they'd gotten the jump on the English.

A loud boom of thunder sounded before the skies opened up with heavy rain and hail. This would make things difficult, but not impossible, with muddy ground and wet powder. To his right on the front line were the MacDonalds, to his left the Frasers, Macphersons, Mackintoshes, Mackenzies, Farquharsons, and Stewarts. If the Camerons were on the front line, Euan would always be happy to have the Frasers next to him because they were well-trained and fierce opponents. Behind him, the Gordon, Ogilvy, and Atholl regiments formed up. Lord Murray came on foot into the fore at the head of the MacDonalds.

"Men at the ready!" Euan shouted out, hearing the order called out from his right and left, then passed all the way down the front line.

The Hanover front lines raised their muskets to fire, but the rain had wet the black powder cartridges and many of them misfired. Euan called a return volley, and the Jacobite lines encountered the same problem when they returned fire. It was then that he saw the dragoon cavalry organizing for what he knew was a charge.

"Camerons!" he called out. "Pistols! Dirks at the ready for the post volley!"

Even through the rain he heard the men drawing behind him and the order shouted down the lines. The Fraser officers heard it and gave the same command as they'd promised they would, as did the MacDonald officers under the direction of Lord Murray. Euan stared down the dragoons as they trotted in the direction of the right flank.

"Aim!"

All of the men raised their pistols.

"Hold!"

As the dragoons came closer, Euan waited. They needed to be closer, within pistol range. The weapons were so small the men on horseback wouldn't see them until it was too late, and that was the entire point. The men beside him stood fast, understanding the same thing.

"Hold!" he shouted again, and as the dragoon cavalry came within range, Euan gave the order. "Fire!"

The lines around him exploded with pistol fire, sending an unexpected and massive volley straight into the approaching dragoon cavalry lines. Some of the pistols misfired, but enough of them didn't and served their purpose. A mass of the dragoons dropped dead on the spot, too close to avoid the pistol fire. The loss of their riders sent horses scattering in every direction and caused three of the cavalry regiments to flee.

"Pistols down, dirks up!" Euan shouted.

The Cameron men knew exactly what this meant and immediately dropped their pistols, gripping their dirks and taking up a crouched position. The action was mimicked down the lines, and as the remaining horses advanced, too close to stop themselves, Euan and the men attacked the horses with the dirks. The collapse of a dead horse brought the rider within range of the same blades, and they were dispatched just as their animals had been. Suddenly, the MacDonalds broke ranks and rushed after the fleeing cavalry, unable to be restrained by Lord Murray.

Euan swore and stood up before he turned to his men. "Fire muskets!"

The men picked up the muskets and fired as Euan crouched. There were more misfires, but that couldn't be helped, and when the volley finished, he shouted his next order. "Camerons! Charge!"

The Cameron men threw down their muskets and pulled their swords, running forward with a scream, followed by the Frasers, Macphersons, Mackintoshes, and Mackenzies. The government forces to the right held firm and regrouped, firing at the charging men but missing most of them as they once again grappled with wet powder, while the Jacobite back lines of the Irish and French prevented an attack on the rear of the charging regiments. As some of the English infantry engaged, the men came together in a clash of bodies and steel.

Euan let the surge of the battle take him over as he fought with government soldiers, not thinking, just acting. If he thought too much, he'd hesitate, and if he hesitated, he'd be dead. He moved fast, taking down as many as he could before he turned to find the face of someone he knew, and it made Euan stop cold: Alexander Munro. He knew this young man. Clan Munro and Clan Cameron weren't usually allies, but they knew each other. Alex Munro was someone he'd encountered many times when Lochiel met with the Munro chief.

"Euan?" the young man asked, his confusion plain even in the midst of all that was happening around the two of them.

"Alex." Euan shook his head, the world seeming to slow and the sounds of battle becoming a dull roar in his ears. "No. No, ye have to get out of here or stand down!"

"I cannae! Ye are a traitor, Euan Cameron!" Alexander shouted as he lowered his bayonet and pointed it at Euan.

"Alex, please, dinnae do this! Dinnae make me kill ye!"

Without another word, Alexander charged him. Euan took a slight step to the side, grabbing the musket behind the bayonet and yanking the young man forward onto his blade with the hope that the force would make it quick and as painless as possible. There was a gasp from Alexander as the blade penetrated his torso, followed by a strangled groan as it exited through his back, and he fell forward against Euan, who caught him and held him up.

"Why! Why did ye have to do it! Damn ye, Alex!" Euan screamed, the tears on his face hidden by the pouring rain. There was no reply from Alexander as Euan let him fall, pulling his blade from the body and then bending down to close the dead man's eyes. There was, however, no time for grief, as the fight was not over.

A blade caught Euan's midsection as he stood back up, just a glance, but enough to make him bleed well. Euan cried out in pain, then screamed in rage as he took a violent and weighty swing at the soldier who'd done it, watching the man's head tumble from his neck as the blade sliced through it cleanly, its eyes still open and mouth gaping. It pleased him greatly to see it was a Campbell, and with great pleasure Euan moved on to dispatch several more of them. A scream then got his attention even as the rest of the Hanover army fled, and it came from the direction of a cluster of his own men. Euan ran toward them to see six of them battling with someone, two of his men dead on the ground, and the combatant still attempting to fight back. Euan recognized the older man as he got closer, and it horrified him.

"Stop!" Euan shouted before one of the Camerons pulled a pistol and shot the man, another hacking at his body as he fell. Euan rushed forward and shoved them away from the man on the ground, who was now a mess of blood and bone.

"He took two of us, but we got him, Euan!"

"Ye have killed The Munro, ye bloody idiots!"

The men's eyes widened with horror, realizing what they'd done … they'd killed the Chief of Clan Munro.

"This one too," one of the others said as he gestured to another body on the ground.

"His brother! Christ, what have ye done! Get out of here! GO!" Euan screamed at them.

The others fled as Lord Murray and some of the Atholl Brigade arrived. "Captain Cameron! Did ye do this?"

"No, m'lord, but it was some of our regiment. I tried to stop them."

Lord Murray shook his head before he noticed the blood running down Euan's torso and turning his shirt crimson. "Christ lad! Get ye back to the others; ye have wounds that need tending!"

Euan bowed and turned, stumbling away. He felt numb, horrified by all of this. It had been a slaughter and a decisive victory for the Jacobites, but he felt no glory in it, not as he had at Prestonpans or Clifton Moor. Once he reached his own men, they wasted no time in ushering him aside to Archibald to see to the cut, which, thankfully, was nowhere near as bad as it could've or should've been. When Archibald poured whisky on the wound, Euan screamed, though it was just as much a scream of emotional pain as it was physical, several men holding him down to prevent him from punching the doctor.

"Sorry, lad, there is no time to numb the pain with drink."

Before Euan could protest, he felt the sharp bite of the needle and the burn of the thread being pulled through his skin. With another tortured scream, his body jerked, and more hands pressed him down to keep him from pulling away from Archibald and the pain he was inflicting. His breathing became ragged, tears streaming down his face, feeling trapped and smothered by everyone holding him there. The pain was intense, unrelenting, and he prayed to go numb or to lose consciousness, but to no avail. Euan suffered the pain of feeling each stitch until it was done, and then he was released.

As many of the others from all of the regiments looted the bodies, Euan found a quiet place in an empty tent at the former Hanoverian camp. He had no desire to participate in looting and never had. It always seemed wrong to him, a desecration the Lord would see and surely punish them for when they appeared before Him. No material object was worth that, and he'd have enough to explain as it was. He stared out in front of him, his gaze distant and his eyes glassy. The face of Alexander Munro and the sound he'd made when Euan ran him through, the way it felt as the blade went in; all of it haunted him. It wasn't the first time this had happened, the first time he'd killed a man he recognized, but it was the first time it had been one he'd known so well. It was easier to dismiss the others, not much easier, but somewhat. It still pained him to charge them as enemies, to look into their faces as he took their lives, but this was different.

Euan pressed the heels of his hands to his eyes, wanting the image to fade, but it wouldn't, and he broke down in tears. Tears for Alexander, for himself, for the country, and all those who were dying for people who didn't care. Tears of rage, sadness, and pain. He'd survived once more, and he should be thankful, he knew that, but he couldn't muster the energy or the gratitude. He wanted to go home, he wanted to see his mother, he wanted to be away from all of this death and destruction. Away from the strangled death groan of Alexander Munro.

"It never gets easier, lad," Lochiel said as he sat down by Euan.

Euan jumped, startled, and tried to hide his tears, but Lochiel shook his head. "Dinnae try to hide it on my account. Any man of war has been where ye are now and cannae fault ye for it."

"I ... Alexander ..."

"I know, lad. I saw it."

Euan sobbed again, shaking his head. "I did nae want to do it, but he left me no choice! I begged him, told him to get away! Why did he nae listen?"

"Aye, he did nae. He did his job, and ye did yers. In this business there are no friends, lad. I saw that ye tried to help The Munro. They will bury him, and the chiefs will go out of respect, a cease fire called for at least that long."

Euan nodded but said nothing.

"I told ye when this all began that ye would never be that young man again, untainted by war and death, and now ye know ye never will be. Do ye remember him, still? I do."

Euan tried to remember what it had been like before, in those three brief years after he'd come home, but found he couldn't call anything to mind but this. "No."

"Ye will eventually, when all of this is over," he said as he patted Euan on the back. "Ye are nae that much different than ye were, I can tell ye that. Ye did well today, Euan. That pistol volley was a brilliant move on yer part, as was the use of the dirks."

"Thank ye, Lochiel," Euan said. Finally, the praise he'd wanted had come, but it had come the one time he didn't want it.

"Ye proved me right. I knew ye could do this, knew ye could lead us and we could be victorious under yer command. If I could convince them to promote ye, I would. Ye are a born warrior, Euan, and I cannae be happier to have ye where ye are. I will leave ye to yer grief but, judging by that cut, ye are lucky to be alive and I am glad ye still are," Lochiel said as he stood. "At least ye sent a fair few Campbells to hell," he quipped before he left Euan alone.

At this moment, Euan wasn't entirely sure he was glad to be alive. Alive meant this pain, a pain he knew would be there until he died, an event he was sure wouldn't be much longer in coming.

CHAPTER 20

AFTER THE BATTLE AT Falkirk, the prince decided not to press their advantage and pursue the fleeing Hanoverians back to Edinburgh, despite the pleading from the chiefs. He wished to stay in Stirling and continue the siege, returning to Bannockburn House with the Lowland regiments while Murray and the Highland regiments were left to occupy Falkirk, something they counted as a small blessing.

Euan marked his twenty-fifth birthday two days later, on the 20th of January. The Cameron officers worked together to procure a small, sweet cake as a gift, and Lochiel provided a cup of ale for each man in the Cameron regiment. The other regiments joined the party, too, wanting to honor a man they respected and who'd just commanded them all to a decisive victory, with their chiefs being kind enough to also provide them with ale. It wasn't the normal way of things to mark the birthday of a common officer in such a way, with nine thousand men toasting his health, but it happened anyway. Even the chiefs joined in. There was plenty of laughter by firelight, jokes and songs and stories. For a moment, Euan was able to forget what had happened and the pain of his still very fresh wound.

"It seems as though ye have a birthday gift from the English!" Murdoch said as he plopped down beside Euan.

"What?" Euan asked with an amused expression.

"Ye have a bounty on yer head, Euan."

There was a sort of gasp from the Camerons around him, and all conversation ceased, but Euan grinned. "Aye? How much?"

"£100," Murdoch replied, dropping his voice low so as not to broadcast the information to anyone who might want to collect that sum of money by turning in a fellow Scot. Though, anyone trying to turn Euan in would likely be killed before he even set foot outside of camp by any of the others.

"Bullshite!" Malcolm exclaimed.

"No, look for yerself," Murdoch said as he handed Euan a piece of paper. "I took this off of the body of one of Hawley's men after the battle and got someone to read it for me."

Euan took it and unfolded it, only to see his name and the announcement that he was wanted for the attempted murder of His Royal Highness, Prince William, the Duke of Cumberland. As he stared at it, he began laughing, with Malcolm and the others joining him.

"Christ would ye look at that! Our wee Euan is a fugitive!" Iain said.

Euan continued laughing so hard it brought tears to his eyes, the merriest he'd felt since the battle. A price on his head, and such a sum! Attempted murder was a laughable offense since it had been in a battle and Cumberland had run up on *him*. It wasn't as though he'd snuck up on Cumberland and tried to pull the trigger. He knew, however, that if he were apprehended, it would mean the Tower for him and death in England, so he'd better make sure he was never caught.

A few days later, Euan stood watch with Iain and Lochiel at Callendar House, where the regiments took turns posting men to look out for the return of Hawley. He was thankful he hadn't been sent out on patrol with Malcolm and the others, as he wasn't sure he could sit a horse with the way he currently felt. He'd taken to barely sleeping now, instead opting to take the watch for others so they might rest. If he slept, the nightmares came, so it was easier to sleep as little as possible. As he turned to walk to the edge of the terrace where they were standing, Euan stumbled and caught himself against the wall.

"Euan, lad, are ye all right?" Lochiel asked.

"I dinnae know," he said.

Lochiel frowned. "Ye are dismissed, lad. Ye have been on duty with little sleep for days. Take yerself to a bed and get some rest. Ye dinnae look well," he said, looking to Iain. "Tell the others Euan is nae well and that I have ordered him to get some rest, so they are nae to disturb him."

"Aye, Lochiel," Iain replied and left to do as he was instructed.

Euan nodded, bowed shakily, and left. There hadn't been a good night's sleep since this had all begun, but it was worse now. The nightmares of killing Alexander Munro, of those he'd killed in battle coming for him, haunted his sleep. He kept his hand on the wall as he made his way down the stairs, needing to stop a few times to regain his balance. It felt as though his body were moving on its own, without his direction, but he didn't care. As long as it took him to a bed, that was all that mattered. By the time he reached the bottom of the stairs, his head felt heavy, and everything seemed to move too slowly. Sound was muffled and far away, and all he could do was stand there.

"Euan?"

He turned his head to look at Malcolm, who'd just returned from patrol, but said nothing as Malcolm moved to his side.

"Lad," was all he managed to get out before Euan's eyes rolled back in his head and he collapsed to the floor.

Euan wasn't aware of anything as he was carried into a room and undressed by others before being deposited into the first true bed he'd slept on in months. They stoked a fire to keep the room warm, covered him with a blanket, and left him to sleep for however long he needed. He had no idea how long he'd slept before he heard someone whisper his name, a woman's voice, familiar and yet not all at once. He opened his eyes, no longer fuzzy-headed and exhausted, and sat up to find the last person he'd ever expected standing at the end of the bed.

"Grace? What are ye doing here?" he asked.

She said nothing, smiling at him as she walked to the bed, before sitting down on the edge of it. Euan didn't move away from her as she reached out and touched his cheek with her fingertips, before sliding them over his lips. It made him shiver, his eyes closing with a sigh before she replaced her fingertips with her lips. The contact flooded him with a feeling so intense it felt as though someone had filled him with the fire still burning bright in the hearth, and he breathed in deeply, pulling her close to him. Turning her across his body even as he continued to kiss her, he felt her join him on the bed to lie beneath him, and her hand caressed his cheek when he pulled back to look at her.

"My love," he whispered. The kiss, the feeling of it, brought the memory of the last time they were together to the forefront. "I have been waiting for ye, and ye have come to me again at last."

She smiled up at him. "Yes, I have. I am sorry I was away so long, but your mind is finally quiet."

"Aye, for the first time in months," he replied.

"You have needed me."

"More than I could possibly say. Ye are the only thing that could banish these nightmares and keep me in this world, as ye have done for so long."

"I am so sorry you must suffer such terrible things. I wish I could take them from you, but I cannot. At least not yet."

"Are ye really here?" he asked, stroking her face, trying to memorize it. His fingertips traced the lines of her cheeks, her jaw, her lips.

"No, I am not here, not truly, just as it always is. You are dreaming, and we are together again in that place that belongs only to us. For a moment you get to see something that waits ahead for you, something your soul has always known would come. You have always waited, have you not?"

"Aye," he whispered. "Even though I did nae know what I was waiting for."

"You have waited for me, just as I have waited for you in my own way. We have always met here when you needed me or when I needed you, but soon it will no longer be in dreams. Neither of us will understand it when we truly meet, but we will know."

"When?"

"Soon. Very soon."

"I dinnae understand how this is happening but, *leannan*, how glad I am that ye have come. I want to stay with ye here, always. Dinnae leave me here alone, in the darkness of death and war."

"You cannot stay, for this is the last time you will see me here."

"What do ye mean?"

"It is the last time I will only be a dream to you, and you to me."

"Thank God, for if ye were to tell me I would never see ye again, I dinnae know if I could take it. Will I know ye when we meet in the waking world?"

"No. Well, not exactly anyway."

"I will survive this war?"

"Not in the way you think."

Euan frowned. "But I will. I have to in order to meet ye."

"Your survival will depend on me, but neither of us will recognize the other by sight; instead, we will feel it. It will terrify us, confuse us, but we will know. When it is time, I will do what I must to bind us together in the physical world as we have always been bound to each other here."

"Do ye —"

"Look like this? Yes. But when you wake up you will have forgotten, as you must do."

"Why must I?"

"You must feel and not see," she said as she placed a soft hand over his heart.

"Do ye love me now?"

"Of course I do, more than I have words for. I love you,

and I always will. There are so many walls around me, but you have gotten through them. I do not know how this happens or why, but I have loved our meetings."

"As have I, and I have loved ye for so long. All of those times ye came to me when I needed ye most, my comfort, my strength, my heart. As I know I have said before, this is yers," he said, covering her hand on his heart. "As I am yers and have always been."

"Then you must live. Fight to live, fight for me, for us. For what waits for you."

"I will," he whispered before bringing his lips to hers again in a deep kiss that once more set him on fire. He could do this forever. No wonder he'd never felt truly satisfied!

She pressed into him, meeting his kiss, flattening her other hand on his back in what he knew was the same desire for him that he felt for her. He could feel the warmth of her skin through her dress, the softness of her hands, her racing heart. All he wanted in this moment was to cling to her, to keep her with him, his light in the blackness that clouded his mind and his heart. He'd begun to secretly wish for death, a wish he was too frightened to admit even to himself. Death would end this, death would set him free from a world he'd so long felt outside of, free from the memories and nightmares that tormented him, free from the life of service that stretched before him, a life he no longer wanted. Though he wished for it, he'd never taken the easy way and stood still in a battle to let someone end him. He'd always fought back, his self-preservation taking over, and perhaps she was why.

"Stay," he whispered against her lips. "Please, stay."

"I cannot, no matter how I might want to, and I do."

"I am afraid," he said, the confession spilling from him. "Afraid of myself, of what I am becoming, of what I have done. I cannae do this much longer, cannae live this way, and though I am nae worthy of it or of ye, I beg ye: save me."

"I *will* save you; I promise I will. Hold on just a little longer;

it is almost time. I know what you want, what you cannot even admit to yourself. Please, Euan, you must be strong. I need you to be strong and not give in to those dark thoughts. You are worthy of everything you would deny yourself. Please do not be afraid; I am with you, always with you. What you have done is not what you are."

Her words brought a gentle sob from him, though he managed to keep the tears at bay. What he had done was not what he was. He'd had no idea how much he'd needed to hear that until now.

"You need to rest. The nightmares will not find you here, for I will protect you."

"To rest means to leave ye and I cannae. Just a little longer."

She reached up and tucked some of his hair behind his ear. "You are afraid I will not come."

"Perhaps, but I also fear returning and what will come with it, what I will be asked to do. I fear the darkness and being trapped within it, unable to get out and ye unable to reach me."

"I will always reach you because there is nothing that can keep us apart. Rest now," she replied.

No matter what else he might have wanted, her voice seemed to control him, and he lay back down beside her. He rested his head on her shoulder and closed his eyes, feeling all the tension leave his body as she wrapped her arms around him. One of her hands stroked his hair, her fingers running through the long strands, and he sighed. There was a perfection in this, in this feeling of her holding him, the way she fit against him. No more questions, no more fear, just rest. He felt her kiss his forehead as he began to drift back into sleep.

"Dinnae forsake me, no matter what comes," he whispered.

"Never. There is nothing you could do that would make me do such a thing. I will stay with you for a while and help you rest. No more nightmares."

Euan nodded, unable to say anything else as sleep claimed him, and when he woke again much later, he felt as though he were coming out of the most restful sleep he'd ever had. Smiling, he rubbed his eyes. There was something there, something just beyond his remembering, a lovely dream he wanted to hang onto but couldn't. It didn't matter anyway, though it had been nice to have a sleep restful enough for dreams instead of nightmares. As he sat up and stretched, he saw his clothes draped over a chair waiting for him. Using the basin left by the fire to clean himself, he dressed and headed out to find Lochiel and the rest of the men.

"Ah, there ye are at last," Iain said as Euan stepped out into the hall. "Ye look much better."

"I feel much better, thank ye. How long was I asleep?"

"About a day and a half."

"So long! Ye should have woken me!"

"Lochiel ordered us nae to."

"Have I missed anything?"

"No. All has been quiet. We can hear the guns between the regiments and the castle, but otherwise naught."

"Thank ye," Euan said with a nod, and he went to find Lochiel, who was standing on the same terrace. "Lochiel," Euan said with a bow when he reached him.

"Euan," Lochiel replied with a nod. "Ye look much better than last I saw ye."

"Aye, thank ye."

"A wonder what rest can do, hm?" he said before he watched Euan offer a weak smile, and he shook his head. "What are ye about avoiding sleep? And dinnae tell me it is so the men can rest."

Euan rested his hands on the stone rail and looked out across the park. "I had nightmares when I slept, so it was easier nae to."

Lochiel nodded. "We have all had those. I am sorry to hear it, lad."

"I think I may be past it now."

"I hope so. We need ye rested and well."

"Have we been called in to relieve the Lowlanders?" he asked, wanting to take the conversation away from himself.

"No, thank Christ."

Euan chuckled. "Still to occupy Falkirk then?"

"Aye, which is fine. It is important to do, so I have no problem with it, and it saves me from dealing with the rest. The prince has apparently been ill but is on the mend."

"Shame. Maybe he is nae sleeping either."

"Maybe he is busy shagging Sir Hugh's niece at Bannockburn."

Euan started laughing. "Aye, maybe."

"Who in the hell is that?" Lochiel asked, narrowing his eyes at an approaching figure.

"One of the prince's aides-de-camp," Euan replied, though seeing the man coming didn't put him at ease in any way.

"Lochiel," the man said with a small bow as he finally reached them. "I have a message for one of your men."

"Whom do ye seek?" Lochiel asked curiously.

"A Captain Cameron, sir."

"I have a few of those, so ye will have to be more specific."

Euan pressed his lips together and cleared his throat to keep from laughing.

"I apologize. Captain Euan Cameron."

Hearing his name, Euan's merriment ceased immediately.

"That does nae help, for there are more than a few with that name."

The aide faltered. "I … he said it was the Captain Cameron who spoke with him at Penrith."

"Who said?" Lochiel asked, not yet revealing that the person sought stood right beside him.

"From His Highness, the prince, sir," he replied. "He wishes Captain Cameron to report with all haste to Bannockburn."

"Is there any particular reason?"

"I am not privy to those details, sir. All I was told was to seek him out and bring him to the prince."

Lochiel looked over at Euan. "Ye had best go, lad; ye dinnae wish to keep him waiting."

"Aye, Lochiel," Euan said, bowing before he followed the messenger.

Euan quickly saddled Absalon and set off for Bannockburn, a trip of thirteen miles. It was quite cold, and he found he wished he were back in that room with the roaring fire at Callendar House, but no such luck was to be his. They made the journey as quickly as possible, though he knew doing so would mean he likely remained overnight in Bannockburn so that Absalon could rest and they could also allow time for any correspondence to be readied to send back with Euan.

As he stepped inside, he sighed in relief at the warmth and the escape from the biting wind outside. Euan was shown to a small study with no chance to freshen up or prepare himself. As the door shut behind him, he noticed the prince at the desk, writing something, though he paused at the sound of the door and looked up.

"Ah! There you are, Captain."

"Yer Highness," Euan said with a bow. "Is everything well?"

"Yes and no, but do not fear, for I am not upset with you. Please, sit," he said, gesturing to a chair near the fire. "You must be freezing."

Euan made his way to the chair and seated himself without delay. "Aye, I will nae deny that the wind was painful just now, Yer Highness."

The prince rose from the desk and made his way over to a table, picking up a tray with tea and other treats on it, and placing it on the table before Euan, who looked at it with curiosity.

"Please," the prince said, "do help yourself to some tea and a bite to eat. It is all fresh."

"Thank ye for yer generosity, Yer Highness," Euan said with a nod before he poured himself a cup of the tea and held the warm china between his hands.

"No titles, please. I have called you here because I have need of your conversation, as I did before."

"Ah, I see. Ye seem as though ye are feeling far better."

"I do, thank you. I heard you were behind our outstanding victory at Falkirk."

"At least partially," Euan said, smiling. "I led the Camerons."

"But it was your strategy, I am told."

"Aye, I helped set it."

"Well done, but then we already knew you were skilled in such things. You have demonstrated it many times over the last months."

"Thank ye for the compliment. It was what I was trained to do, after all."

"That is true."

"What is really troubling ye?"

The prince looked at him curiously. "What makes you say so?"

"Ye dinnae hide it particularly well."

"Or perhaps you are skilled at seeing otherwise."

"That is also a possibility. There are also the reports that ye drink often."

The prince sighed, closing his eyes and rubbing his forehead. "Who else knows?"

"Everyone. Ye surely must know that nothing will stay secret long."

"Yes, I do drink, perhaps more than I should of late."

"Why?"

"I seek an escape. Sometimes I find it; other times I do not."

"An escape from what?"

"All of this. I … no, I cannot say that, for you would not understand it and it may get back to the men."

"Ye would be surprised at what I understand, and I will say naught to anyone."

The prince regarded him in silence for a moment, as though he were weighing the options in his head before he spoke. "Have you ever wished to be out of a situation so badly that death seems welcoming?"

"Many times, unfortunately. Is that what ye feel?"

"At times lately, yes. We are doing well, but I cannot help but feel pulled in so many directions, and I hate it. I miss my old life, where this was all talk and I was not expected to know everything."

"I understand that quite well, but at the same time, it is nae so. This is where ye are now, and all ye can do is keep moving."

"And if I do not want to?"

Euan sighed, taking a drink of his tea. "Ye have no choice. There are nine thousand men out there who are depending on ye to lead them. They are looking to ye. What do ye think will happen if ye fall by yer own hand or by getting yerself killed in a battle? Who would lead us?"

"I am sure someone would keep going and fight to bring my father back to his throne."

"I understand that yer spirits are low, but ye cannae let that cloud yer judgment. Instead, be buoyed by the fact that we have won another battle and done so decisively. Think about what ye wish to do next and where ye wish to go."

"That is part of the problem. I am pulled in every direction by my advisors."

"But ye dinnae meet with the chiefs."

"Why should I?" he replied, his tone becoming angry. "They do nothing but object to everything I say and do their best to undermine me."

"No, they dinnae. They are trying to get ye to understand the best way to move forward in this country. Yer advisors dinnae know this place or the people here, and it shows."

"I have no wish to discuss them."

"As ye wish," Euan replied, though the dismissal irritated him. "I understand where ye are now, what ye feel. There was a time when I was in France that I wished for naught more than death to save me from the torture I endured daily. What stopped me was the thought of all those who would be hurt by my death, my mam first amongst them. For ye, the stakes are even higher. Who would be hurt by this? Ye would abandon those ye claim as yer subjects? They have followed ye this far only for ye to abandon them in yer melancholy. What would yer father say? If someday ye wish to be king, ye must know that this is naught compared to what ye will face when millions of lives depend on what ye decide. Being in power is nae easy, but it was what ye were born to, what ye were raised for. Ye cannae hide from that responsibility, no matter how much ye might wish to."

"But I could if I —"

"No," Euan said, the word and tone firm. "Ye know better than that. Think with yer head and push back against those shadows that beckon ye."

"How did you manage it?"

"Whenever I was at my lowest, I sought for the light to guide me, the feeling that I had much to do, and that if I only persisted, something perfect awaited me."

"What was it?"

"I dinnae know, for I have nae found it yet. The light is always there if ye seek it. It could be something small, a memory perhaps. Think of something that ye can call back on that pleases ye. The thought of seeing yer family again, the pride of yer father when ye succeed, a beautiful flower in a garden, or the way a summer wind sounds in the trees. Whatever it is, think of returning to it and let that thought pull ye out."

The prince nodded. "It is good advice, just as you gave me before, but perhaps more difficult than it sounds."

"Of course it is. Naught is ever easy, but all can be overcome if ye try."

"Thank you," the prince said, a small smile on his lips. "I knew that if I spoke to you, I might find my way."

"I will always do what I can."

"You do more than you know. Come, finish your tea and tell me about the battle, then you can get some rest."

Things remained quiet at Falkirk and Stirling until the 30th, when word came that Cumberland had reached Edinburgh, regrouping with Hawley's survivors and advancing on Stirling. Broughton arrived in Falkirk to demand Lord Murray help draw up a battle plan, which Lord Murray refused to do, instead sending Broughton back to the prince with a letter explaining they'd been quite weakened by desertion while spending time at Falkirk and were thus in no state to engage with Cumberland. Lord Murray's intent was to retreat to the Highlands for the winter, where the various clans could spend the time seizing government forts and reducing their ability to send reinforcements.

Word came back that the plan was accepted, in part because de Gordon had made a complete mess of managing the artillery, leaving it open to the castle guns, which immediately destroyed it. The remaining guns at Stirling were spiked before daybreak, and the regiments withdrew in silence from Falkirk to meet the rest of the army at St. Ninian's as the area around Stirling Castle fell silent for the first time in two months.

When they reached St. Ninian's, the prince ordered that the stockpiled ammunition be destroyed so it wouldn't fall into Cumberland's hands when he arrived. The work began quickly, with carts being taken out to the waste ground where it would be detonated. What none of them noticed was that one of the barrels had spilled some of its contents, and as Euan and some of the others stood with Lochiel while Cameron men loaded the next cart, it was accidentally ignited. There was no time for anyone to react, the blast sending people and stone from the church in every direction. Euan felt himself leave his feet, and he hit the ground some distance away with punishing force before he lost consciousness. When he came to, his ears were ringing, so he couldn't hear. Lifting his head, he saw people running every which way, the church itself in ruins, and the unmoving bodies of some of his clansmen.

Euan's body ached, he knew he was bleeding, but nothing felt broken. His head spinning and his vision blurred, Euan pushed himself up and stumbled forward to check them, finding many of them dead. He then saw Lochiel, his eyes going wide in horror as he rushed toward his chief. Lochiel groaned, still alive, but Euan had no idea how badly he might be injured. Those men who could move on their own did so and helped others get out. The Cameron men pulled Lochiel away and found Archibald to tend to him.

"He is lucky to be alive," Archibald said. "All of ye who remain alive are lucky. Every last one of ye should, by all rights, be dead on the ground with the others. His arm looks to be broken, and he has a fair few cuts, but he will live."

The men present breathed a sigh of relief and said a silent prayer of thanks. Euan rested his head in his hands, his head and body aching, feeling nauseated. It hardly registered when Archibald came to him next after checking out some of the other men.

"Euan? Can ye hear me?" When Euan didn't respond, Archibald gave his shoulder a gentle shake. "Euan!"

"What?" Euan said, his voice too loud as he looked up at the shake, seeing Archibald saying something but unable to hear it.

"Can ye hear me, lad?"

"I cannae understand ye. Ye are whispering."

Archibald sighed and shook his head. "I am sure yer hearing will return soon enough. Where are ye ailing?" he said with a raised voice closer to Euan's ear.

"I feel sick. My head hurts terribly and …" Euan managed to get out before the nausea caught up with him and he turned and vomited, which only made his head hurt worse.

Archibald frowned, and when Euan turned back to him, he could see the bleeding cut near his temple. "Christ."

He reached out to examine it, but it did not seem deep. The same side of his face had abrasions on it from where he'd hit the ground, but the young man seemed remarkably unharmed.

"I swear the Lord is on yer side, Euan Cameron," he muttered.

"I swear to Christ I am going to kill him myself!"

Archibald turned as his brother yelled and saw his men holding him down. Rolling his eyes, he hurried back to him. "Donald, ye are going nowhere at the moment. We need to tend to yer arm, and ye cannae kill the prince's advisors."

"I can! I bet it would be easy! Euan could do it!"

"Ye are angry and in pain. Stop speaking nonsense."

"They have put me and my men in danger for the last time this winter! We are nae going north with him and the others. The Camerons are returning to Achnacarry to see to our business there and recover!"

There was a sense of jubilation that swept through the Cameron men at this order. They were *finally* going home.

CHAPTER 21

"MY GOODNESS," SPECIALIST GEORGE said.

"Which part are ye referring to?"

"All of it, really. I'm so sorry you were forced into the situation with Alexander Munro."

Euan sighed. "So am I, but that is what war does. It makes enemies of friends. He made his choice, and I made mine."

"But it still bothers you a great deal."

"It was nae even a year ago."

"That's a very good point. Do you still have nightmares?"

"All the time. I still had them even when Grace came to get me. When I have them now, she is there, always there, to help comfort and calm me. She will sit up and talk with me until I feel I am ready to rest again. Her presence is the one thing that is sure to help."

"You had another dream, you said. After Falkirk," George said.

"I did."

"Do you remember any of it, or is it like all the others?"

"The same. I remember the feelings, but I cannae remember the dreams themselves. All I know is that she once again came to me when I needed her, and that is all that matters."

"Let's discuss the lead-up to the battle. How did it feel when Lochiel asked you to command the men?"

"It was an honor, and still is."

"It seems a sharp turn from where he was," George noted.

"Aye, it does, but he was nae always as I know he seems to ye. It felt to me that this was his way of showing me he was proud, that he trusted me, that he had faith in me," Euan explained.

"Do you still feel that way about it?"

"Aye, in a way. Maybe it was nae pride, but he was certainly telling me he had faith in me, or he would nae have entrusted the men to me."

"Were you concerned about your ability?"

"No, it was the one thing I was sure of. I could do it; I knew I could."

"And you were quite successful."

"I was, and while I should have been elated, I found I could nae be."

"Because of Alexander?"

"Aye."

"You were also wounded yourself."

"Aye, and lucky it was nae worse. That bastard got the worst of it," Euan said, his smile dark.

"It's shocking to me that they tended to you with no sort of provision for pain," George said.

"There was nae time for it, and there was nae enough to drink as well as treat with. They used it for cleaning wounds, and it was the right choice, no matter how painful it was."

"You mentioned that the prince was said to often be drinking."

"Oh aye, he was, which only made things worse. Some of the common men were starting to resent him; he was losing support left and right but refused to see it. He took no care of anything or anyone, save himself at that point, at least that was how it seemed, and he left much of the planning to his advisors, who knew naught. As ye can see, that was a disaster for Stirling."

"Did you ever find out if he was with Sir Hugh's niece?" George asked with a wry smile.

Euan laughed. "Nae absolutely, but she was a comely lass, and he was royalty. He would nae have had to try all that hard."

It was George's turn to laugh now. "I suppose that's fair."

"Then, of course, ye had the refusal to press our advantage at Falkirk, which was a mistake."

"Indeed. And the murder of Chief Munro."

"Ach, Christ, I promise ye that was the reason they came after us in the aftermath of Culloden."

"I don't doubt it. Were you surprised to receive the summons from the prince?"

"Aye, I was indeed."

"He seemed quite willing to confide in you."

"Aye, and I am nae sure why, if I am honest. He barely knew me."

"As we discussed before, perhaps he saw someone his own age who was worldly and educated enough to be able to understand him in ways others might not."

"I had nae thought of it that way, but perhaps."

"In this case you were very able to relate."

"I was. It was strange to see someone who had so much be mentally in the same place I had once been and still sometimes find myself. I knew he was a man the same as any other, no matter his title, but it is always strange to see it from someone ye believe should have no cause for it."

"Every advantage brings its own problems."

"Aye, that is true enough."

"Did it seem to help him?"

"Aye, oddly enough, it did. He seemed to rally a bit and made the decision to head north. Though we did nae go with him there, they were successful in battle, destroying the castle in Inverness after a siege."

"But that didn't extend to Culloden?"

"It did, from what I understand. I know I have made him sound disinterested, nae a leader, and that is a mistake on my part. He was at those battles, all of them except for Falkirk, far closer to the action than he should have been, watching and directing. As I said before, he was nae a stupid man, nor was he incapable of being in command. He was often willing to listen and take direction until the fracture happened, and I saw him correct something his advisors had set out more than once. When he was nae in the midst of melancholy, he inspired the men, walked with them, talked with them. Once, he even held a contest to see who was the better shot, giving any man who wished to try a chance, allowing them to use his own fine sporting rifles. He won, however, and nae because they let him."

George chuckled. "That sounds far different from the man I've heard of so far."

"Aye, and as I said, that is my own fault. I have told ye all the bad and none of the good, and there was plenty of good. After our first meeting in Penrith, he would often greet me if he saw me or sometimes have me translate for him when we were talking to the men who spoke only Gaelic. He would tell terrible jokes," Euan said, pausing to laugh, "but on purpose. What the English did to him was nae fair, but war never is."

"What do you mean?"

"I have read the 'history' that is out there, and all of it makes him look terrible. All of it. Now things are coming out to contradict that, but the damage was done. Once he shed his princely distance, he was a decent man. I am told that, at Culloden, he was again watching from far closer than he should have been, and when he saw it starting to go wrong, he actually tried to charge in with us but was prevented from doing so. Watching us be slaughtered broke him, and I am nae sure he ever recovered. He spent months on the run afterward with Lochiel and other chiefs, desperate to get to France, and was almost caught a few times. He suffered physically and mentally, nae divorced from it as many leaders are. Once he returned, he discovered there was no more support left for him and the cause was as dead as the men on the moor. Word came to him of the destruction Cumberland had wrought upon the Highlands, and it only served to crush him further.

He sank into depression and drink after that, and I cannae say I blame him for it. What do ye do when yer entire life's work is destroyed? How do ye move on and find a new purpose? He could nae, and I feel badly for him because of it."

"That's the most complimentary I think you've been of him."

"I realized the impression ye were getting, and I did nae want to add to it. I wanted someone to know it was nae all bad."

"That's very noble of you, but that you should wish to do so doesn't surprise me. So, you helped him and returned to Falkirk where Lochiel and Lord Murray awaited you."

"Aye, I returned with correspondence, and when they asked why I was sent for, I told them it was because he wished to hear the details of Falkirk directly from me."

"Clever. You were then called to meet the prince at St. Ninians, and the explosion followed."

"Aye, the explosion. We were lucky there were nae more dead, and those of us who lived were lucky to do so."

"So, Lochiel decides to return home."

Euan smiled. "Aye. Home."

Though the prince tried to talk him out of it, Lochiel remained insistent and refused to travel north. Many of the other chiefs concurred, following his lead and taking their forces home for the rest of the winter so that they might rest, recover, and regroup for a spring and summer campaign. The winter would prevent any further hostilities on either side, as travel with so many men, wagons, and artillery would become impossible. The Camerons were quick to get on the march for the one hundred mile trip from Stirling to Achnacarry. They would have to cross some difficult ground to avoid the route that would take them past Perth and thus too close to Edinburgh, as well as the route that would take them past Fort

William. There were Hanoverians massed in both locations, and the Camerons were in no shape to get into conflict with any of them. It would take longer due to terrain and weather, but they would manage it as swiftly as they could.

As they neared Achnacarry after a week on the road, there were smiles on the faces of every man in the regiment. Home was in sight; loved ones, rest, and a bit of peace awaited them. The drummers began playing, as did the pipers, and the Cameron regiment broke into song for the final push to the castle. The sound brought people from their homes, shouting and cheering to see Lochiel and his men return. When they marched into the castle yard, people poured out, cheering and crying, an emotion shared by the weary warriors. They might have been dirty, wounded, and exhausted, but none of that mattered as wives and children rushed into the arms of long-gone husbands and fathers, and sons were welcomed home. There was lament as some discovered their kin hadn't returned and never would. Euan dismounted and said a prayer of thanksgiving as his feet touched his native soil for the first time in seven months. He hadn't expected to be here, and probably shouldn't be after all he'd lived through, and he was grateful he'd been wrong. His own mother wasn't here, and he knew she wouldn't be. She didn't work at the castle and would've had no reason to be here, and it wasn't as if anyone had known the men were coming. Euan took the initiative amongst the reunions to lead his horse back to the stables.

"Euan!"

He stopped to look as someone called his name, turning just in time to catch Brenda as she flung herself into his arms and hugged him while she cried in relief. He returned her embrace; it felt good to have someone welcome him in such a way.

"Thank God ye are safe!"

"Aye. I have much to thank Him for."

"What happened?"

Euan shook his head. "I cannae tell ye and dinnae wish to speak of it. Please, dinnae ask me," he replied.

"If that is yer wish," she said before moving to kiss him.

Euan turned his head away and stepped back, keeping her at arm's length, taking her hands and squeezing them with a smile before lifting one to kiss it. He saw the hurt in her expression, but he had no interest in such affection now.

"Thank ye for the welcome," he said before releasing her hands and walking away with his horse.

Once he made sure Absalon was rubbed down and taken care of, he bathed, shaved, and then sought dismissal from Lochiel, which was quickly granted. Euan started the walk toward home with a smile on his face, his heart light. The weight sitting upon him for months was gone, at least temporarily, and it was a relief. As he reached the cottage, he could see his mother inside as she struggled to reach something. He smiled and very quietly made his way inside.

"I dinnae know how I will get ye down, damn ye, but I shall! I should have had Euan bring all of this down before he left," she grumbled.

Euan reached over the top of her head and pulled the basket down.

"Ach, thank ye, Son. I could nae have reached it without —" she began, then froze. After a long moment, she turned around.

"Hello, Mam."

Aileen screamed, a mixture of joy and shock, before she pulled Euan into her arms, all while still screaming. "Ye are home! Ye are safe! Praise and thanks be to the Lord God for bringing my boy home!"

Euan laughed, hugging his mother in return, and it wasn't long before his laughter dissolved into tears. It was a mix of happiness and sadness, of relief from months of stress and anxiety. Aileen held him, crying with him, so happy was she to have him home with her again.

"Oh, my sweet bairn. It is well; ye are home now. Ye are safe here."

After a long few moments, the emotion slowed, and he took a deep breath. "I have missed ye, Mam."

Aileen pulled back to look at him, seeing the still healing cut on his head and the abrasions on his face. "Christ, what has happened to ye?"

"Ammunition exploded as we were leaving Stirling. I am all right, but others were nae so lucky."

"It is more than that, love. Ye look exhausted, nae at all the son who left me," she said as she stroked his cheeks. "There is such pain in ye; ye are haunted by it."

Euan nodded. She wasn't wrong about any of it, and he wouldn't bother trying to hide it from her. He couldn't even say he was the same son who had left here seven months ago, because he absolutely wasn't. "I dinnae think I can speak of it, or that I want to. Perhaps someday I will tell ye, but nae now."

"Is the war over, then?"

"No. We will carry on in the spring and summer. The weather is too bad for us to do anything now."

"So ye will leave again."

"Nae for quite some time. We may be gone for a week here or there, but we will come back. We will nae depart for true battle until the spring."

"Are ye at least winning?"

"I would say we are rather even at this point."

Aileen sighed. "Let me treat those cuts for ye, and then ye can get out of those clothes so I can wash them."

"They probably need it desperately," Euan admitted, chuckling.

"Aye, they do. Ye are in luck that I spent my time while ye were gone making ye a new set. I thought ye might need them, and I was right. These will be good for naught but work now."

"I can wear them when we resume and leave the newer ones here to wait for me."

"Whatever ye wish to do, love. Come, let us get started. Ye can eat and then go to sleep."

Sleep. Sleep sounded like the grandest thing in the world. Sleep at home, in his own bed, on his own land, where it was safe for now. Euan didn't resist her and sat patiently while she treated his cuts, helped him to undress, and got him into a clean shirt. She cried out in alarm at seeing the scars on the once smooth skin of his torso, the one from Falkirk still healing. He was thankful she had the restraint not to ask him where they'd come from. A bowl of stew was placed in front of him, and he ate it so fast he hardly tasted it. After that, he crawled into his bed, asleep before he'd even fully settled himself.

When Euan finally stirred again, he found it hard to open his eyes, and every part of him felt heavy. But the panic came quickly. Where was he? What was happening? It was too quiet! He sat up with a gasp of shock, his heart pounding as he looked around him. It took a moment for his mind to catch up to his body before he remembered he was home, and he closed his eyes, forcing himself to breathe.

"Ye are all right, Euan," Aileen said.

"Mam. Thank God."

"Forgot where ye were?"

"Aye. It has been so long since I have woken to such silence."

Aileen smiled. "Ye needed the rest."

He opened his eyes and looked at her, then looked at the light outside. It was mid-morning now. "Ye should have gotten me up to help ye with the morning work, Mam," he said in admonishment.

Aileen looked at him, arching an eyebrow. "How long do ye think ye have been asleep, Euan?"

"The night?"

She shook her head and laughed. "Ye have slept for two days, Son."

"Two …" he began before his eyes widened. "I need to get back to see what they need from me!"

"There is no need. Someone came while ye were asleep to convey the order that ye are at yer ease for at least a week and have no need to report to the castle. It seems Lochiel is aware of how worn his men are."

"It has been near-constant movement, but I am sure it has much to do with how weary he is as well. He was gravely injured at Stirling in the same explosion," Euan said as he dropped back onto his bed.

"I know ye dinnae wish to speak of what ye have done, but can ye at least tell me where ye have been?"

Euan smiled and turned his head toward her. "Aye, I can tell ye that, but I think ye will nae believe me."

Aileen chuckled. "Go on, then."

"From Glenfinnan we went north, then we went to Perth. From Perth to Edinburgh."

"Edinburgh!"

"Aye. We took the city and held it for six weeks."

"I am sure the English did nae like that."

"No, they did nae," Euan said, chuckling. "From there we went into England."

Aileen's face went pale. "Ye went …"

"Aye, into England. Took Carlisle and went through Manchester all the way to Derby."

"Where is that?"

"About four days' march from London."

"Christ, so close to them!"

"We turned back then, as we knew we had nae the strength to face them yet. We may still go back if we are stronger, which is what Lord Murray wants. After we retreated, we went to Glasgow, then to Stirling and Falkirk."

"Who was with ye?"

"Macpherson, Murray, Clanranald, Glengarry, MacDonald of Glencoe, Appin, Atholl, Fraser, and others."

"Well, at least ye had close allies in the Macphersons and Frasers."

"Aye."

"Did ye see the inside of the palace at Edinburgh?"

"No," Euan replied, deciding not to mention that it was his own choice in solidarity with his men. "I was nae allowed inside, as I had no business to be there."

"Ye have been so many places I never could have dreamed ye would have gone."

"And will likely go to more still."

"Nae just now ye are nae. Get up and dress yerself so ye can eat and then do as ye please."

"If do as I please means helping ye as I should, then aye," Euan replied as he got out of bed, stretched, and reached for the fresh clothes Aileen had put out, happy to return to the ordinary for a while.

Euan spent the rest of the week helping Aileen in whatever ways he could, seeing to things she couldn't do herself or things he saw needed repair. It was a much-needed balm for his soul to just exist and put the war from his mind, and the normal work of living made it easy to let go of it. He took time to walk and take in the beauty that was present, even in winter. It was good to keep his endurance up, for he knew he'd have need of it soon enough. At the end of it, he reported back to Achnacarry and learned that the plan was to lay siege to Fort William in a few weeks' time after joining the others in a siege at Fort Augustus. The Campbells had been raiding Cameron land out of the garrison, and Lochiel wanted to put a stop to it. Men were called back and drilled, to keep them sharp, but it was nowhere near as intense because it didn't need to be. If they kept up with drilling during the break, they could remain battle-ready with no change in their efficiency from a winter off.

Aileen wasn't pleased at the thought of Euan leaving again, but he assured her it wouldn't be long, and they would only be at Forts William and Augustus. When the Cameron men departed once more, they were rested, healed, and ready for a fight. That they had the chance to go against the Campbells was a bonus.

"Are ye ready for this, lad?" Lochiel asked.

"Oh, aye," Euan said, smiling. "It is time for a bit of revenge."

"Fire!"

The men watched as yet another mortar sailed toward the walls of Fort Augustus but caused no real damage, groaning in irritation.

"Reload!"

Though the walls of Fort Augustus were not impressive by any means, the cannons the Jacobites currently had at their disposal had thus far been ineffective against them. Their reconnaissance had told them that the walls were feeble, the artillery installations set in plain view, and defended by only three companies of men. One of those companies had already been neutralized by a straightforward assault on the barracks where they'd been hidden by the governor of the fort. Now, all that remained was breaching the wall and taking the fort itself, something they'd been attempting since the day before.

"Fire!"

The men of Cameron, Glengarry, and Keppoch watched the newest shot make its way toward the fort, the trajectory just a bit different as it carried on the wind.

"Wait, that one is going over and nae at the wall," Iain complained. "That is a waste."

"I dinnae think it was supposed to miss the wall, but the wind gusted," Euan replied as they watched it crash through a roof inside the fort.

In the next instant, a massive explosion rocked the fort and the ground, sending out a shock wave that threw the watching Scots to the ground. Euan lifted his head and surveyed the damage, then started laughing hysterically.

"What is it?" Malcolm asked.

"The shot landed in the magazine! Oh, that is a thing of beauty!"

The others scrambled up to look.

"Sweet Christ, it did!" Malcolm said as everyone standing there joined Euan in laughing.

When the dust cleared, the breach was seen, the fort now open to an easy and swift assault. The Scots massed into their regiments, all fifteen hundred of them ready to storm the breach, but before they could a white flag was waved, bringing a groan of disappointment from those gathered. The fort was surrendered, a small garrison of their own left in place, cannons taken, and then the army took to the road, heading for Fort William. Before they departed, both Lochiel and the Keppoch chief wrote to the prince to alert him that they had together declared war on Clan Campbell for war crimes. The siege of Fort William was personal for the two clans, who were determined to take it or kill as many Campbells as they could in the attempt.

Upon arriving on the 20th of March, the Jacobite army opened fire on the fort. To the dismay of Euan and others, the attack was entrusted to de Gordon, who'd so badly managed the siege at Stirling. In the hope that the governor might surrender, a drummer was sent with a letter requiring that he do so. It was returned with the response that they were prepared to defend Fort William to the last. All the men could do now was to wait for the mortars and cannons to do their work while they guarded the batteries. The sounds of mortar and cannon fire seemed ceaseless as each side worked to outgun the other but got nowhere. The battery on the ground above the governor's garden began firing round shot, grapeshot, nails, and red-hot pieces of iron; the last were intended to lodge in the timbers and set them alight, something the army had become quite specialized in since Stirling. This action was enough to spur the fort to send a sortie of one hundred and fifty men out to assault the Jacobite batteries. The Jacobite relief forces were unable to make it in time, and the soldiers spiked two mortars and a cannon. They'd then charged the battery above the garden, where Euan and his men held them back even as two waves of reinforcements were sent to bolster the government forces.

Lochiel and Keppoch were furious when word came that the prince refused to reinforce them or send the larger guns they'd need, and on the 2nd of April, Euan was summoned by his chief.

"Euan," Lochiel said as the young man approached him.

"Aye, Lochiel."

"It is time to do what ye do best, lad."

Euan raised an eyebrow. That statement could mean a good many things, and he wondered which one it would be this time.

"The prince will nae reinforce us, so there is no possible way for us to win here. All we can do is take as many of them as we can before we go."

A small smile appeared on Euan's face. "I think I can manage that for ye."

"I know ye will. Go."

Euan bowed and headed out. "Malcolm! Iain! Duncan! I need ye!"

Within an hour, the four men were waiting, hidden in the darkness. Fort William didn't have a dedicated water supply, and that meant the soldiers had to leave the fort for water on a regular basis. Euan, Iain, Duncan, and Malcolm waited as a small group made its way out to fetch water, giving the party a few moments to feel at ease before they struck. They yanked their targets into the darkness created by the shadow of the fort's wall, preventing any possible chance to shout for help by a knife into the throat of the unlucky victim.

"Die, ye Campbell son of a whore," Euan whispered into the ear of the man he'd gotten his hands on before letting his body fall to the ground in a heap.

Weapons were confiscated from the bodies and Euan gestured them out before the garrison could realize something had happened. Their next targets were any sentries stationed along the way back to Achnacarry. When they returned hours later, he went to Lochiel, who looked at him and his bloody clothing and nodded. The regiments retreated from Fort William under the cover of darkness, with Keppoch continuing on with the others toward Inverness. Lochiel intended to rest his men, and they reached Achnacarry by dawn. Euan didn't stop and departed for home.

Aileen had just risen for the day when she saw Euan come over the crest of the hill, covered in blood. Her face went white, and she screamed in panic, rushing out to him. "Euan! Oh God, what has happened to ye?"

"None of it is mine, Mam," he said, his voice tired and flat.

She recoiled and looked at him in shock. "What have ye been about?"

"Dinnae ask," he said coldly as he walked past her to change and clean himself off.

Aileen crossed herself, saying a prayer for his soul. This man was not her son.

In the hours that followed their return from Fort William, Euan slowly returned to himself, much to Aileen's relief. She continuously begged him not to go with Lochiel and the others when the call came for the spring campaign, but he refused to promise such a thing, saying only that he'd consider it. When word came that he was to report back to Achnacarry that evening for a meeting of officers, his heart sank. They were only a day back from Fort William, but he knew what this summons meant. He took leave of his mother that evening with the excuse that he was going to dine with Malcolm and his family, and upon arriving at the hall, he sat down with the others. Lochiel looked stern but didn't keep them waiting long. He picked a letter up from the table, and Euan recognized the seal instantly, confirming what he'd already suspected.

"Lads, we are called back to the prince at Inverness," he said. "He intends to face Cumberland there."

Euan closed his eyes and dropped his head. They'd all known this would be coming, but it had come far faster than any of them wanted. The other officers beside him sat stone-faced.

"I have sent the others to call yer men back. Ye have ten days, and I need ye prepared to leave by the 12th so we can meet the prince and the others by the 14th. It will be a tiring trip, but we should have a chance to get a day's rest in when we arrive. I dinnae want to leave before we absolutely must in case there are reprisals from Fort William. Are orders clear?"

"Aye, Lochiel," they all replied in unison.

"Good. It is back to bloody war we go, gentlemen."

CHAPTER 22

EUAN AVOIDED TELLING AILEEN about his leaving again by going out early to hunt with Duncan and some of the others. They'd been successful even though Euan's mind wasn't on hunting. He was troubled at the thought of leaving again, and his old feeling that he wouldn't live through this war returned with a vengeance. He was ready to be done with war and ready to be done with everything. He was lost in his own thoughts when he heard Duncan's voice.

"Euan," Duncan called out in a loud whisper. "Euan, come here. I see something."

Euan, snapping out of his own head, looked up from the trap he was setting for rabbits. "What?" he asked as he stood up and made his way over to where his friend stood.

"I see something there by the loch."

"Do ye know what it is?" Euan asked as he approached. "A buck, I hope."

"I dinnae think so," Duncan replied as he raised the musket he carried.

Euan gave him a curious look as he stepped up beside the man and followed his gaze as well as the aim of the rifle. His eyes widened. "Duncan, wait!"

But the words came too late, and the crack of the rifle sounded before he could even get the words out of his mouth. A woman's scream came back to them, and Euan heard Duncan swear in fear behind him as Euan took off running toward the woman Duncan had shot. He burst out of the tree line in enough time to see the young woman push herself up to her knees and touch her shoulder, her hand coming away covered in blood.

"Really?!"

"Christ, lass, are ye all right?" Euan said as he reached her and knelt at her side.

"Yes, no thanks to you," she sniped.

Euan couldn't blame her for her tone. She'd just been shot while she was minding her own business, after all. "I was nae the one who shot ye," he replied as he glared at Duncan, who arrived out of breath and looking dismayed.

"Well, it does not matter who shot me — just that one of you did," she huffed. "Help me up, would you?"

Euan and the other men looked at each other in confusion. The woman in front of them should be dying, or at the very least screaming in pain, but she was doing neither of those things. In fact, she seemed to be in no pain at all and was coherent enough to be incredibly irritated with the entire situation. He'd never seen anything like it, not even in battle when the blood was pumping and he felt invincible. If someone had been shot, they were down regardless. Euan held out a hand to help her up, and she fashioned a sling out of the length of wool around her waist once she was standing.

"We should take her to Lochiel," one of the others said.

"Aye," said the rest in unison.

"No, thank you," she replied. "I have had quite enough of your help."

Euan continued to survey her in curiosity. Who in the hell *was* this woman? "No, I will take her to my mam. She would be sent for by Lochiel to help the lass, so I might as well just take her straight there."

"Ye are nae going to tell anyone I shot her, are ye?" Duncan asked.

"I will nae lie if questioned further than this, but I will say ye thought she was a poacher, Duncan."

"Thank ye, I can at least get out of that if asked," Duncan replied.

Euan bit back a laugh as the young woman rolled her eyes, fed up with all of them and the ridiculousness of anyone thinking she was a poacher, but he kept himself in check. It wouldn't help the situation and would only serve to make her more cross. She was beautiful though, he'd give her that, but he also knew she didn't belong here. There was, however, something so familiar about her, something that called to him and pulled him to her in a way he found unsettling.

"If we are to go to a healer, could we please make our way there?" she asked, making no attempt whatsoever to mask her impatience.

"Aye, of course. Lads, get ye gone from here and say naught," Euan said before he picked up the bag near her and draped her good arm about his shoulders. The young men dispersed, and the two of them walked back into the woods. "What is yer name?"

"Grace."

"Grace, hm? An English name, but ye dinnae sound English. Well, nae exactly anyway," Euan said.

"Because I am not."

"Where are ye from, Grace?"

"Someplace you have never heard of. What is your name?" she asked.

"Euan. Euan Cameron."

ACKNOWLEDGMENTS

Dr. Chris Robinson of the West Highland Museum – Thank you so much for your invaluable help, from all of the books I purchased while researching this book, to answering myriad questions and sending me scans of original maps and reports to geek out over.

Professor Christopher Duffy – Thank you for answering random and obscure military questions and setting me on the right path when I realized I needed to change something.

Paul Macdonald – where do I even start? From the beautiful cover photo to answering questions in the middle of the night Edinburgh-time, your help has been a blessing. Your Thursday lectures are always fascinating and always teach me something new, so much so that I *had* to put Big Duncan in this story. I didn't really know you well when I started out, but I feel fortunate to call you friend now. *Tapadh leat mo charaid.*

Wardruna – your atmospheric albums were the perfect backdrop for writing this tale, and they were on constant repeat during the writing phases. It always helped me get into and stay in the proper headspace to write about a man in the middle of a war for not only his chief, but for the fate of his entire country.

And always, to my wonderful husband, for understanding how his wife works and her need for historical accuracy while not complaining too much about having to find space in bed to sleep around stacks of books and research material.

Grace kept her hands clamped over her mouth to stifle the scream welling up inside of her chest, her body shaking with silent sobs. The only way this would be worse was if she'd marched him there herself or pulled the triggers of the muskets that they'd executed him with, and as far as she was concerned, she might as well have. It may be a different Euan in a different timeline, but fundamentally he was the same. He was the man she loved, the one who'd so captivated her that she'd broken the cardinal rule for him. The man who, even this morning, had brought her a cup of coffee in bed but let it go cold because he was too comfortable snuggled up under the blankets with her to let her to sit up and actually drink it. The same one who'd saved her life by pretending to betray everything he'd once stood for.

Grace stood up, the speed with which she did so tipping the chair over, and then began pacing to try and calm herself down. Once she felt she had sufficient control over her emotions, she hurried out of the archives, requesting entry when she reached Council chambers. She was inside as soon as the doors opened wide enough for her to squeeze through, not bothering to wait any longer than necessary.

"Watcher Cameron? What are you doing here? Is everything all right?" Councilwoman Rochford asked as she stood up, looking concerned.

"I need to speak with you right now. *Alone.*"

Rochford's concern seemed to deepen, but she nodded, gesturing toward the door Grace now knew led to the private gardens. Without another word, Grace walked over to them and outside.

"What is this about, Grace?" Rochford asked as she came out behind her, letting go of the formality now that they were alone.

"Why didn't you tell me?" Grace asked, turning to look at her.

"Tell you what?"

"That day when I woke up and asked you about Nairn; why didn't you tell me I'd actually been the cause of his death?"

Rochford sighed. "Why would I? You were upset enough, and it made no difference at that point. Why add to it?"

"It makes a difference to *me*!"

"It should not."

The sound of derision Grace made was cold and bitter. "Easy for you to say, hm? *You* didn't kill your Companion before you met him."

"Grace —"

"No! Don't you *dare* try to excuse this or excuse me. What I did caused him to be captured and shot! He wasn't supposed to be there, Alice! You didn't tell me he was there!"

"Because it no longer mattered! He would never experience any of it again in any timeline. Once he joined with you here it became as though he and his mother never existed there or anywhere after the point where we changed things to be as though he left with you, and that was the night before they left again for Inverness. He would never go back to that field to die."

"But he did then! The time I ran that mission he did!"

"The *only* time, Grace. The potential success of that attack never happened again because he was no longer there, then or ever. It can never happen again."

"I want to see it."

"What?" Alice gasped out, aghast as she looked at Grace.

"I want to see what I did. I need to see it."

"That seems very unwise."

"I need to see what I did to him, what I caused. Send me as an observer so I can't do anything."

"Grace, why? I am not sure you understand what you are asking, and perhaps if you took some time to think about this then you would see that this isn't what you really want."

"Because what I did had a price, Alice, and someone else paid it, someone I love more than myself or anyone else. I need to remind myself that there are costs to this, costs I never see. I need to brand that into my soul, so I'll never forget or take for granted that what I do affects real people."

Alice sighed. "You are not going to take no for an answer are you."

"No, I'm not."

ABOUT THE AUTHOR

Eilidh Miller, FSAScot, has a BA in English and studied history as an undeclared minor to better inform her literature studies. A recent winner of the Robert Burns Literary Award and a Fellow with the Society of Antiquaries of Scotland, Eilidh was very active within Southern California's Scottish community, spending a great deal of time volunteering with the charitable organization St. Andrew's Society of Los Angeles.

A long-time historical reenactor, Eilidh loves research and educating the general public about historical events, as well as entertaining them with tidbits no one would believe if they weren't documented. She extends this same energy to her work, extensively researching the historical periods she includes in her writing to ensure that the information she presents is correct, even going so far as to travel internationally to access archives and scout locations.

She resides in the Pacific Northwest with her husband, daughter, and feisty Shiba Inu sidekick while working on her master's degree in the history and politics of the Highlands and Islands.

You can keep up with Eilidh on TikTok – @authoreilidh – or her Facebook page to keep up to date on the next release, special content, and information on appearances.

Facebook: eilidhmillerauthor

OTHER BOOKS BY THE AUTHOR